Gordon Parker was born in Newcastle on Tyne in 1940 and has lived all his life in the industrial belt of Northumberland. He was educated at Blyth Grammar School and Newcastle Polytechnic and has been intimately involved in North East industries in his capacity as a representative for a large engineering firm. He has written short stories for local radio and has a deep interest and affection for 'Geordieland' and all its characteristics. This is his first novel.

Gordon Parker is married and has two daughters. They live in Holywell, a picturesque village which in the past was populated almost entirely by mining families and is only two miles from the site of the Hester pit.

Gordon Parker

The Darkness of the Morning

Foreword by
Sir Derek Ezra MBE

Futura Publications Limited
A Futura Book

A Futura Book

First published in Great Britain in 1975
by Bachman & Turner

First Futura Publications edition 1976

Copyright © Gordon Parker 1975

ISBN 0 8600 7315 7

Printed in Great Britain by
Hazell Watson & Viney Ltd,
Aylesbury, Bucks

Futura Publications Limited
110 Warner Road
Camberwell, London SE5

To all who helped and encouraged
and to the miners of Britain
for whom I have the greatest admiration.

FOREWORD

by

Sir Derek Ezra MBE

Chairman of the National Coal Board

Over the years, the coal-mining industry has provided the backcloth for many novels. Its closely-knit communities, all dependent for their livelihood on the success of the local pit, have exerted a fascination on some of our greatest writers.

With *The Darkness of the Morning*, Gordon Parker adds his name to this distinguished company. He describes with great warmth the passion and humanity of a mining village, and the bitterness of a strike in 1844, a strike occasioned not only by the natural desire of the miners to better their standard of living, but also by their concern that safety standards should be improved, a concern eventually vindicated when the pit was flooded out. When we read the vivid account of the struggles and sufferings of those days, we cannot but be thankful for the profound change in attitudes that has occurred since then, and grateful to the early trades unionists for helping to bring this about.

A regrettable feature of coal mining which is inevitably highlighted in many novels is the colliery disaster. Even today, when they are thankfully on a much smaller scale, such occurrences draw the eyes of the world to the pithead. Through television and newspapers, the groups of anxious relatives standing against the sombre silhouette of the colliery headstacks become part of our lives. In retelling the tragic events of the Hartley Colliery disaster of 1862, when two hundred and four men and boys perished, Gordon Parker brings back with great clarity those harrowing scenes, as the whole country (including, as we know, Queen Victoria) waited hourly for the better news that was not to be.

The Epilogue tells also of the aftermath of the disaster: the public outcry, and the swift legislation requiring the construction of two shafts at every mine. Out of tragedies such as this grew the great reforms of the Mines and Factories Acts of the nineteenth century.

In this, his first novel, Gordon Parker brings to life the colour and the basic qualities of the people in the old mining communities: their comparative isolation from the outside world: their concern for each others' welfare; their desire for the education and betterment of their children. It was through the labour of such people that the industrial life of Britain prospered, and all who are interested in obtaining the flavour of those times—as well as all who are looking for a good story—are strongly advised to read this book.

DEREK EZRA

Book One

SHIREHILL

CHAPTER 1

A.D. 1820

The door of the Black Goose swung violently open, spilling weak yellow candlelight and heavy smoke-filled air into the darkness of the night. Rose Simpson followed, propelled almost head first, her feet clawing wildly at the cobblestones as she tried in vain to control her unnatural movement. Peals of laughter came from the faces that appeared at the doorway as her spindly legs buckled then tangled, causing her to fall in a heap into a conical pile of horse droppings that was soft and sodden from the constant rain of the last two days.

"There now, you old bitch. Take your foul mouth somewheres else," shouted a man from the doorway. "And your lousy body, you're not hawking yourself in here. Now go on, bugger off."

Rose Simpson slowly dragged herself up on to her feet to the accompaniment of more laughter and jeers from the doorway. She turned to face her tormentors half grunting, half sobbing with anger; her eyes wide and glazed as she wiped the dung from her face and hair.

"You bloody rats," she shrieked. "You vermin! You're nothing more. You work down a bloody hole don't you—well it suits the lot of you—you should effin well live there. You're not worth a peck of this." She bent down and scooped up a handful of dung and threw it with all her remaining strength toward the oblong of yellow light that framed the silhouetted faces. Some vanished. Others weren't quick enough and the missile splattered against its several targets.

There were deep throated howls from the doorway and it was Rose who laughed, defiantly, hands on hips and head thrown back. Two men advanced, but were pulled back by a hand at the scruff of their necks and the harsh feminine voice of the landlord's wife.

"Leave her be you pair of brutes—leave her be! She's only a bloody woman—not much of one I'll grant you but if you want to grapple with a woman, try me—if you fancy your eyeballs on the floor!"

The two men protested but retreated. The landlord's wife pushed them back into the saloon and turned again to Rose.

"Get yourself home Rose—go home and sleep it off. Don't cause any more trouble—we can do without your kind of trouble."

"Yah!" shouted Rose. "Those iggorant bastards don't know how to treat a lady. They're rats every last one of 'em. I should know, I've had 'em all—including that pig of a husband of yours."

She threw back her head and laughed again.

The landlord's wife shook her head sadly. "Go home Rose," she said quietly as she turned and entered the saloon.

She closed the door behind her and the yellow shaft of light shrank to a narrow slit, then was lost to the darkness of the night.

Rose stood for a moment staring vacantly at the door, her cheeks rising and falling as she fought back the tears and listened to the muffled derisory laughter still coming from within. Finally she sniffed and turned and staggered along the mud-filled lane toward her cottage.

The rain still fell with a constant hiss and the acrid stench from the pit heap hung heavily in the cold night. She drew the edge of her soaked shawl tightly to her throat as she bowed her head against the weather. Bloody men! she thought. What's wrong with me? I'm as good as their women—better than most; yet they turn their dust-filled noses up at me. I've got a right to live, haven't I? My bloody husband gets blown to smithereens down their soddin' coal hole and what do they care? Surely they could spare a few pence for a change of thighs, the miserable bastards.

Almost instinctively she turned the corner at Bessie Lambton's shop then raised her head to squint through the darkness of the lane. The rain stung into her face and the remaining horse dung ran down her hollow cheeks and between her withered lips. She spat loudly as the taste reached her tongue and her gin-filled stomach retched convulsively.

It was almost twenty minutes before she finally reached her hovel. She felt weak and her head still swam with the gin and her body, chilled with the cold rain felt stiff and somehow detached from her head. But there was still a spark of awareness which registered immediately she saw the faint flickering light from the window.

Robbers! she thought, or perhaps a customer after all! She crept stealthily along the last few yards of lane keeping close to the wall. Finally, her heart fluttering madly, she peered cautiously through the glass. The rain pattered against the small panes, sending rivulets cascading down and her heavy-lidded eyes could only register a distorted maze of colour. Gently she pulled the sodden shawl down over the palm of her hand and wiped quickly at the glass. There was only a second or two before the rain twisted the scene back into a blur, but it was enough. Her eyes widened then closed to thin lines before she threw open the door.

Daniel Simpson jumped from his kneeling position in front of the great black iron fireplace, sending the fragment of mirror that was balanced on top of a stool up and over and into the ashes as his small arms swung wildly with shock. The draught from his movement whipped the candle flame into a frenzied dance causing the shadows of the room to see-saw back and forth in eerie turmoil. There was a silence as his mother closed the door behind her, her eyes never leaving him. The candle regained its composure and there was a metallic clatter as the scissors were released from the sweating hand and hit the stone floor among the curls of blond hair.

"So!" Rose whispered between her teeth as she took a step forward.

Daniel's face twisted into a horrified grimace. "No! mammy no—please!" he shrieked, his eyes bulging and his feet rooted with fear. He lowered his gaze with a mechanical jerk of his head and stared at the pile of severed hair. "I couldn't help it —I don't want long hair—the lads at the pit never leave me be. They call me Jessie and pull at my pants to see if I'm really a lad. Please mam—please don't hit me."

Rose ignored him. She didn't even hear. She lunged forward and grabbed him by his remaining ragged locks and they both

13

screamed in unison. "You cur!—you little swine. I'll teach you to cut your hair," she snarled as he danced like a puppet under her clenched fist. "I warned you what I'd do if I ever caught you cutting your hair. I couldn't have a girl—it had to be one with a pod on didn't it, so you'll pay for it you little bugger —you're my little girl."

She flung the boy to one side and he crumpled in a corner, sobbing from the searing pain that burned from his brow to the nape of his neck. Rose staggered to a rough wooden chest that served as a table and with one swipe of her thin arm cleared the mugs and plates that had lain there for days. She lifted the lid and rummaged for a moment then triumphantly held up the dress of greying white.

"There now Daniel—there's a pretty thing? This is for my little girl. It's nice is it not?—Is it not!" she screamed; Daniel nodded as he sobbed. She thrust it toward him. "Wear it!" she commanded.

"Mammy please—not again, don't make me wear it again."

"Wear it!" she shrieked.

Slowly Daniel unloosened the string from around his waist and pulled off his pants, then his shirt. Still sobbing he took the dress and pulled it over his head.

Rose stared at him, her eyes becoming glazed once more. She slowly lowered herself on to the stool and sat silently for a moment before beckoning him towards her.

"Come here my little Margery," she sang gently. "Come to your mammy my little angel."

Daniel began to cry again as her grasping fingers curled around his arms. She drew him slowly closer.

"Don't cry little Margery—come to Mammy—you're safe now."

She took his head between her hands and rested it against her flat chest. At the same time she began to sway slowly from side to side, her mouth mumbling a cracked song.

> Go to sleep me bonny bairn
> Divvent have nee fear
> Yer mammy's by yerside agen
> So wipe away yer tear

Daniel struggled to get his breath as she held him to her.

He could smell the dank stench of horse dung on her clothes and he felt sick with the disgrace of wearing a dress. His head still throbbed with pain and a new sensation crept through him. His fingers began to tremble and a strange tingle rippled up his arms, down his body to his legs. His mother continued to sway. It had happened so many times before but never had he felt such an agony of pain in his head or the strange twitching tingle in his body.

He was scarred that night, deeply and inwardly; a scar that was to manifest itself many times during the rest of his life.

CHAPTER 2

March 1844

Daniel Simpson was awake in an instant. The unreal light of dawn began to pick out the low ceiling, the hearth and the scant furniture that made up the only room of his cottage, as he blinked his eyes into focus. It was cold and his excited breath billowed out as a ghostly vapour but the chill air had no effect on him; he felt no cold, only elation at the thoughts of men united in a common aim, wielding their collective voices into a force that all but the dead could hear and fear and take heed of.

"Dossie—up!" he grunted as he swung his legs out of the bed, "I've important work this day."

His wife yawned then coughed and finally released her swollen body from the tangle of bed clothes. She wrapped a shawl across her shoulders then waddled slowly to the fireplace and poked at the ash in the grate.

"Hurry up woman, I want summit to eat. The lads'll be ready soon," he barked at her.

She stopped poking and turned. "Surely even you will agree that at nine months the weight of this slows you doon—just a bit!" she mumbled, pointing to her stomach.

"Shit!" he shouted back. "That's nowt to concern me. That was all your doing and don't you forget it."

"You had a part in it," she whined, then suddenly cackled insanely, "in more ways than one you did!"

He stared at her for a moment, the fire of hatred smouldering in his eyes.

"Get a bloody move on you bitch," he hissed between clenched teeth. She turned back to the hearth and pulled a

16

derisory face at him. She wondered how she could have been such a fool to get tangled up with this man and why she had bothered him in the first place. It was her fault entirely, she granted herself that, no one could be blamed for it. Plenty of people had warned her and even Daniel himself was farthest from blame, and in a sarcastic sort of way she felt sorry for him. Just nine short months ago she had been free to choose any eligible man in the village. She had been widowed almost a year when the quiet sullen man who never bothered with girls suddenly began to interest and attract her. Dorothy Laidler widow of Matthew Laidler and aged twenty years three months suddenly recovered from the nightmare of seeing her husband's charred body unceremoniously dangling from a rope at the mouth of the pit and realized that she was still a woman, a young woman with an appetite for other than food. At first the challenge intrigued her. Daniel Simpson was well known to have no interest in women—in fact he shunned women. Some said it was because he was frightened of them, others that he was deformed and God had left out of him the normal desires of a man. The challenge was overwhelming. He was big and broad, not handsome but masculine and his quiet manner and solemn face with the sad, ice-blue eyes, stimulated her feminine curiosity. Each day when his shift at the pit suited, she would watch from the window of her father's bakery for him coming and her heart would pound at the thoughts that that might be the very day she would make a breakthrough. He would enter the shop, black with coal dust from the top of his shaven head to his feet and those cold penetrating eyes would almost stop her breath.

"Two pasties," he would grunt.

In her most charming and demure manner she would serve him, chatting about this and that and fluttering her eyelashes, yet for months he seemed oblivious to her presence. He sometimes grunted in answer to her questions other times he would stare straight through her, his bottom lip sagging open and swimming with saliva.

Finally after a long time she gave up, hurt at her failure as a woman to spark even a flicker of interest. She decided to act cool and aloof when he came into the shop. It took only two days for him to react. On the second day after the pasties had been thrust into his hand, he turned, then turned back knotting

17

his brow as he did.

"Yes, Mr. Simpson was there something else?" she enquired, haughtily.

"Why are you mad at me Miss Dorothy?" he whispered. "I liked you better the other way."

Within a week she was chatting to him like an old friend and even if his conversation was still cool and hesitant, she had made the breakthrough—now she could really turn on the charm!

It took several more weeks before she managed to entice him into the back room next to the ovens, "for some of her father's special cake" she said, and it took several of these visits before she realized that he was unbelievably naive. All her joking and slightly improper chit-chat brought none of the expected double-edged answers designed to test her true feelings on sex; just innocent replies without a hint of embarrassment or excitement in his quiet voice. One day she decided that the only solution was the direct approach. Once drawn out of his shell he would be as normal as any other man, of that she was sure. She laid her plans carefully making sure that her father would be well away from the shop when Daniel called, and when he did arrive she was in her prettiest and most daring dress, the neck being cut so low as to just reveal the cleavage of her breasts. Her breath came quick and she tingled with anticipation as she led him to the back room.

The heat from the ovens made the room doubly hot and oppressive on that June day as Dorothy looked at him. "Daniel, I've been thinking," she said coyly, "you and I are friends are we not?"

Daniel nodded, a puzzled look on his blackened face.

"Do you ever feel the desire to kiss me, perhaps?"

His brow tightened. "Kiss?—no Miss Dorothy, kissing's sissy."

She put out her hand to hold his, but he quickly put them behind his back. "Daniel," she whispered, slightly chiding him, "you're thirty years old—kissing a girl is not sissy."

"It is," he mumbled, feeling all the uneasiness and fear flooding back. She realized then that she must use the most drastic plan that had come to her mind and trust her intuition, for if it failed she would be shamed for life. The room was gloomy so she lit another two candles then turned toward him, the

18

heat from the ovens adding to the excited beads of sweat on her brow.

"Daniel—look at me," she commanded.

She stooped down and lifted the hem of her dress up to her chin. She was naked underneath.

"Do you like what you see Daniel?"

He stood transfixed, with sagging jaw and eyes bulging. Suddenly, uncontrollably, his latent animal instincts were unleashed. With a roar he was upon her, ripping and tearing at the cloth, rubbing his blackened dusty face against her white belly and down to her trembling thighs. Like a practiced seducer, he unbuckled his belt and pulled down his trousers and was in her, thrusting wildly as she responded to the sensation. My God in Heaven, she thought, he's a man all right—no mistake, he's a man, as she cried with success and the ecstasy of its reward.

Their new found relationship was short-lived. A month later she announced she was pregnant and the whole village sniggered and Daniel became his old self again. They were married "to keep things right" as Dorothy's father had put it and Daniel became more and more embittered as he realized how he had been seduced; the outcome being to lose his freedom to a woman and the prospect of sharing his cottage with someone who was the same sex as his late unlamented mother.

It was a grey morning. Cold, still and overcast with the smell of snow in the air. The four straight lines of terraced cottages that made up the village of Shirehill seemed even lower and dirtier against the neutral sky as the smoke from the newly kindled fires billowed loosely from their chimneys and hung low over the sloping rooftops. The villages looked desolate in the quiet of the dawn. Its regimented simplicity offered no beauty to the surrounding countryside. It existed for the pit that loomed like some surrealistic junk pile in the distance and viewed together they were complementary to each other. The same blackened, rough workmanship. The same utilitarian coarseness. The same abject ugliness.

A dog yawned and looked blankly toward Daniel as he strode importantly down the row, dressed in his Sunday best

19

and shouting the men out. In dribs and drabs they responded until fifty or more were gathered behind him when he reached the end. Sidney Garrett was at his side, his dense, curling beard still spattered with crumbs and droplets of tea. The pair turned when they reached the last cottage and Daniel held up his hands to silence their murmuring chatter.

"Good lads—everyone of you. Anybody missing?"

There was a few seconds of head-swivelling before somebody shouted, "The whole row's here!"

"Champion lads," Sid shouted, "we'll meet up with all the rest down the lane. Now howay, let's away to Newcastle and show the bastard masters that this time we mean business!"

There was a cheer from the crowd that sent clouds of vapour billowing up from their eager mouths and set every dog in the neighbourhood barking as the men marched off around the corner and out of sight. They hadn't gone more than a mile before a breathless young girl tugged at Daniel's sleeve.

"Mr. Simpson—Mr. Simpson," she gasped.

"What's up?" he growled.

"Your missus—she's got the pains—she's gonna cowpe."

He pulled her hand away from his sleeve. "So what—bugger off, there's nowt I can do. It's woman's work."

The girl stopped jogging and was left behind. Daniel turned his head.

"Get Hetty from next door—she'll know what to do," he bawled reluctantly down the road. Blasted woman, he thought, what does she expect me to do—deliver the damned thing for her? It's her fault she's in that state, now let her suffer for her sins. The thought flashed through his mind that she might die and he would be back where he was before, but then, she might be taken and the baby might live. He tried to imagine what it would be like with yet another unwanted person invading his cottage that last year at this time was quiet and peaceful and his own to do with as he wanted. Now he had a female that shared his bed and made his flesh creep and the prospect of a child that would cry all night and mess itself and grow up to be a . . . boy! A son! he thought. It'll be a son and it'll be me— Daniel Simpson! At least a son wasn't a female that would wear ridiculous dresses of lace and ribbon and smell of perfume like the minister's wife and have long curling hair. Long hair! by God no! His son wouldn't have to put up with the degrada-

20

tion he had known. He would be a man and treated as such. Men were the only thing that mattered in the world. Men, strong and determined. No frills or fanciness. No scheming cattish ways. No long hair or dresses that set your teeth on edge as they rustled. Yes, Daniel Simpson's son would be a man and as a boy he would have everything that Daniel missed.

Sidney made to speak when Daniel barked at the girl, then thought better of it. What Daniel said and did was his own business. He had often wondered why he was so harsh and unbending about women but was so used to it now that it had become just part of his character like being jolly or grumpy or religious. Sid knew nothing of Rose Simpson's treatment of her son, only that she "had him like a lass" as his mother would tut and whisper on seeing him with his long blond locks hanging down to his shoulders. No wonder he shaved his head now; Sid could well understand that. He had even joined the others in calling him names and playing tricks when they were both door-boys at the pit, but now they were men and their foolish childish confrontations were forgotten. Daniel was his friend, at least they hewed coal together, drank together and out of all the men in the village Daniel spoke to him most of all— that was comparative friendship. He was a deep, quiet man and knowing him as he did Sid knew that his few words were always well chosen and he meant them and Sid respected him for it. There was only one thing in the world that could change Daniel Simpson and that was his work and matters about it and the men that laboured with him. Injustice and bad conditions at the pit magically transformed him almost to the point of extraversion and he forever rowed with the overman, the viewer and anyone else who might in some way alter the conditions in which they slaved. Even that morning he had strutted down the row lustily shouting the men out when usually he slunk to and from the pit in silent solitude. He was a complicated man, Sidney concluded, and knowing the background to his marriage, could not find fault in him if he chose to treat his wife less than the dust.

The procession arrived at the Town Moor Newcastle and a cheer went up from the miners already assembled when they saw the banners and recognized the collieries from whence they came. To Daniel it seemed as though every

21

miner in the country had turned out to hear the speeches. They were in their thousands, all orderly and dressed in Sunday best and he pushed through them with gladdened heart toward the cart in the centre of the mass from which a man was shouting to eager ears.

"And I say men, that the only way for the masters to take heed is for us to strike, no matter what hardships we may have to endure—strike to better ourselves me lads, and drag ourselves out of the mire of oppression."

A loud "Aye" resounded across the moor and then a cheer. Daniel felt his pulse quicken. This was living; to feel the determination of your comrades like a thousand tributaries gathering into an insuperable force to frighten even the bravest of adversaries.

The man on the cart waved for silence. Daniel nudged Sid. "That's the Union talking Sid. Think of the power it's got now with all these lads behind it," he whispered. Sid nodded, overawed.

"It will not be long my friends before the annual binding is upon us," the man continued. "I say, if the masters do not give us a say in the contract or relent on our other grievances we should not enter into a new bond. We will withhold our labour until such times as the masters recognize us as human beings with a will and a way of our own."

There were loud, long cheers from the crowd. Sid stood almost hypnotized.

"Dan, how does one become so educated as these lads?" he asked.

Daniel shook his head. "It takes brains and hard brain work Sid," he said softly, "but these men are self made—they take in schooling like we take in pints of ale."

Sid nodded profoundly.

"Let me give you examples of our treatment," the man shouted to the crowd. "We'll start with West Holywell. They work for 4½ pence a tub. They are fined for sending small coals to bank, which means sometimes they work all week and owe the masters money!"

An angry roar rippled over the crowd.

"What is more the masters sell the small coal for six shillings a chaldron!"

It took several minutes for the boos and angry cries to die down.

22

"Let's go on to Elemore colliery. They pay the lads there fortnightly on a Friday. Last payday our beloved masters refused to pay on Friday and said they would pay on the following morn. The lads were there at eight of the clock—do you know what time they were paid? Five of the clock in the afternoon. Nine hours awaiting in this weather, lads. What sort of animals do they think we are?"

The crowd erupted into angry shouts of derision and shaking of fists, and the examples of injustice kept coming and coming. Every pit in the counties of Northumberland and Durham seemed to have similar grievances and they were all aired. Several men got up to speak and the booing and the cheering went on till well into the afternoon.

Daniel stood drinking in every word and, roused by the fine speeches, conjured up a glowing future for himself and his workmates. Suddenly as one speaker prepared to leave the cart amid loud applause, on an impulse Daniel jumped up to him.

"Canna speak?"

The man looked puzzled for a second then smiled and turned to address the crowd again.

"Here's a lad wants to say some more. Give him your ear men—he's a son of the pit if ever I saw one."

Daniel opened his mouth, then he faltered. He was taken aback by the immense sea of faces, all hushed with expectancy. Then he took hold of himself and let his voice ring out and carry, he hoped, to the very edges of the crowd.

"I'm not educated like the gentlemen that have been giving us counsel here today. Like he says I'm one of you, weaned on coal dust and stythe, and what I wanted to say was, having been gassed one or twice myself, as I know most of you have, it's an awful thing to have to bear. And there's something else—what about the fiery pits; it's only nine years ago that 102 of our mates were blown to kingdom come at Wallsend. We need better ventilation, men. If the masters want us to work we need air and if we need air we need better ventilation! I heard tell of a miner who was compelled to work in a certain seam or be fined 2 shillings and 6 pence. The seam was full of stythe but he went. It took only half an hour for him to collapse. He was carried out and lay on a sick bed for three days and when he returned he was set on in the same

23

place. He collapsed again and was idle for fifteen weeks with his face and limbs all swollen." The crowd erupted into violent cries of "Death to the bastards," and "All coal owners are swine."

Daniel waved for silence, surprised and strangely elated at the effect his speech was having on the men but the last thing he wanted was violence. "Lads, I can see your anger at my tale—and justly so, but let me finish my piece with a warning. Remember the strike of '31 over boys' hours and 'Tommy shops' and whatnot."

There were loud "Ayes".

"Then remember well the trouble we got into. Smashing gins and hoyin' tubs and machinery down the shaft got us nowhere. The Militia were in weren't they, and by God the sight of them huzzars bearing down on you with a bloody sabre swishing through the air was enough to keep me in by the fire I'll tell you."

The crowd laughed.

"All I'm saying lads is if this strike comes off—keep to the law, turn the other cheek against all hardships and we'll have the sympathy of every working man in the country behind us."

The cheering and whistling took almost two minutes to subside. People gathered round him and slapped him on the back, the first being Sidney, amazed and proud of his friend. "How the hell did you do it, man?" he gasped.

Daniel looked around him dazed, "I don't know," he mumbled.

One of the previous speakers approached and held out his hand. He was dressed in a long black frock coat and his rounded face with the steady eyes radiated level-headedness and honesty. "Well done, sir," he said in a calm exacting voice, shaking Daniel's hand, "and whom have I the honour of addressing?"

Daniel seemed embarrassed. "Daniel Simpson, sir."

"Daniel Simpson is it? Good speech, man. Y've got a way with the lads, they like listening to you, I could tell. My name's Judd, Martin Judd. Shall we find somewhere to talk?"

Both Sid and Daniel nodded together.

"My cousin's got a tavern down by the quay," said Sid. "We'll get some ale and bread there."

"Champion, lead on," said their new-found acquaintance.

The snow that had threatened earlier now began to fall slowly. The meeting began to disperse and someone wound up the speeches by thanking the mayor for allowing them to meet on the moor.

The three men walked slowly along Percy Street past the city populace rushing here and there, with the unending clip-clop of horses' hooves on the slushy cobbles. There were hansom cabs drawn by Clevelands, drays drawn by majestic Shires and fine men carried on ponies and each time one passed, Daniel winced; another thing he disliked was horses. They reached the George after about half an hour and after Sidney had greeted his cousin and they had been warmed at the fire, three pints of ale and a large plate of bread and cheese were placed before them. Martin Judd made to pay but the landlord stopped him. "First lot's on the house. It's almost five years since I've seen this bugger." Sidney beamed.

They ate and drank and chatted about the resolutions that were proposed to be put to the owners and the consequences of their being ignored. Finally Martin Judd came to the point.

"Daniel, as I said before, you've got a way with the men. If this strike comes off—and it's almost certain to do so, will you and perhaps your mate Sid here help the Union?"

They both nodded, then asked how.

"I would like you to keep the men pacified. It'll be a long hard struggle will this one and the lads'll get restless and violent and they'll weaken." He shook his head sadly. "You've got to be somebody strong, to be keen on continuing the strike when the wife and bairns haven't had a decent meal for three or four months."

"Do you think it'll take that long?" said Sid, raising his eyebrows.

"Maybe longer," Daniel said before draining his mug.

Martin continued. "I want you to go around the area, keeping up the lads' spirits—can you do that?"

Daniel looked him straight in the eye. "What if I weaken?"

"Not you, mister—not you."

They shook hands and it was agreed.

"By the way," Martin said, "there's no need to go on foot. There's a friend of mine at Killingworth'll lend you a horse."

Sidney laughed out loud. The strong ale had weakened his inhibitions. "Y'll not get Dan on a horse Mr. Judd—he'd

25

rather walk. Two things he can't abide—women and horses, eh Dan?"

Daniel glared at him, but Martin intervened.

"Ah, a woman hater eh? A lot of people find out their dislike for the opposite sex when it's too late," he said with a little laugh. "Are you wed?" he added.

Daniel nodded.

Martin threw back his head and his mouth formed an oval, not wanting to pry further into dangerous territory. "But come, man, what have you against horses? Without them industry and commerce would flounder."

Daniel looked at the table. "Dunno," he growled. "They stink. I don't like the smell of them."

"Tell him what happened at the pit t'other week, Dan," Sid said, following with a hysterical laugh.

"When?"

"You know, when the galloway took fright in the ways."

Daniel looked sullenly at him. "You tell him," he said flatly.

Martin looked toward Sid.

"Well this galloway took fright in the ways, see. The little bugger wouldn't budge. Every time someone went near, its lip went back and its great brown teeth started snapping at everything. After upwards of an hour it had the bliddy pit almost at a standstill, then somebody sent for Dan here."

"What did he do?"

A smirk came to Daniel's face. He was enjoying having a tale recounted about him to such an important man.

"Well Daniel picks up a short pit prop—about a yard long and gans straight up to the galloway and bops it one—right between the ears." The ale had him now and he gave a ridiculous giggle. "The poor owld galloway's knees just buckled and the lads carted it out the way like a side of beef."

"Was it dead?" Martin asked with a frown.

Sid laughed again and Daniel choked on his ale.

"Dead?—naw, just stunned—anyhow it was as right as rain in a couple of minutes. Dan clowted it and Dan brought it round."

"How?"

"Well man, he takes out his cock and pisses straight in its ear. It jumped up like it had had a shot of powder under it!"

26

Sidney had been shouting out the tale and one by one the tavern was listening. Suddenly the place erupted into shrieks of laughter.

Soon Martin Judd bade them farewell with the promise of another meeting or instructions about the strike and they parted company. Sid and Daniel headed north out of town and as soon as the busy roads of Newcastle were left behind, it became obvious that the snow was lying in the fields and on the less-used roads and lanes. It had stopped snowing however, and the sky was clear and it was bitterly cold. The sun had already set and faintly the brightest of the stars appeared. The two men felt elated. The day's success and the ale had put them in a good mood and as they plodded their way home to Shirehill they felt only a warm satisfaction inside them. It was eight o'clock when they passed the Hastings Arms at Seaton Delaval.

"Have we any money, Sid?"

"Two-pence—how about you?"

"Same—let's have a couple of pints before home, eh?" Sid nodded and eagerly opened the door.

There were more cheers from the men in the tavern when they recognized the new arrivals and cries of "Good old Dan" and "What a speech" from the miners who had been with them and had arrived back sooner. Their praise was gratifying to him. He glowed inwardly with a satisfaction that seemed to melt his returning shyness. He felt flooded with confidence for the first time in his life.

His breath came quick and he cautiously laughed and joked with the men. He had felt a sensation of power up there on the cart, a power to motivate men by the words from his lips, to make them believe or disbelieve, to do or not do; an intangible power so unlike the only other he had ever known which emanated from his broad back and muscular arms and caused the black gleaming coal to split from its prehistoric grave. But the same satisfaction was there; it exhilarated him and rejuvenated his soul. Suddenly the tavern door opened and the little girl who had tugged at his sleeve that morning shouted out his name. Through the smoky atmosphere Daniel turned, a smile still locked into his face. There was silence.

"What is it?" he whispered.

"Your lass—she's had the bairn."

27

Daniel's eyes lit up. "What kind?"

"It's a lassie," she said and was gone.

Daniel's mouth twisted savagely and his eyes closed. "Ye Gods!" he screamed and smashed his mug into a thousand pieces on the bar-top.

CHAPTER 3

Hetty Charlton was an old woman. No one knew how old; even she had forgotten but she had a son, who said he was fifty next birthday and the pair of them lived next door to the Simpsons and shared the same earth closet which stood across the back lane.

Because she was so old, yet so active, the people in the village were amused by her rantings and old-fashioned ways but they held a deep respect for her because when there was some midwifery to be done or a corpse to be "seen to" for the undertaker she was always called; or if little Johnny had a raging pain in his belly which half a pint of castor oil hadn't shifted, Hetty usually came up with an "old-fashioned" cure. She was witch-like in appearance. Thin, stooped and always dressed in black, she had a shock of sparse white hair, a deeply wrinkled face and one large brown eye tooth which protruded well down from her collapsed mouth. She had a high-pitched strangulated voice and her alert immortal eyes took in everything through the barest slit of her eyelids. She looked at you in fact, like a contented cat.

It was this woman with the rough but gentle blue-veined fingers who first touched Margaret Simpson. Her withered lips were the first to touch her lips as she blew life-giving air into the tiny lungs and she was the first to bathe the slime of living from her body. To Hetty Charlton it could have been the very first child she had ever touched because as she fondled the new born girl she marvelled at the tinyness, and her twisted old body and slothful mind drew some of the vibrant new life into herself; she felt reborn herself and she gave thanks for the miracle of life. Funny she thought it's only two

29

days since I laid out Meggie Stone, all cold and old and ravaged by time. How could this tiny being be the same one day, just like Meggie Stone, just like herself. She dismissed the melancholy thought from her mind as she wrapped the baby in clean linen and placed it snugly in the tiny wooden cradle near the fire. She turned to Dorothy and gave a wild cackle as she took the piece of leather from between her teeth.

"There now bonny lass, we'll clean you up eh?"

Dorothy's head fell to the side and she moaned gently. Hetty tapped her sweating cheek.

"Come on, wake up and see your daughter. She's been worth the eight hours hard work—she's a little beauty."

Hetty brought some hot water in a bowl from the fire and in ten minutes had made the new mother feel as fresh and comfortable as possible. She had brought the cradle to the side of the bed and lifted the baby out for its mother to hold and caress and admire.

Hetty cackled again. "She's all there, she's got all her bits and pieces so don't worry about that."

Dorothy held out a hand and grasped the old woman's. She was too weak to speak but Hetty read the thanks in her eyes.

"Well, y'll be having no more after that eh? It's not as nice as puttin' them there is it?" she croaked. "Aye, they all say that. Said it mesel'—but I had eight." She nodded towards the wall. "Only one left and one younger that lives in Shields. Delivered a few bairns y'kna—hundreds on them—aye an' laid a few folks oot." She gave a wide grin and her single tooth stood out like the tusk of an elephant.

"I help them into the world but mind I've seen plenty bugger off out of it!"

She turned and shuffled to the window.

"Snow's stopped. Your man should be back b'now." She nodded knowingly.

"Union's more important than this eh? Wait'll I catch him. They're all the bliddy same—just dick and grub—that's their lot, and none of the consequences."

She pointed toward the wall.

"That silly son of mine would have gone if I hadn't threatened him with the brum—and him just gettin' the feelin' back in his legs after that bliddy mountain fell on his back down below." She sniffed and shuffled back to the bed.

"They'll be on strike an' we'll all starve. Just you watch, our Billy'll get fit again and they'll be out on strike anyway."

She poked a bony finger at Dorothy's nose. "Daniel Simpson's got them all het up!—just wait till he's got no beer money and that bairns screamin' 'cos your milk's as weak as water."

She bent over and cackled as she patted the baby's head. "Keep her on the breast as long as y'can mind. Y'll not fall wrong again while she's on the breast—remember now."

Dorothy's eyes flooded with tears. She knew she wouldn't conceive again. How could she with a husband who lay beside her as cold and stiff as a statue and who only tolerated her in bed because there was no other blankets and no other bed. She wondered if he knew about the baby yet. She had heard the old woman despatch the wide-eyed young Isabel who had been hovering around all day, with instructions to search the street corner cliques and try the taverns. She imagined he would still be at Newcastle if he hadn't arrived at home by now. Surely, she thought, the very least would have been for him to come straight home. She looked down at the tiny groping face. The eyes were as blue and penetrating as Daniel's and the tiny head had a faint growth of blond hair. It was Daniel's daughter and she was happy and proud but deep down she wished it had been a boy, for nothing else than to hope Daniel would take an interest in him as he grew. She had longed for a son. She had prayed for a son. She knew that nothing would rekindle his interest in her; she had committed the unforgivable—eight months of silent tolerance had proved that and she was resigned to spending the rest of her life suffering and paying—but if only she had had a son!

Hetty lit her clay pipe and spat into the fire. "I'll just nip next door and see if Billy's all right, and I'll be back—want another candle lit?"

Dorothy lay back against the pillow and shook her head. The old woman nodded and shuffled to the door. "Rest now. I'll be back shortly. If you want me urgent, hoy that mug against the wall."

She opened the door and a cold blast of air sent the candle flames shivering. "Snow's stopped," she mumbled, forgetting she had already said it. "Keep that bairn covered, it's freezing hard now."

She pulled the shawl from her shoulders and covered her head. The door closed gently.

Dorothy looked around her and examined the room through the fragile glow of the tallow candles. The simple poverty of it did not register with her. It was all she had ever known. Riches and finery were contained in tales of fantasy and in fine houses like the home of the Delavals down the road. The breathtaking splendour of the shape and size of their house triggered off her imaginings of the inside. The great home of the Delavals was the size of their colliery row, and so remote from the colliers that it might have been Heaven itself. Her father had told of delivering bread there once, in preparation for a feast but his tales of sides of beef and deer and game birds hanging there in a kitchen twice the size of the church brought peals of disbelieving laughter from his listeners. One man knew a girl at Seaton who had worked as a maid there and he told a captive audience about carpets on the floors and fine paintings on the walls and plates and cutlery of solid gold. But then he said, the wench was made pregnant by one of the fine men of the house, and the spell was suddenly broken; they were the same as ordinary mortals, needing the basic necessities of life and succumbing to the basest instincts of the animal world.

She must have dropped off to sleep for a few minutes because when she opened her eyes the big shoulders of Daniel were hunched over the fire as he sat on a stool warming himself.

"Daniel," she whispered. "Have you seen the bairn?"

He ignored her.

"Daniel—it's a little girl and she's like you. She's your spittin' image."

He allowed himself a derisive grunt.

Her voice revealed her fear. "Please, say you're pleased—don't blame her for what happened between us. She's a lovely little lass. What should we call her Daniel? What do you think? I like Margery."

His shoulders stiffened as though an invisible knife had been pushed into his back. Slowly he swivelled on the stool. His eyes were wide and wild and burned with the reflection of candles and fire. The dome of his stubbly head was lowered toward her and his teeth bared themselves like a frightened dog. The memory of that night long ago came flooding back in all its vivid reality. A pain seared across his head and the strange tingle began to radiate through him. He lifted himself up and walked slowly toward the bed. Dorothy held the baby closer to her.

"Daniel what's wrong?" she bleated.

"If you call that bairn Margery, I'll throttle the pair of you—unnerstand?" he hissed.

Dorothy was frantic. "Margery—all right—we'll call her something else—what's wrong with Margery it's a nice name. We'll call her Margaret, how's that? Yes, Margaret's a nice name as well."

She gave a frightened moaning shudder and burst into tears. Daniel blinked, then seemed to sag. He stood for a few seconds breathing noisily then turned back to his stool. Dorothy sobbed. The baby began a tinny faltering cry. The door latch rattled and Hetty's wizened features appeared. She let out a cracked gurgling sound that was a cry of surprise and triumph rolled into one.

"Well, well," she cackled. "If it isn't the fine fellow who thinks more of the Union than he does of his wife and his firstborn."

Daniel ignored her. Hetty turned toward the bed. "Had a few tears hinny? Take no notice of the sulkin' great hulk. Get the brum to his backside and he'll be washin' nappies in no time."

Dorothy cried again. The old woman took the baby from her and shushed it, then put it in its cradle. She took Dorothy's hand. "Easy lass," she whispered. "All men are pigs dressed in suits." She winked, "he'll come round. He'll be house-trained in no-time."

She cackled again and shouted toward Daniel. "I say you'll be house-trained in no time you big bugger—won't you?"

Daniel looked over his shoulder. His voice was calm and his words slow and flew from his lips like polished icicles. "Get out, you stinking old hag. Your work's done—y'll get

33

paid at the pay day."

Hetty stood dumfounded, her ancient head wobbling on frail shoulders and her lips stretching and pursing as she fought her fuddled mind for the right abuse to answer him. But nothing came. She released her grip on Dorothy's hand and moved to the door. Silently she opened it and with a sad look at Dorothy, she was gone.

When the caller rapped on the window, Dorothy was already up. The baby had squeaked then started its weak wailing call for food an hour earlier and had tugged at her breast with amazing ferocity. Thankfully Daniel had done no more than turn over, so she sat quietly in front of the faintly glowing embers of fire still weak from her ordeal, her eyes still tight from the tears, but with a dull contentment growing inside her, as her child drew its nourishment. She tried not to think of her future or of her daughter's. It was like a bad dream, a nightmare that she hoped she would suddenly wake from and laugh with a joyous sense of relief. The caller made her jump even though she heard him approach. The baby was changed and asleep. Daniel grunted as she began to poke at the ashes. She rekindled the fire and placed the big black kettle on the hob. Silently he swung his legs out of the bed and pulled on his work pants. He finished dressing and stood warming himself in front of the crackling fire, watching her as she cut bread for his "bait".

"What're you doing up?" he gurgled, before hawking and spitting over his shoulder into the fire.

She stopped cutting and looked solemnly at him. "Making your bait same as always," she whispered.

"You've just cowped haven't you—get back to bed—stupid bugger."

She was overjoyed at his smattering of concern. "I had to get up to feed the bairn. Have a look at her Daniel she's just . . ."

"Get back into bed woman!" he snapped. "No bugger's going to accuse me of ill treatin' you—I can get me own bait for once."

Dorothy sighed and put down the knife. She walked unsteadily to the bed and got in, pulling the covers up to her neck. She lay there watching his great form, illuminated by the fire, move surprisingly quietly around the room. He went outside and she heard his feet crunch through the frozen snow and the closet door bang. He reappeared and took his overcoat from where it was draped as a blanket at the foot of the bed. Soon the sound of a single pair of feet crunched past the window, then another, then two more and then some more. Daniel was dressed and ready. He lifted the latch, opened the door, then closed it. He turned toward the bed. "You're frightened of me Doss—aren't you?" he whispered.

She nodded slowly and cautiously.

"Try not to be—it's a hellish thing to be frightened."

She heard the hiss of exhaled air as he closed the door behind him. Daniel walked down the back lane and Sidney who had been waiting against his door fell into step beside him. He was bursting to discuss further the meeting of the previous day, but sensed from his firm step and the resolute hunch of his shoulders that it wasn't a time for speaking. Daniel had shaken off the euphoria of the meeting and Sid was disappointed. It was the beginning of a new week of toil and it was as though in their silence they mentally prepared for the ordeal ahead. The sky was clear and moonless and the crisp freezing air seemed to bring the stars within touching distance. There was no sound other than feet rasping through the frozen snow and away down the road the dull thump and thud that was the pit awakening. The two men turned at the end of the back lane and took the footpath skirting the edge of Johnson's farm. The path was lined with a black tangle of naked hawthorn bushes which seemed in a petrified frenzy to release themselves from the white blanket beneath.

Daniel switched his four picks from his right shoulder to his left and he put his numb right hand into the relative comfort of his coat pocket. He looked away to the East across Johnson's fields. There was still no sign of dawn. He knew he wouldn't see the light of day again until the next weekend but it didn't bother him. In the winter the limp sun shone only at weekends for the miners and for that he was sometimes grateful. The darkness seemed to form a barrier between himself and the rest of the world. He was relaxed in the darkness, just as he was in pit. When he was tucked away in some narrow seam with nothing but the blank face of coal to observe him, he was content. He struck at the coal with his pick and enjoyed the way it broke from its lair. The feel of it, the smell of it were his life. Now he sensed another contentment; success over the masters who held life and labour so cheap. The bloated, unfeeling owners who grew fatter and happier on the sweat of him and his mates, were due for a rude awakening. He had an important part to play—Martin Judd had said that. He felt his pulse quicken when he thought how he would be instrumental in getting the men better conditions and eliminate injustice and he savoured again those precious moments on the Town Moor when he held the emotions of thousands in his hands. Suddenly his thoughts went to his wife and child. He felt nothing—no love, no hate, only a neutral awareness of their existence. They were there, they were a fact of life; they would be tolerated. He wondered why he had bothered to speak to his wife before he left that morning. Perhaps for the first time he sensed the fear in her. Perhaps subconsciously he had recognized the ether of fear that was always there to greet him each evening when he came out of the pit and walked into his mother's cottage. How he had hated trying to love her as the other lads loved their mothers; yet when she died, white, pitifully thin and diseased from head to foot he had felt a strange desire to cry. She was no more; she was gone and there was a great void in his life. He was fifteen and all alone.

Soon they rounded the bottom of the pit heap which grew daily like some giant cancer out of the grassy field and the Lovat pit reared in front of them. The tall brick building of the winding house and the two square chimneys rose out of the ground transforming the gentler contours of the surrounding land into the scab of industry. Behind the chimneys there was the high black lattice work that supported the big winding wheel and straddled the shaft.

At the pit-head the miners stood around in small groups and the odd greeting or peal of light-hearted laughter broke the silence. The big wheel above them spun in its housing and the miners prepared to descend. There were a few joking comments as they shuffled along in the queue. Someone shouted, "Got your fur pants on Willie, it'll be enough to freeze your nuts off down there with the air movin' and all."

36

"Let's hope the effin air's moving," Daniel growled, "I'd far rather freeze than chowk with stythe."

Suddenly the rectangular cage appeared out of the Earth and eight of the men moved into it, four above and four below. Daniel and Sid rode in the bottom section. The shaft was open to the sky and the stars still shone brightly around them. The air was clean and cold and sweet and the men in the cage looked up and around and filled their lungs. Then there was a shout of "Rap her away lads!"

The engineman pulled on the great lever. The engine punched out its exhaled steam into the oncoming morning and the cage slid down, down into the primeval entrails of the Earth, away from the dawn and the snow and into a claustrophobic world of shadows and dripping water, where Daniel Simpson hid from himself.

CHAPTER 4

It was a nightly ritual where the eldest bathed first and the youngest last, and as Sidney Garrett immersed his blackened body into the soothing steaming water, his two sons John aged ten and Robert aged nine stood, equally black, waiting their turn. Luckily the boys were still small and were able to bathe together but in a few years Robert would have to wait until John had finished, then he and his brother would carry the bath full of filthy grey-blue water to the door and with an almighty heave send it gushing across the lane to run down the channel behind the earth closet and into the stream that crawled sluggishly past the lane end. At the moment however, the boys although working in the pit all day, were allowed the childhood luxury of having their parents labour after them. By the time Sid was washed and dried and dressed, the boys were white again and he and Martha his wife, ejected the contents of the bath into the lane while they hurriedly dried themselves.

Sid was a squat, thick-fingered man with a ruddy farmer-like complexion and a beard of curling red hair that matched the mop he carried on his head. He was a proud man, not in the sense of being independent, but proud of his two growing sons and his two younger daughters and proud of his few possessions. He had a wife who accepted her position with mute dutifulness and who had courted him and loved him and produced his children with predictable conventionality. She kept the cottage clean and tidy; she cooked delicious pies and bread and Sid never for one moment regretted their match. Eleven years of marriage had however, degenerated almost imperceptibly slowly into the dull routine of habit, and any spark of novelty or excitement at their being together had long

38

since dulled, then vanished completely. Their co-habitation was entire and absolute and each respected the other for what they were. Life for Martha was bringing up her children, looking after the cottage and her husband and satisfying his physical and sexual needs. She was content knowing that she was successful in doing that. The children were strong and healthy and her husband was uncomplaining, so with a sort of smug boastfulness that she managed to radiate to the neighbours, she modestly and constantly praised herself at her achievements. Sid was not quite so content. As their relationship became predictable he began to feel that something was missing from his life; that undefinable uncertainty that adds interest to intrigue was non-existent and it nagged at him like a sore tooth. His wife looked to his every need—but it wasn't quite enough.

Sidney felt good after his bath. His clean shirt rubbed pleasantly against his skin and the fresh soapy aroma that surrounded him was an invigorating change from stale sweat. He stood carefully combing his beard and hair and silently admiring his features in the mirror while his wife scolded the boys for wrestling in front of the fire and his daughters cleared the dishes from the table. Yes, he thought, extracting an elusive bit of coal dust from the corner of his eye, Thursday again—at last; the best night of the week is here again, thank God. A little quiver of excitement spread upward from behind his knees and he smiled at himself in the mirror. He carefully fitted a collar to his shirt and tied his maroon cravat into position. He stood back and stuck his chin up and smoothed his beard. Yes, he would do. He looked good. He picked up his jacket from the chair and his wife bustled across the room. She took it from him, a smirk of satisfaction on her face. He turned his back and stuck out his arms to receive it.

"There now Sid, you look smart as anything," she whispered, smoothing down his shoulders.

He turned and smiled at her. "You mean that Martha?"

"'Course I do. You're a fine man Sidney Garrett—always said so."

Sid winced inwardly. Each week the same routine, the same comments, the same answers. He mentally asked himself, "What's the practice tonight?"

"What's the practice tonight?" asked Martha.

"Dunno, we might do a run of the whole piece," he said, as he bent down and groped under the bed.

He dragged out an oddly shaped box and opened it. The children gathered around and stared at the gleaming trumpet.

"Canna have a blow Dad?" Robert asked.

Sid smiled and ruffled the boy's hair. "When you're older son and got a bit more wind."

He checked the mouthpiece and gave the trumpet a quick rub with a piece of soft cloth, then closed the box. He turned and kissed the two girls in turn, then his waiting wife. "Don't wait up hinny—could be a long practice with the contest coming up and all," he said light-heartedly as he walked to the door. Martha nodded. Suddenly there was the sound of hooves in the lane; the slow clip-clop of a walking horse, a gentle snort as it was reined to a halt, then a heavy hammering on the door. Martha frowned as Sid opened the door and peered at the dark figure standing there. The four excited children crowded around their father's legs.

"Daniel Simpson?" asked the voice.

Sidney was immediately disappointed. It was a rare occasion for anyone in the colliery rows to have a visitor on horseback and for an instant he felt important that the caller was at his house, irrespective of whether the reason for his visit was good or bad. Already the neighbours within earshot of the horse's approach were at their doors and straining their eyeballs to see the mysterious horseman, Alfie Mennem, four doors up, stood with his hands cupped to his eyes like blinkers and his little fat wife peered between the crook of his arm. Alfie Mennem was a born worrier, he also couldn't abide an event taking place that he didn't know about. He was the village "nose" and ably assisted by his wife, managed to know almost all of everybody's business. He was a lean round-shouldered character with a sunken pallid face and all that remained of his hair was a horseshoe that ran from ear to ear with two or three wisps of the former adornment stubbornly growing across his bald pate. He was a miserable man with an almost permanent sour look to his face. There was always an aura of misery around him as though in a constant state of regret for being alive. He worried about anything and everything and the more he worried the more miserable he looked. As a child he could remember worrying if his father was late from the pit. When he himself first went to the pit he worried constantly about the roof coming down or the cage rope snapping. When he was an adolescent he heard a frantic but discreet revelation from an acquaintance that masturbation could turn one blind. He worried about that; but it was peculiar, that particular worry evaporated each time he did it. He stood now nervously grinding his toothless gums together, bursting to know the reason for the horseman's visit and worrying in case it could remotely mean trouble for him. Finally he could stand the suspense no longer.

"It is for me Sid?" he shouted casually.

"Naw it's bloody well not," Sid snarled, before telling the stranger that he was not Daniel Simpson. He could see a folded paper in the man's hand and as his mind worked overtime thinking of why he wanted Daniel, it suddenly clicked.

"Daniel lives about ten doors down. Are you from Martin Judd?"

"Aye, I am."

Sid couldn't get the words out quick enough. "I'm his mate; if its a message y've got I'll take it."

"What's your name?"

"Sidney Garrett—Dan's friend. I was with him when we spoke to Mr. Judd."

The man nodded. "Yours was t'other name mentioned." He held out the note.

"See he get's it bonny lad. The die is cast."

He put his foot in the stirrup and mounted the horse. He pulled it around in the lane.

"Is it about the strike?" Sid asked eagerly. "We've waited near a month."

"It is that mister, the instructions are all there. Good Luck to you all."

He dug his heels into the horse's belly and the clatter of hooves became merged with the distance and lost.

The neighbours muttered among themselves as Sid closed the door with a flourish of superiority. He felt a wave of glee at the control he showed in ignoring Alfie's final agonized croak of "What's up Sid? Is there something wrong." He felt a glow inside him as his wife and children fussed around their so important father. Sid thrived on things like that. He was the first to realize and admit his inferior position in life. He was like thousands of other miners and workmen, but he often dreamed of riches or high position and having a fine house. He could neither read nor write, he tended to get muddled easily if he thought about more than one thing at a time but he had his dreams and his ambitions and however improbable, they constantly reminded him of what the world beyond Shirehill had to offer. Now the Union, through Martin Judd had need of his services. True, Daniel was more forthright than he when it came to Union matters; he was the natural leader, and Sid was quite satisfied to be his assistant. Such was the true measure of his simple aspirations.

"It's about the strike is it?" Martha said in a whisper, her hand at her throat.

Sid nodded, looking down at the still folded note. "It's come Martha. This is what we've been waiting for. It'll be hard on us but it'll be worth it. We've slaved long enough, this time we'll get justice."

"When do you start?"

Sid opened the paper and stared for a second at the unintelligible writing. He blinked and smiled a sickly smile at his wife. "I forgot to ask him—and I forgot to tell him I can't read—and neither can Dan."

Martha patted his hand. She could see her husband's vision of fame disintegrating. His chest that had been swelled with pride just a few seconds before, deflated and his shoulders sagged. "Take it to that creature Simpson and let him sort it out," she whispered.

Sid nodded and picked up his trumpet case. "Don't wait up," he murmured as he closed the door.

His mind raced as he walked slowly down the lane; he knew Daniel should have the letter as soon as possible and he realized the information contained in the letter should not be made known to all and sundry. It was for the miners only, but who did he know that could read? He could think of no one at the pit other than the overman and the viewer and they certainly weren't seeing it. Suddenly, it came to him and a thrill of excitement ran through his body—of course! Why hadn't he thought of it before—it was staring him in the face. Happily he thought of how pleased Daniel would be—and amazed, when he also looked blankly at the letter, then Sid would show him—he would spout out all the information and watch the respect pour from Daniel's wondering face. He walked quickly past Daniel's door and with a carefree gait set off down the road toward the Hastings Arms and the crowded upstairs room, full of thick tobacco smoke and beer fumes, where he and a couple of dozen of his workmates would blow enormous blasts clear up to Heaven.

As was usual on a Thursday night Sidney waited until the rest of the men had dispersed. As their goodnights and raucous laughter diminished, he set off alone toward home. He had enjoyed himself that evening, he had blown up a good thirst and with three pints of best ale inside him, he felt good. He savoured the taste of the cool beer—it might be the last for a while, he mused, and remembering Martin Judd's prophesy, added—a bloody long time!

He walked slowly and steadily down the slight hill toward the rows of colliery cottages. He forced himself to walk slowly—it was good mental training and made the delightful anticipation last longer. Soon he came to the cottages; silently he passed the dark shape of a couple of men lounging against a closet wall. He tried to keep his trumpet case still and hidden against his side. He breathed again when no call of recognition came. He passed the end of the next row. A dog barked, and a few doors up, the sound of a heated argument permeated the air. He came to his own row but walked resolutely on. At last the end of the cottages. He turned opposite the track up to Johnson's farm and keeping near to the hedge he made for the small house standing back from the road. His breath was quicker now as though he had been running and his eyes pierced through the darkness. Yes—there it was—a dull candlelight playing on the green bedroom curtains. He took a deep breath and stole quietly up the path. Thursday again— how wonderful. Thank the Lord for Thursdays. Everything in his life was perfect.

Elizabeth Drummond was a heavy-boned woman. She was tall and rather muscular, with powerful arms and thick ample thighs. She was not fat; her flesh was firm yet supple and her large round breasts still supported themselves quite nicely for her thirty-seven years. She was convinced that years of humping heavy boxes and sacks around her husband's shop had

43

kept her body in such good condition, but she was a little sad that a by-product had been to hunch her otherwise smooth contours into ever-so slightly protruding muscle, especially at her calves and arms. Still, whenever she examined her naked form in the full length mirror she was pleased with what she saw.

She sat now, gently rocking in front of the fire, an amused smile on her face as she waited for Sidney and imagining his gulping ardour and fumbling amateurism. These Thursday nights had become a tonic for her—a break in the never ending dullness that was steeped into every wall of the house. Each Thursday her husband Henry took his horse and cart and made the journey to Sunderland, to his brother's wholesale business. Each Thursday night he slept at his brother's. Each Friday he brought his groceries and other paraphernalia to the large shop they had bought from Percy Lovat when "Tommy Shops" were abolished. Each Friday his wife greeted him with a vibrance and keenness that slowly evaporated again during the next seven days.

She had often cursed herself for ever marrying Henry Drummond. He was a dour business man with little time for anything but his shop and his endless accounting. At night he would tuck himself into a corner of their living-room and for hours on end the only noise was the scratch of his quill pen and the dreary ticking of the grandfather clock. Elizabeth longed for excitement. Life was nothing like the girls at school had said it would be. They forever dreamed of dancing, and handsome soldiers sweeping them off their feet to some far off mysterious place where they would be waited on hand and foot and meet all the kings of the world. Perhaps some had achieved it. She thought she would herself. Even when Henry came along, he was young and dashing and full of absolutely exciting ideas of going to America or India and trading with the natives. But she was in Shirehill where nothing ever happened and nobody ever came who had been within a hundred miles of a royal personage.

She glanced up at the grandfather clock as the inside suddenly started to whirr in preparation for striking 10.30. Slowly she got up, smoothed her dress and checked the lock on the front door. The door was bolted firmly. She then went to the scullery and checked the back door. With a gentle up and

44

down movement she unbolted it. She climbed the stairs and entered the bedroom. Carefully she placed the flickering candle on the chest in front of the window and began to undress. She imagined Henry lying snoring and snorting in Sunderland and then she imagined that in a few minutes some dark handsome Captain would stealthily pad up the stairs. But she knew it would be Sidney—keen, eager Sidney. Sidney excited her, he was strong and rough and virile and for sixty or so glorious minutes she would be dominated and left recharged for another week.

She pulled the covers over her naked body and lay on her back.

Soon the back door opened and the noise of cautious foot-steps came up the stairs. Her chest rose and fell quickly and the pulse in her temple became noticeable. She bit her bottom lip. Perhaps, just perhaps, it would be a gallant soldier.

Sidney walked silently across the room and blew out the candle. He stood in the inky darkness and she could hear the rustle of discarded clothes. The covers lifted and his cold naked body touched hers. Her arm curled around his neck and pulled him to her. She didn't care about the coldness of him, in a few moments it would be warm.

"Mrs. Drummond," he whispered in a trembling voice as he buried his bearded face among her breasts.

"Mr. Garrett," she said with gentle pseudo-surprised purr.

The formality they used to each other was deliberate and lent an extra thrill to their surreptitious meetings. Carefully she wrapped her legs around his, then let his eager muscular body overpower her with a savagery she enjoyed.

He almost forgot the note from Martin Judd. It was in his jacket pocket and as he bent to pick up his trumpet case he remembered it. Elizabeth lay still and quiet, her forearm resting across her brow, the blankets tucked up around her neck and her eyes staring sightlessly toward the ceiling.

"I've an important note here Beth—it's from the Union. Will you read it to me and not tell a soul?" he whispered, reverting back to familiarity. A faint curiosity stirred in her. "Bring the candle and let me see," she said in a toneless voice.

She unfolded the crumpled paper. She read the first couple

45

of lines to herself then began again out loud.

"My Dear Mr. Simpson,

No doubt you have waited impatiently for my communication and for that I thank you. After the national conference at Glasgow where all the grievances were once again aired it was voted that no strike should take place in Northumberland and Durham. However, since then my colleague Mark Dent has written to the owners reminding them that the annual binding is nigh and asking that deputation from both factions should meet to discuss the terms of the bond. I wish to inform you that the owners have taken upon themselves to ignore this, as they did the first circular. It is obvious from the contempt these men have for their workers that the only course of action is to strike. I ask you to pass the word to your workmates at all the pits in Shirehill, Holywell, Backworth and Earsdon, and to request them not to enter into a new bond. Believe me, when I say that all the miners of Northumberland and Durham will be of the same mind. We will strike until the owners relent and I am relying on you and your workmate Sidney Garrett to keep the men in good cheer until the battle is won. May I remind you of your words, that any violence will be detrimental to our cause and I know you will do your utmost to promote this thought. The fifth of April is the day. You will be contacted again.

Martin Judd."

Once more Sid stuck out his chest with pride at having been named in the letter. "There now Beth," he said, "what do you think of that. The Union knows my name you know. I'm one of the officials during the strike," he added, exaggerating slightly.

Elizabeth nodded thoughtfully. "So it's to be a strike after all is it," she said flatly.

"It is that. We'll make Lovat pay for getting rich."

"What about us?"

"Who?"

"Henry and me. A strike means no work doesn't it—and no work means no pay. No pay and nobody buys food. What about us—we've got to live on nothing as well have we?" Her voice became louder and more irate.

Sid shushed her.

She felt anger, she felt despair. She saw Henry scratching

46

with his quill pen and bemoaning their fate. She saw numerous creditors hammering at their door and people begging at the counter. She disliked unpleasantness, she couldn't abide whining persuasiveness and she was revolted at the thoughts of these people in their stubborn hundreds perhaps causing them to suffer foreclosure. Shirehill was nothing to her, but debtors prison was worse.

"Get out Sidney," she shouted, "and don't come back until you go back to work."

Sid beat a hasty retreat. He grabbed the note, his trumpet case and was down the stairs in a flash. Funny woman he thought, always the same. Always find something to fall out with me for after she's had her oats. She'll be all right by next Thursday though. Of that he was positive. She always was.

After a quick glance around him Sid stole down the garden, through the gap in the privet hedge and was soon casually walking along the row towards Daniel's cottage. He recited the gist of the message over and over again and with a happy heart he knocked heavily on the door. He knew Daniel would be pleased that he knew the contents of the note. He knew that he would be pleased that at last the strike was underway. Yes he thought, Thursday—thank God for Thursdays.

CHAPTER 5

April usually meant peace of mind for Percy Widmore Lovat. With the winter behind him and the fullness of spring bringing calmer seas and favourable winds, April was the harbinger of a busy season of trading. His three ships plyed continuously between Newcastle and London, leaving the Tyne low and steady, with holds full of coal for the ever growing appetite of the Capital and returning with tea, fruit and vegetables. The warming weather meant less absenteeism at his mine and that meant greater output and that meant regular profitable journeys for his ships. Yes, usually April was a time when he would sit in the sumptious lounge of his great house at Tyne-mouth and watch the ships leave the river, their sails swollen in the wind, their decks alive with activity: Some bound for far off ports, others for London or Aberdeen or Hull.

It was a great occasion for Percy Lovat when one of his ships was about to enter or leave the river. If his four grand-children were in the vicinity he would gather them to his side; gleefully he would point it out to them, show it to them through the telescope and gloat and rant about it with an egotistical delight as though the ship, in being his, was a symbol of supreme power. His wife or their children would look and smile a smile of tolerant amusement. They knew him of old and were used to his excitable ways, but his grand-children were different; they were relatively new on the Earth and to them their imposing, overpowering important grand-father was the epitome of power and success. They watched with wide eyes and open mouths as he boasted of his posses-sions and with dramatic sweeps of his arms, told them over again how he had built his empire from virtually nothing. The truth was in fact that his father had left him a small but thriving warehousing business on the river edge at Newcastle and with a typical exaggerated sense of importance he set about expanding the field of activities with visions of greatness and an eventual knighthood.

He worked extremely hard, abounding in nervous energy. He slept only three or four hours a night and was constantly plotting, planning and making himself known to the businessmen of the city. His keenness and unstinting efforts did not go unnoticed and within five years he was the owner of a successful trading company. He had a giant sign mounted along the length of his warehouse broadcasting his name in enormous letters and was supremely overjoyed when he heard that some visiting dignitary on approaching the city from the south had asked if Percy Widmore Lovat was the city's new name.

Soon, instead of paying inflated prices for coal to export, he invested in some land and sunk himself a mine. It took a few years for him to break even, a few frightening years when a slump in trade reduced his net profit to a trickle, but eventually with almost frantic effort he managed to steer his companies on the road to success. He went from strength to strength. Labour was cheap and plentiful and other than the odd outrageous applications for more money or better conditions the profits kept climbing. He bought a large house on the green banks of the Tyne, near the sea and near the river and it was there, watching the ships go to and fro, he thought of his own fleet. Immediately he saw a dozen or more ships all with white sails and golden masts. He saw a pennant fluttering from each mast-head. A bright red pennant with a large white "L" superimposed. Yes! he would cut out the ship-owner's profit, he would have that for himself. He would buy his own ships. Why not? His credit at the bank was excellent. And so he bought the first of his ships, then another, then another and with growing peace of mind, he watched them from the window of his large sumptious lounge.

That particular April day however, Percy Widmore Lovat did not have peace of mind. He was a worried man. He had a problem and as was usual, when he was troubled, he sat staring vacantly out of the window, tapping his thin, tight lips with the forefinger of his right hand. Mark Jessop, the son of his cousin and manager of the Lovat pit, stood nervously fingering his cap and awaiting an answer.

Mark Jessop was a stout bow-legged man, thirty-nine years old and a bachelor. He had a round bloated face with a great walrus moustache bending down from his top lip, and his nose was enlarged and an angry red. He was in poor physical shape from being overweight and his great flabby belly hung sloth-fully over his wide leather belt. He had a chronic asthmatic condition that made him wheeze constantly and during a bad bout of asthma his face coloured to match his nose.

He was the son of Lovat's cousin, Caroline, and when her husband died of consumption when the boy was only two, Lovat had felt a strange attraction toward her. She had been improved with marriage and Lovat had taken it upon himself to impress her. He had the boy educated and promised his mother he would have a good trade. She had suddenly married again and moved south when Jessop was fifteen. Lovat had been furious. In his anger he had taken Jessop out of the office in Newcastle and for ten years had had him learn the ways of the pit during its development at Shirehill. Lovat received a weak satisfaction in writing to Caroline and informing her of his actions but there was no reply. Finally Jessop had been given the job of managing the Lovat pit and Lovat delighted in the way he had moulded himself on his benefactor.

Finally Lovat swung around in his chair and faced his visi-tor. His usually immaculate grey-blue hair was slightly askew and his usually bright alert eyes seemed clouded slightly. For the first time in his life he felt old. He continued to stare, still not speaking, still tapping his lips. Finally after a full minute he slowly raised himself to his feet and turned to the far wall of the lounge, where an assortment of guns were mounted at varying angles. There were rifles with long barrels and short thin stocks, neat compact pistols, big heavy pirate-type pistols. There was a shotgun and a blunderbuss, and they all gleamed down at him with a silent lethal foreboding. He stood looking at them for a moment, hands clasped behind his back, then he swung around and stared toward Jessop, the left-hand side of his mouth twitching involuntarily as it always did when he was angry and excited. Mentally he tried to stop it for he knew it revealed his true feelings and he did not want Jessop to know his true feelings. He wanted a devil-may-care attitude; after all, Jessop shouldn't see that a bunch of ignorant greedy miners could rattle him.

"So," he breathed out. "It is as we expected. They will not sign the bond."

He strode forward, hands still behind his back. "They have refused to work, but believe me Mark, it will not last—it cannot. They will have no money for food"—he gave a half-hearted laugh—"A hungry belly mellows the most resolute mind, eh Mark?"

Jessop nodded quickly, anxious to please, hoping his uncle, as he called him, would not think he was in any way to blame for the miners' action. "The whole of the two counties are out you know," he blurted, as if to take some of the seriousness from their own dilemma.

Lovat smiled weakly. "Give them a fortnight and the bastards'll come crawling back—begging to work." He laughed slowly through his nose, "You'll see my boy, I've dealt with these creatures before. They've got no damned sense, man—they live from hand to mouth—they've got to." He held out his hands—appealing fashion. "What would they do if we paid them more?—I'll tell you—they'd have more money for drink and tobacco—they'd play more of that infernal game—pitch and toss or whatever they call it. You see Mark they're not like us. We save, we, we invest, we think of the future, we try and better ourselves. I mean look at . . ."

Jessop cut him short. "Their pay's one point but it's the conditions they work in as well. It would cost thousands to make them happy. They've been shouting about another shaft for years now. The gas is bad in places but hell, another shaft just to pump air down!"

Lovat's eyebrows shot up. He smirked. "Just what I was saying—they're ignorant. They think I can just go and lay my hands on money and just for their benefit, sink another shaft."

Jessop sighed. "I hope you're right uncle—about the hungry bellies I mean. There's something about them. I don't know how to describe it, but you can see it in their faces. I think they mean what they say."

Lovat turned and slammed his fist hard on the desk top. "Dammit man," he shouted and then quickly controlled himself. He walked over to Jessop and put his hands on his shoulders; his mouth twitched and he silently cursed it. "It's your

51

imagination son, remember, I've seen it all before—they'll be back, don't worry." He nodded condescendingly. "Look—tell you what I'll do. Get back to Shirehill and tell the men there's to be a meeting at the pit-head on—let me see—how about Saturday—yes, Saturday morning at say, eleven—then I can take Sarah straight to Newcastle for the shops. Tell them to turn out, each one of them—tell them Mr. Lovat wants to speak and has something important to say."

He smiled broadly, pleased that he had turned Jessop's misgivings to his own advantage; he wanted an excuse to talk to the miners, to try and make them return to work—for his sake, but he hoped with a little of his skill at talking they would think it was for their own sakes.

Jessop nodded. "All right Uncle, if anyone can get them back you can." He turned at the door. "I'd bring a few bodyguards—just in case." Lovat frowned and tapped his lips. "Good idea —just in case. See Aunt Sarah before you go—and don't worry lad—they're like sheep, they'll be guided in the right direction."

Jessop turned again to leave.

"Oh Mark, what was the name of the men who are the leaders?"

"Daniel Simpson and his mate Sid Garrett."

"How do you know?"

"Henry Drummond says that his wife overheard it mentioned in the shop."

Lovat nodded grimly. "Point them out to me on Saturday would you?" The door closed and Lovat gave a long forlorn sigh. The pretence had exhausted him, he felt numb and cold. His mouth began twitching again. Deep down in his stomach there was the gnawing fear that he could share with no one. The strike could only last about two weeks. It mustn't last longer. In two weeks his reserves of coal would be gone. His ships would have nothing to carry to London. The cost of trading would soar. There would be harbour fees for his immobile ships; there were bills—big bills awaiting the rich summer profits before being paid and there was the instalments at the bank. He still owed three thousand pounds on his ships. In two weeks he would have to draw on his reserves; in two weeks his empire would begin to shake. He had built his castle without adequate foundations. The strike had to finish in two weeks!! He slumped down in his chair and faced the window overlooking the river. It was a bright day with clouds billowing from the north-west. Seagulls hung in the wind then swooped or soared to a different position. The river mouth was blue and choppy and its movement seemed to lull him, calm him, pacify him. He nodded off to sleep. Sarah, his wife, crept up and with a smile, placed a blanket around him. She patted the top of his head very gently. My poor Percy, she thought, he's getting old—but still as handsome as ever. Percy did not wake, but his body gave a great shuddering jump before settling down to breathing that was almost imperceptible.

On the Saturday the men of Shirehill, primed by Daniel and Sid, gathered around the pit-head and waited for the rare appearance of Lovat himself. At five to eleven Jessop paced nervously up and down glancing at his pocket watch every twenty seconds or so. He wondered how the men would react when they saw him. They seemed in a good enough humour at the moment but perhaps they had something planned for when Lovat arrived. He wished he would hurry and get his speech-making over with then get away to Newcastle.

Daniel and Sid were at the front of the crowd of about 150 men and boys. It was unusual to see them all gathered clean and dressed in what decent clothes they had. Some of the womenfolk were there to see and hear from the man who provided them with a living and all in all they stood patiently waiting in groups or singly to hear what they already knew he would say.

Jessop had left his uncle's house and travelled straight back to Shirehill, that day. He had gone direct to Daniel's cottage and found him and Sid squatting at the door.

"Well, I've got the pair of you together." he said, his chest straining for air.

"So what?" Daniel sneered.

"I've got a message from Percy Lovat himself. He asks that you pass the word to the miners. He wants a meeting at the pit-head on Saturday at eleven."

"Tell him to piss off," shouted Sid.

Jessop's lips thinned. "Watch it Garrett. There's still such a thing as civility."

"Then why doesn't that bastard use some and give us what we deserve," Daniel growled.

"You'll get all you deserve—you two—be sure of that. Now I've given you the message, if you think anything of your mates you'll tell them."

"Why us?" Sid asked before spitting clear across the lane.

Jessop smirked. "I know you two are the ringleaders. You don't fool me."

Daniel's face broke into a wide grin. "Is that a black mark against us Mr. Jessop."

"It could be if you don't go back to work."

They both laughed loud and long. Jessop turned and walked quickly back up the lane, a faint whoop coming from his throat as he angrily fought for breath.

A carriage pulled by two gleaming black horses and guarded at each corner by a hefty horseman, rounded the pit heap and drew up in a cloud of coal dust beside the winding house. The crowd gasped at the richness of the carriage and the finery of the man and woman sitting there. Slowly, with rehearsed dignity Percy Widmore Lovat rose to address the gawking faces. Jessop dashed across and stood, smiling bravely beside him. Lovat bent down and he and Jessop whispered for a moment before Lovat surveyed the crowd and noted the faces of Daniel and Sid. He cleared his throat, glanced reassuringly at his wife who smiled demurely at him, then at the crowd. He held up his hands for silence but it already was silent. He put them awkwardly to his side before nervously fingering his signet ring.

"My friends, I have made the journey here today to speak to you about this ridiculous strike."

He opened his mouth for the next sentence, but he shut it again abruptly as the crowd broke into a chorus of boos and jeers. The horses started a nervous stamping and the four mounted bodyguards had to rein their steeds. Lovat blew angrily through his nostrils. The fresh glow disappeared from his cheeks. He hadn't bargained for such antagonism so soon, but he persevered.

"Listen!—Listen to me! I speak on your behalf. I have your own interests at heart. Forget this strike—go back to work and feed your women and children. Forget the rubbish that is pumped into your heads by this Union. Unions are evil my friends, they can do you naught but harm."

Lovat waited patiently until the jeering died down, but Daniel's voice rose as the others faded.

"What about your own Union Mr. Lovat. Haven't you coal owners formed your own Union to protect your interests?"

Lovat stared at Daniel and felt his mouth beginning to twitch. They were better informed than he thought, these miners. They were more aware of developments than he imagined. He thought quickly. "Our Union was formed to make sure you pit-men get a standard wage. None of you can get less at one pit than at another."

"And no bugger can get any more either," shouted Sid.

"Here!—Now here," said Jessop, moving forward a pace. "There's a lady present."

"She's no lady—she's a fat old cow," came from somewhere in the crowd. Lovat turned white with rage. His mouth twitched violently. "You damned fools," he screamed, "think of your families—think of your starving children."

Daniel turned and beckoned into the crowd. A man approached carrying a boy who clung shyly to his neck. The crowd went silent as he gently stood his feet on to the ground and supported him under the arm-pits. The boy was about nine, and stood staring blankly at the carriage. His stomach was swollen badly, his head was broad and enlarged and his soft flabby legs buckled at an almost impossible angle. Lovat winced. Sarah turned away.

"Yes, turn away my fine lady," shouted Daniel. "Turn your head and your heart from this boy. Don't think about it, because this lad was fed as much as his father could afford with your wages. He has rickets from malnutrition."

"Is that his father," roared Lovat.

"It is."

"Do you drink man, or smoke, or gamble?"

The man shook his head. "I'm a chapel man sir. Anybody'll vouch for that."

Lovat sagged, he was getting nowhere. "Then it must have been an act of God," he whispered.

"Do you want to see more Lovat. Do you want to see an old man of twenty-five, gassed so badly he'll never work again," shouted Daniel. "Your pit is no good and your wages are no good and we'll strike until you and your kind give in."

A tremendous cheer rent the air. Lovat stared hopelessly at his wife. When the cheering faded he held up his hand. "All right, you will not listen to reason. I have come here today to try to help you, but you will not listen. You must bear the consequences. Jessop—draw the horses from the pit. These men do not want to work. Let them starve."

The crowd booed and jeered as the carriage was turned around. A rotten egg flew through the air and hit Lovat square on the temple. Another hit his wife's hat. Lovat turned from white to purple. "You'll pay the lot of you—you'll damn well pay!"

The carriage gathered speed and turned out of sight at the pit heap. Jessop stood dumbfounded, hoping and praying that his uncle did not mean what he had said. He had convinced him only three days before that the strike would end in a fortnight, surely he didn't mean to bring out the galloways just for a paltry few more days. He decided there and then to visit Tynemouth again that night and see what his uncle had to say after he had calmed down.

"Is it right Mr. Jessop. Does this mean that he intends us to starve?" Jessop turned, Alfie Mennem stood, shoulders hunched, chin stuck forward wringing his hands nervously.

He looked into the shifty darting eyes. "It's right Alfie Mennem. You've cooked your own goose now, the lot on ye."

Alfie's face twisted. "God, we'll all starve, and me with three lassies and four strappin' sons. What's to be done?"

Jessop weighed up the genuineness of Alfie's ploy. "Do I take it you're not agreeable to strike."

"I don't want to, but I've got to. I'm worried sick about what's to happen to us."

Jessop walked away. There was a curious smile on his face. His mind worked overtime. Yes he would definitely go to Tynemouth that evening. It was as important for him to survive the strike as the miners themselves; after all hadn't his uncle promised him a nice legacy if he showed himself as a good viewer and kept the productivity up.

Lovat and his wife did not go to Newcastle, that day. They

returned home as quickly as possible to wash the stinking mess from their skin and clothes. Lovat was silent for the whole of the journey, and his wife sat, head bowed, sniffing the eau-de-cologne from her handkerchief and whimpering every few minutes. After they had washed and changed Lovat took his usual seat at the lounge window and sat staring blankly out over the river. He tried to think straight but could not, he had a hollow feeling of despair in his stomach and his mouth twitched irritably. He tried to think what he could do to make the men return. Had his threat of drawing out the horses made them realize he meant business? Were they bluffing? It was as Jessop had said. There was no half-hearted barracking. They seemed more determined than ever. Suddenly, anger mixed with despair welled up inside him. What was he to do? What was to happen to his business, his status in the community, his family who regarded him so highly? He let out a shuddering sigh and his six-foot frame seemed to crumple under the weight of his problems. Slowly he raised himself out of his seat and called for the maid. He ordered a large brandy and a bowl of warm water and soap. He looked down at his trembling fingers. They felt dirty even after his earlier wash. They felt clammy and sticky with the rotten eggs of Shirehill. When the maid brought the brandy he downed it in one gulp. When she brought the soap and water he washed his hands slowly and deliberately, a glazed triumphant look in his eyes. The soap and water radiated an intangible comfort through him.

When Jessop arrived that evening Lovat was in a much better frame of mind. "Yes, yes, my boy—draw out the horses —give the pigs a fright, but that will only be the beginning. I've sent messages to Hobbs, Walker, Foggett—the lot; all the mine-owners in the area."

He walked back and forth across the room in quick succession, staring wildly at the carpet and occasionally flinging out an arm for greater emphasis. "I've a job for you lad. We're going to teach these creatures a lesson they'll never forget. They'll think twice—no three times before they strike again. Pack your bags Mark, you're going on a journey."

"Where to Uncle?"

Lovat stopped in his tracks. "I'm not sure yet. We'd better wait until we hear from the others."

Jessop frowned then shrugged his shoulders. Lovat walked

over and slumped down in his chair.

"By the way Uncle, there's someone who I think will help us at Shirehill." Lovat spun around, eyebrows lifted. "Oh, and who is that?" he asked sarcastically.

"It's a miner, name of Alfie Mennem."

CHAPTER 6

It was warm for April and that was a good thing for the miners. Coldness sharpened the appetite, by making demands on the body to restore the energy expended in keeping warm. Coldness also reflected despair and uselessness and foreboding. But this April in 1844 was unusually warm and the miners after being on strike almost three weeks were still in high spirits and confident that they would defeat their masters. It was a busy time for Daniel and Sid. It was almost as exhausting as being at work. After their meeting with Lovat their days were spent travelling around the pits in the area, calling on the miners, laughing and joking with them, recounting the tale of Lovat's visit and generally trying to keep them all convinced that success was only a matter of time. Both of the men enjoyed their new task; to Sid it satisfied his craving for importance and he felt good explaining that he was a chosen Union official inspecting the striking men. To Daniel it did something else: seeing so many people united in one cause, and seeing them all suffering the same hardships and doubts and fears made him realize in a way that he was not the singular outcast he had always thought he was. It did his ego good and instead of only coming out of his shell to discuss Union matters, he found himself talking to them about more mundane things, such as how were they off for food and tea and had they any special hardships, where they might be able to help. The task however, was bound to become harder as time went by. The small store of food that they had all saved was disappearing or going bad in the warm weather. The few coppers they had managed to put by in case of an accident or a death was dwindling and the wives and mothers first began to feel the effort of putting on a brave face.

It was three weeks to the day and Daniel and Sid were returning to Shirehill from Earsdon. They were walking along a path lined with high bushes that spread the evening sun in a mottled red pattern against their sides. It was bright and their forward movement caused a flashing scarlet light in the corner of Daniel's eye which annoyed him. He turned toward the cause of the trouble and through the maze of budding branches he could see the headgear of the Lovat pit. He stopped sharply. Sid almost tripped over him.

"What's up Dan?" he asked trying to shade his eyes and follow his gaze.

"The pit—look at the wheel—its turning," he said flatly.

"So it is. Somebody's using the shaft!"

"Come on, let's see what the buggers are up to." Before Daniel had finished his sentence he had parted the bushes and ploughed through. Sid followed and they ran as swiftly as possible across Johnson's freshly seeded field.

Before they reached the pit they could hear the cracking of whips and loud annoyed shouts of:

"Howay, howay, ye little bastards—get a move on."

They walked now, slowly and deliberately toward the pit-head and to where Jessop and a couple of strangers were guiding the galloways into the cage.

"What's this then Jessop," Daniel shouted. "Puttin' the horses back eh? You expecting us at work tomorrow?"

Jessop stopped and looked startled for a moment. Quickly he composed himself. "You're trespassing you two—this is Lovat land—now eff off sharpish.'

Sidney moved forward uttering a curse under his breath, but Daniel pulled him back.

"Take no notice Sid—remember, no violence. We'd be playing straight into their hands."

Daniel turned and Sid followed. They walked slowly toward the village. Sid was angry and highly agitated. "But what can it mean Dan—why put the horses down for nowt?"

Daniel shook his head. "I'm not sure, but we'll be back tomorrow to keep an eye on Mr. Jessop and company."

"Do you think they've got blacklegs?"

Daniel was becoming angry now, mainly because he couldn't think of an explanation. He took it out on Sid. "Shut up for hell's sake Sid. I'm not a bloody mindreader. We'll just have to wait and bloody well see," he shouted.

Sid shut up and they walked the rest of the way in silence, each with a heavy heart and a wondering befuddled mind.

Daniel didn't sleep that night, he tried but could not, so he sat quietly in front of the dying fire listening to the dogs howl and the occasional girlish giggle coming from the lane. His mind raced and a dozen possibilities came to him why Jessop should be putting back the horses. He wondered if he should report to Martin Judd. He wondered if the strike had been called off and the news had been delayed. The baby began crying but he ignored it. Dorothy got up and took it to bed with her. It became silent again. Outside, the lane had settled down and the stillness of early morning took over. Perhaps Daniel had fallen asleep, he didn't know, but slowly, ever so slowly, away in the distance he heard a noise that became louder. When he became aware of it, the faint greyness of dawn was playing on the curtain. At first he couldn't place the noise. It was something like the distant roar of the sea that could be heard at Shirehill on a calm night, but then again it was different; he could hear voices, singing voices, now overpowering the other noise. Gradually the noises became more distinct. He sat up in the chair. Dorothy woke up and asked what they were. Daniel ignored her. There was a sudden banging on the door and a commotion in the lane. People's voices rang out in all directions. Daniel threw open the door. It was Sid.

"They're marching Daniel—marching to the pit."

"Who are?" Daniel asked.

"Men—hundreds of them with soldiers to guard them, and they're carrying picks and shovels!"

Daniel grabbed his coat and ran down the lane. He could see the thin line of men now spread out along the narrow path at the edge of Johnson's farm. The leaders were already turning at the end of the pit heap and the tail-enders were just entering the pathway.

"Jesus," Daniel whispered, "hundreds of them!" He turned to see Sid and about twenty of their workmates following him.

"Come on lads," he screamed, "they're not going to ruin our strike—let's get them."

"What can we do against that many—and soldiers?" Somebody asked.

Daniel looked wildly about him. Suddenly he calmed down. "That bastard Lovat and his soddin' relation Jessop," he growled. "Come on men let's see what these blacklegs have got to say."

They reached the pit-head where the strangers totalling about ninety in all, stood about in groups.

Daniel cupped his hands to his mouth. "Men, tell me what you want at this pit?"

The men looked at each other, puzzled at the question. "Why do you ask?" came the counter question, in a strange accent.

"Because this is the pit we work at, but we are on strike for more money and better conditions."

There was a murmur among them.

"We did not know that there was a strike called. We have come from Wales because we were told that there was a dire shortage of labour."

"Lies, all lies," Daniel screamed. "The masters have deceived you. Did you not wonder why there are soldiers here to protect you?"

"Yes, but we were told that the local people do not like miners. They think of them as scum and vagabonds."

"It's all lies men, we are miners—we live in the village there. Please I beg of you don't work for Lovat he's trying to break the strike."

The Welshmen formed a circle and muttered to each other in their own tongue. Finally their spokesman said, "What are we to do? We have no money to go home, Mr. Lovat paid our fares here."

"How much did he promise to pay you?"

"Fifteen shillings a week."

There was a peal of laughter from the Shirehill miners.

"He's a blackguard is Lovat. The most anybody earns at this pit is eleven shillings," shouted Daniel.

The Welshmen talked among each other again, then the man shouted. "If we get our fares we will return home."

A great cheer went up from the locals. Jessop almost wept. He knew it was useless to argue. Dejectedly he wandered home and saddled up his horse for the trip to Tynemouth.

Daniel was overjoyed. "Wait here men, within an hour you shall have your money."

The two leaders shook hands and Daniel and his followers returned to the village. They went around each cottage asking, begging coaxing for every penny that could be spared and at the reckoning they had almost sixteen pounds.

"God that's a lot of money," Sid whispered reverently.

"There's a lot of them Sid," Daniel said sadly, "let's hope it's enough."

They made their way back to the pit, where the Welsh miners sat around or lay in the sun, waiting. Daniel found their spokesman.

"Well, here you are," he said thrusting forward a cloth bag, "there's fifteen pounds nineteen shillings and twopence farthing, more money than I've seen at one go in all my life. Will it be enough?"

The Welshman took the bag and weighed it mentally in his hand. He stood for a moment as though wondering what to do then finally said, "It'll do."

Another cheer went up from the locals and the Welshmen began to pick themselves up and start off down the path toward the pit heap.

"You've done us a great service—you brothers in toil. We won't forget you," Daniel shouted after them as they marched off on to the main road at the far end of the village.

"Whoopee," Sid shouted. "We did it Dan—we beat old Lovat at his own game."

There was a great deal of back slapping and laughter and merriment in the village, that went on into the early hours of the following morning, but for Daniel and Sid it did not; they knew they had a long day ahead of them. They had to walk to Newcastle and find Martin Judd.

True to the rest of the month the next day was fine and warm. Daniel and Sid left at 5 a.m. and began their trip to Newcastle. Sid silently wished that Daniel would get to like horses because he knew the journey could be quicker and easier if they picked up that mount at Killingworth; but he also knew it was useless trying to persuade him. He didn't like horses, horses didn't like him, as he always said, and he had a scar on his side to prove it. So, happy at the events of the day before, Sid fell into step with Daniel and they set out on their task to find Martin Judd.

When Shirehill woke itself fully it was like any other day. The village was more crowded than usual with the striking men and boys standing around or playing football up the lanes. The women stood at their doors and chatted to their neighbours or filled their poss-tubs and possed a few clothes in the back lane while they shouted the latest gossip to each other. The men were becoming bored at being inactive for so long. They began to get under their wives' feet and inevitably there were more domestic rows than was usual; but still their spirits were high and the warm weather tended to make them forget their ever growing hardships.

It was about 10 a.m. when it started and the news spread through the lanes like wildfire. Jessop with a band of thirty policemen and as many swarthy looking roughnecks began the job of evicting the miners and their families. They started at Bella Finch's cottage. George Finch her husband stood bravely barring the door.

"Will you get back to work?" shouted Jessop.

"No!"

Jessop nodded and the policemen prised George Finch from the door. Two of them held him while his wife led their two young children across the lane. The children screamed. Bella sobbed into her apron. A colliery cart was backed up to the door and their possessions roughly thrown into it. Bed, clothes, ornaments from the mantelpiece; kettle, pots, pans, the clippy mat from the hearth. Everything that was theirs was cleared from the house and trundled away from the lane and dumped. Bella screamed hysterically and her children joined her. Soon the commotion brought out all the miners of the village. There were angry scenes of shaking fists and oaths and curses but the men, well schooled by Daniel and Sid took no direct action. They knew immediately that this was Lovat's retaliation for his beating the day before. They knew he wanted them to start a violent reprisal which would do more harm to them than good. So they took it. They took whatever Lovat had in mind. Lovat had in mind evicting them all. One by one the police knocked at each door. No one would work. Everyone was evicted. Cissy Heslop, ninety-three years old and bed-ridden for the last ten years, was carried out into the street by two of her sons while the bed that was her sanctuary was tipped on to the cart. The boy with rickets, Daniel's wife with a month-old baby, Hetty Charlton swinging at her unwanted guests with a poss-stick, were all dragged out into the street. Dogs barked, babies cried and men shouted obscenities but it was no good. No one was spared. Lizzie Chapman started her labour pains an hour before they got to her cottage. Her water broke as she stood watching the bright new cot her husband had made cartwheeling down the lane as it fell from the cart and broke into pieces. The baby lived for three hours in the make-shift open-air room made out of blankets hung between bits of furniture.

Alfie Mennem hesitated then said, "No," to their request and like the rest he suffered the same fate. His wife was down on her knees sobbing into the ground with her daughters beside her. One of the roughnecks pushed her out of the doorway with his foot. George her eldest son could stand it no longer; he surged forward and kicked the hefty man with all his might, between the legs. The man's eyes almost popped from his head. He let out an agonized bellow and sunk to his knees, holding his crotch with both hands. George was quickly bundled to the back of the crowd before anyone noticed. A policeman eventually saw the man lying there and walked quickly toward his prone figure.

"What happened here?" he barked.

"He tripped and fell over the step," someone shouted.

The policeman seemed to believe it. He whistled for help and they carried the man away amid jeering and laughing from the crowd.

It took all day to evict the whole village. By five o'clock it was completed. Everyone was turned out into the street and all their belongings were scattered like some long drawn out junk pile on the roads running alongside the lanes. When Jessop and his party had finished, threats to his life came from everyone he passed, but he took no notice. He knew his uncle would be pleased that his orders had been carried out satisfactorily and he knew the miners after a few days under the stars would submit and come crawling back to work. But it would do them good; they had to be taught a lesson and that was just what they were going to get. They wouldn't get their jobs back, not for a time anyway, and when they did, they would hang on to them as though their lives depended on it.

When the shouting and crying had died down, there was a sort of anti-climax to the whole event. An air of peace and tranquillity descended on the village as people numbly hunted for what was theirs. Occasionally there was a peal of hysterical laughter and women stood helping the very young and the very old while their husbands gathered their possessions together. Daniel and Sid made their way home as quickly as possible. They had found Martin Judd and told him the events of the previous day. He was delighted but warned them that the same was happening all over the two counties. He also told them of the evictions to enable the owners to house their blackleg labour and of how the miners were showing no violence. Already the other trade unions were supporting the miners in their struggle. Each day their cause was becoming more widely known and better supported. Now Daniel and Sid hurried home, convinced that there would be no evictions at Shirehill because of the Welshmen's decision to go home, and anxious to tell their mates of the latest developments.

Their shock was indescribable. It was one thing talking about evictions and another seeing the misery and degradation it actually brings. Sid let out a shuddering moan and set about looking for Martha and his children and his few loved belongings. Daniel walked silently among them, listening to their whispered talk and whimpering cries for help. He was sickened. He thought of Lovat standing there in his fine carriage with his fine clothes. He imagined Lovat and Jessop laughing at their success and toasting each other. He hated them both. Gradually he picked his way through the maze of furniture and clothing and found Dorothy. Already she had formed an enclosure with the chest of drawers on one side and the wardrobe on the other. She had placed the bed at right angles to the drawers and hung coats and blankets around to give some privacy. The cot was beside the bed and she had made a canopy over the lot with the two largest blankets held in position on the drawers with the fire irons and on the wardrobe with an axe and a heavy poss-stick.

"When did it happen?" he whispered.

Dorothy fought back the tears. "S'morning' about 10 it started."

Daniel nodded and looked around. "Lovat's done this because of yesterday, but he won't gain a thing. Any violence?"

She shook her head. "Not that I saw."

"Good. Did they leave anybody?"

She shook her head again. "Everybody's out on the street." Her voice began to falter and she started to cry.

Daniel sighed and sat himself on the edge of the bed. "We've got troubles Doss, big troubles, the men'll get sick of this, soon as hell."

The next day he had more troubles. The Welshmen returned, having spent the miners' money in Newcastle and having been offered sixteen shillings a week by Percy Widmore Lovat.

It was a joyous day for Lovat when Jessop reported the mine back in production. He clapped his hands with glee and slapped Jessop heartily on the back. The world suddenly seemed brighter to him, as though he had been in constant twilight for the past weeks. The strike had lasted longer than the two expected weeks and he had suffered a set-back when the Welshmen were bought off, but now they were back, they were housed in the Shirehill cottages, the mine was working again and he was making money. Not profit, he kept reminding himself angrily, but money enough to pay the overheads and pay some of his bills. He had rashly promised the Welshmen sixteen shillings a week and he paled when he thought of how stupid he had been in his anger to offer them so much. They would have probably travelled north for twelve, he thought, and then accepted thirteen not to go home, still by the time their efforts were "laid out" for being small or having stones and the inaccurate weighing machine weighed out much less than was being hewed, it would probably reduce the overall

67

price to twelve. It was still a highly unsatisfactory state of affairs. The pit was not producing its old output and some of the imported labour worked until a pay day then got drunk for a week afterwards. Sooner we get the locals back to work the better, he thought. I'll bet they're rueing the day they tangled with Percy Widmore Lovat. Suddenly he remembered the other reason for Jessop's visit. "Have you brought him?" he asked. Jessop nodded his head toward the door. "He's outside. Shall I bring him in?"

"Yes, let's have a look at him."

Jessop opened the door and Alfie Mennem shuffled in, his nervous shifty eyes blinking at the richness of the room. It was like a palace to him. He had dreamed of fine places but never had his imagination stretched to luxury such as this.

Lovat nodded grimly at him. He despised him immediately, even though he would be another tool in his campaign. He was a spineless cur who hadn't the courage to stand with his friends and suffer if they suffered. Jessop smirked as Alfie whipped off his cap and almost bowed in front of his uncle.

"Well now Mennem, Jessop here says you don't agree with the strike?"

Alfie smiled painfully and his Adams Apple shot up then down in his scrawny neck. "No sir," he whispered.

"Why?" Lovat's voice boomed across the room.

"I—that is, we don't want to starve," he whispered looking at the floor, "and the missus is expecting."

Lovat couldn't abide him. "Give him three shillings a week and tell him to get among the men and persuade them to go back—now get him out of my sight"

Jessop took his arm and guided him out of the door. Lovat felt suddenly nauseated at the whole wretched business. His stomach turned. He broke into a sweat. His hands felt clammy and sticky and filthy. Quickly he rang for the maid and ordered some soap and water.

The strike dragged on into May, then into June. It was an exceptional year for weather; the sun shone almost every day and the low rainfall kept the miners relatively comfortable. But the heat brought swarms of flies to the open ditch that the evicted families were using as a toilet and the stench became almost unbearable. Food and money were things of the past. Trips had been made to Newcastle with small family valuables but the pawnshop dealers, knowing the desperation of the owners, paid them in coppers for what was worth pounds. Some of the less proud tried begging, first at Drummonds then at other outlying shops, but they got nothing; perhaps some sympathy but no food. They existed on the occasional fish from the sea at Seaton or a snared rabbit or a turnip filched from Johnson's field where it had been left from the previous year for the sheep to nibble at. A pigeon sometimes filled a few bellies and a hedgehog baked in clay was a delicacy. Someone suggested butchering one of Johnson's sheep but Daniel stopped them. "You'll hang for it you silly bugger,' he had said.

Sid was doubly upset. He could see his children thinning. He noticed their bulging haunted eyes and their stomachs swelling. Henry Drummond, because of lack of business saw no reason to visit Sunderland which meant Sid had no chance to visit his wife and that left him more depressed than ever. But he tried to keep cheerful remembering his official job and he and Daniel kept up their rounds at the various pits and found conditions much the same everywhere as in their own village. There were bands of soldiers encamped near each mine, the ones at Shirehill being billeted at Johnson's farm. Their duties were boring however, because other than a few jeers and boos the miners allowed the Welshmen to go to and from the pit unmolested. In return they kept well away from the villagers and spent most of their spare time drinking and gambling.

The people of Shirehill were determined to keep cheerful and win the battle against their masters. No one gave a thought to ending the strike, or if they did they kept it to themselves. No one that is except Alfie Mennem. He wailed and moaned most of each day and half into the night, saying that they were all fools and should be back at work; but nobody listened; Alfie was Alfie.

Cissy Heslop died on a Friday night. She had been in her bed quietly resting after a meagre dinner of soup made from pigeon bones with a few bits of turnip and potato peelings added, when a rat had jumped up on to the bed. She opened her eyes to see the rat's face an inch from her nose. Her old heart just gave up. She died without making a sound. One of her sons had seen the rat gnawing at the blanket where she had spilled some soup. They called for Hetty Charlton and she came, fussing and complaining, but with a look of amused flattery on her face. She did her job expertly. She consoled the relatives, then stripped and washed the old woman, tutting loudly at her bony, wrinkled frame, then she tore up strips of cloth for the job of plugging the orifices of her withered body.

"Where's the layin' oot gear?" she shouted through the curtain of mats and coats.

"It's in the bottom drawer," whispered a voice with a faltering sob.

Hetty opened the drawer. She held up the plain white smock that had been washed and folded for so many years, ready for its singular occasion. "Lovely—lovely," she crowed. "Ooh she'll look beautiful in this."

Finally with a loud cackle she pulled back the curtain. "Ye's can come in now—she's lovely, she's just asleep—pretty as a picture."

She smiled and nodded with satisfaction as the mourners squashed into the small enclosure and her long eyetooth was given a full airing. She made her way slowly back along the edge of the camp. She felt good. She had done a good job but she felt weak and weary in her soul. Her own thin wiry body ached constantly and she felt cold even during the day. She sighed and thought about Cissy; another lifetime acquaintance gone, she thought, not many left. Poor Cissy—at least in the midst of all the troubles she's well prepared to meet her maker.

She pulled open the blanket that bounded her own little quarters. Billy, her son was sitting on a stool, his elbows on his thighs and his head in his hands.

"What's up wi'ye son?" she asked.

"Nowt—just fed up."

"Aren't we all, ye silly bugger but we've got to mek the best on't."

She gave a wild throaty cackle. "Cissy Heslop's gettin' away —ah've just laid her oot."

Billy nodded sadly. He got up and sighed. "She might be lucky."

Hetty grabbed a broom and shook it above her head. "Don't you ever let me hear ye say that, ye big sod or I'll crown ye. There's nobody in this hoose weakenin'—d'ye hear?"

Billy smiled, "All right, ma, anything you say."

He pulled back the curtain then chucked his ancient mother under the chin before he wandered off to meet some of the other men. It was dark now and the stars shone out of a clear sky. Hetty sighed and started to undress for bed. She muttered irritably as she pulled her long nightdress over her head and cursed her own weakness at the effort it took. She looked up through a crack in the sacking that served as a roof. Another clear night, she thought. Lovely—no soakings tonight either. She opened the gap in the sacking wider and struggled into the bed. It was nice lying watching the stars. They seemed so close and brilliant and for a fleeting instant her tired cloudy mind felt the vastness of the Universe. Her bright eyes watched as a star seemingly fell from the sky. Suddenly she felt glad she had had her life. The simplicity of it, the parochial limitations of it, the hardships and struggles, the rewards of her family and helping her friends. She had felt the richness and fulfilment of being needed. The sky looked beautiful to her. She saw some beauty in everything. The sky was black and studded with light. She snuggled down in the bed as a shiver went up her spine. The bed felt damp and she was cold again. God has been good, she thought as her eyes flickered shut.

She never opened them again.

CHAPTER 7

Sid knew he was taking a chance but he couldn't help himself. It was over two months since he had seen Elizabeth and he wanted to see her again; just to see how she was and get an assurance that after the strike and things had settled back to normal they could return to their usual Thursday meetings. For the first time since the troubles began he felt a warm sense of excited anticipation as he walked casually along the dusty rutted road toward Drummond's shop. He had had a bellyful of their make-shift village with its reeking atmosphere and the drab depression of crying children. He had sickened himself of acting hale and hearty to the other miners and he was sickened by the unending misery that exuded from every village in the area. The air was heavy with it, the faces, lean and haunted were twisted with it. Sid was weakening in spirit as well as body. He cursed Elizabeth's bewildered looking husband who had greedily accepted their hard-earned money, yet now they were on the point of starvation, would still not give them so much as a penny's worth of credit. He cursed him for that and for not going to Sunderland. Fondly and sensuously he remembered the nights he had crept up the path to their house; the tingle of delight when he softly pressed the latch and the door opened; the almost delirious thrill of climbing the stairs to find her silently waiting for him. But that was years ago and now he was thin, weak and old.

Henry Drummond was still trading—the Welshmen used his shop for a few things, but business was nothing like it used to be. He had resolutely refused the miners credit and in a way he was glad that Lovat had warned him of the consequences if he did. He loathed credit and hated the idea of debt. It ruined his book-keeping and it worried him that he might not be paid. He preferred everything cut and dried and exact, even if it meant suffering himself until the strike finished. So in an aggravated sort of way, he contented himself.

Sid wondered who he would see first. Perhaps Drummond would be there. In that case he decided to try a begging act— that, he concluded would arouse no suspicions in him. It must happen twenty times a day. He wondered if Elizabeth would know he was just acting and that he had only come to see her, or would she feel repulsion at his cringing cry for pity.

Cautiously, with a feeling of guilt, he pushed open the door. The bell rang out, somewhat incongruously to its surrounding, like a trumpet in a church, and the heavenly smell of smoked bacon mixed with nutmeg and tea and new sackcloth invaded his nostrils. His mouth flooded with saliva and his hands trembled. His dull sunken eyes were filled with the brightness of new kettles hanging in clusters from the beams, tin baths and basins lying against the walls, clean cream broom-shanks, shining picks and lamps and bunches of tallow candles and sacks of beans and peas and flour. It was almost too much for him. He felt his remaining strength drain through his boots and his knees buckle. Then he saw her. As the ringing bell became silent the dark brown door that led to some mysterious back room opened and Elizabeth appeared. He made to speak but no sound came. She looked warily at him for a second then the recognition came with a quick hand-to-mouth movement. She looked good to him. A little sombre perhaps; a sort of rejection to her mouth, but still tall and strong with her white unblemished face and her rich black hair parted in the middle and combed back into a roll. Her lips were red and alive and her dark eyes flashed in the dimness of the shop. In an instant she regained her composure. She gave two quick upward nods of her head, indicating that her husband was in the back room, then moved along the counter toward him. She stopped when she was level with him and the eighteen inches of counter separated them. Sid could smell the divinity of Lily-of-the-Valley and after the appalling stench of the village, her perfume almost made him faint.

"Mr. Garrett," she breathed, "what has happened to you— you look so ill?"

The sound of her voice made him ache for her; and she

was playing their intimate little game of formality.

"Mrs. Drummond," he croaked, "I had to see you—it's been more than eight weeks."

Her eyes closed and her hands groped over the counter and touched his for a second before she withdrew them. "Oh, Mr. Garrett, it's been so long. These weeks have been terrible," she whispered, "when will it end?"

Sid swallowed and shook his head. "I don't know. I hope it's soon, but we'll never give in."

"Make it soon, make it soon," she pleaded.

There was a noise from the back room. The door opened and Henry Drummond appeared, dressed in a dark brown apron, his hair plastered down with Bay Rum and his eyes squinting painfully through his little round glasses. "Who is it dear?" he asked cautiously. Elizabeth raised her voice.

"It's a miner Henry—begging again. Trying to get food without paying. I've just told him to begone."

Drummond nodded quickly. A pained look crossed his face. "Get out!—yes, get out. You'll get nothing here. I keep telling the lot of you—you'll get nothing here. Get back to your work and earn some money and you'll get some food—now get out!"

Sid couldn't help an amused smile. He backed toward the door.

"Surely Mr Drummond, surely sir. Just trying me luck. I can't wait to get back to work—believe me sir."

Drummond looked pleased. He smiled at his wife.

"They're sickening, eh Bess? That what's his name—Alfie Mennem, and now this one. It's catching."

He gave a triumphant sort of laugh.

"The sooner you're at work the sooner we'll all feel better. Pity you weren't all like Mennem and put a few shillings aside for a rainy day. He's got money to spend. He's a wise man. He's not starving—Salted away a few coppers every pay day instead of drinking it all. He's not starving."

Sid's brow furrowed, but he forced an unconcerned look to his face immediately after.

"Is he still buying food?"

"'Course he is. Now you get out and earn some money yourself and you can have the pick of the shop."

Sid's stomach turned as suspicion about Alfie Mennem

flooded his mind, but as he opened the door and the bell clanged again, Drummond's remark about the pick of the shop riveted his eyes on Elizabeth and the faint amused turn of her mouth spoke volumes. She lowered her eyes slowly as he closed the door and he offered a silent prayer that it wouldn't be many days before he could immerse himself into the intimacy of her again.

He was troubled as he made his way back toward the village. The more he thought about it, the more obvious it became. Alfie and his family hadn't waned like the rest of them. They had remained relatively strong and healthy looking. But how? he thought. Surely Alfie couldn't have saved money enough to carry him through all these weeks. He was the same as the rest of them, and with seven children to feed, by rights he should have been one of the first to be penniless. Suddenly the thought ran through him that only two days before, Alfie was shouting out his fears that one of his daughters was near death from starvation, but no one took any serious notice of him. Then he started his bleating persuasive cant about returning to work before the Welshmen brought women to the village and really settled down.

Sid's suspicion became an almost certain conviction and when he reached the encampment he was angry—very angry.

He stalked determinedly toward a large group of villagers who were gathered around in a circle. He recognized the voice from the middle of the human enclosure and pushed his way through searching at the same time for Daniel.

Henry Gilpin, the Methodist Minister was in the middle of an impromptu sermon. He was a tall imposing figure with white flowing hair and a long white beard and had his arms stretched and his chin raised toward Heaven as he shouted hoarsley to the silent congregation, while his eyes were kept tightly shut to give the impression of divine guidance. The saliva at the corners of his mouth was whipped to a white cream from the action of his lips and his face was red and sweating from his exertion. He had entranced himself and the threats and promises and guidance came unhesitatingly from his tongue.

"Hear me brothers and sisters. To work is to live the good life. The Lord in his love has provided you with work and shelter and children. If you flaunt his goodness and turn against your masters it will be a sin in the eyes of the Lord. You will enter the gates of Heaven only to be flung into the eternal fires of Hell, there to cavort for ever more with the evil wrongdoers of creation. Return to work brothers—cleanse your souls now and return to your honest and holy occupations for just as you are toilers in the Earth so was Jesus a toiler among men and all honest work is Holy in the sight of the Lord."

One or two lay preachers from the surrounding area were in attendance and shouted pious "Amens" at regular intervals as did some of the listening crowd but Henry Gilpin knew he was wasting his time. He had toured the area for weeks, spewing forth every fearful threat of Hell he could imagine or promising eternal reward but the miners had ignored him. Still, he soldiered on convinced that if anyone deserved a place in Heaven, he did.

Sid searched the sea of faces for Daniel but he wasn't to be seen. Then he caught sight of Alfie Mennem's sickly features nodding furiously in agreement with the Minister. Sid smiled grimly. He nudged the man standing next to him. "You seen Dan Simpson?"

The man shook his head.

"Has anybody seen Dan Simpson?" he screamed, drowning out the preaching voice.

Henry Gilpin stopped his sermon and blinked himself back to reality.

"Has anybody seen Dan Simpson?" he shouted again.

"He went fishing at Seaton," somebody murmured.

Sid turned and pushed his way through the crowd as the Minister regained his composure and pointed Sid out as a disciple of the devil and that all who listened to him were as bad. Sid ignored him and with blood boiling, set out for Seaton to find Daniel and inform him of his suspicions.

The loose sacking that served as a door to the Mennem camp was pulled roughly to one side as the large form of Daniel entered and stood with wild staring eyes piercing the twilight and into the startled faces of the Mennem family. Alfie's camp was bigger than most. He had three beds for a start. One for the boys, one for the three girls and the other for himself and

76

his wife. His two youngest sons aged four and three were already in bed. The three girls were sitting on their bed, playing with dolls and the two eldest boys Tom aged fourteen and George, sixteen almost, squatted opposite each other with their right arms held behind their backs and attempting to push each other over with their left. Mary Mennem sat on a stool folding some of the girls' clothes. They all stared silently at Daniel's penetrating eyes, sensing that his visit brought trouble or bad news.

"Where is he?" Daniel snapped.

"Who?" Mary asked.

"Come on, come on, you know every bugger's business—where's Alfie your own husband?"

Mary looked at her two eldest sons.

"What's the matter Mr. Simpson?" George asked standing up. He was normally a quiet, mannerly boy, broad and muscular for his age and with a little of his mother's plumpness. Since his action during the evictions, which had surprised even himself, he had been treated like a hero by some of the villagers. He had suddenly grown up and now he felt he was able to protect or speak for the family.

"Where's Alfie," Daniel repeated, emphasizing the words, "and that's a strenuous game you two are playing—where's all the energy coming from. Your Ma must feed you good."

Mary Mennem guessed immediately. Her podgy hands went to her eyes and she cried. George and Tom and all three girls ran to her. George turned angrily. "What are you saying Mr. Simpson—Why is Ma crying?"

"She knows why son and so do you, I'll bet my britches. Now come on, where's the money coming from to keep you all better fed than anyone else—all bloody nine of you. How has he done it?"

"It's savings—he saved it," George shouted as his mother sobbed louder.

"What's it go to do wi' you anyway."

Daniel took a step forward and Sid followed him into the enclosure.

"You're a lying set of buggers," Daniel roared. "He's in the pay of Lovat—isn't he?"

"You're mad," George screamed. "He saved the money—it's his life savings—isn't it Ma?"

Mary Mennem moaned and sobbed into her apron.

"Why has he kept it such a good secret—why hasn't he come out and told someone?" Sid asked.

George looked wildly at the two inquisitors. "Because—because he said if anyone knew, they'd pinch it—that's why."

"Where's your father now?" Daniel asked again.

George looked bewilderedly around him. The two small boys woke up and began to cry and the three girls clung timidly to their mother.

"He went out," George mumbled, "he said he was going for a walk. Usually does at nights."

Daniel nodded solemnly. Then his lip curled into a snarl and he beckoned with his finger. "Come with me son and we'll find out just what he's about."

George followed them numbly, glancing at his mother with a puzzled look. Daniel and Sid walked slowly and silently along the path that by-passed the pit and led to the house of Mark Jessop.

Jessop stood with his back to the fireplace, his hands clasped behind his back, gently rocking to and fro, attempting to emulate his sophisticated uncle. His asthma was bad that night and it took a severe physical effort to force air into his lungs, but he was determined to act aloof and superior, and other than the loud rasping of his breathing, there was silence as Alfie Mennem gave his nightly report. He told him about the visit of the minister and the reaction of the crowd, but that did little to cheer Jessop, nor did the rest of Mennem's tales. All he could say was that they were surviving, their spirits appeared to be good and there seemed no sign of a desire to return to work. He mentioned that two of the miners had caught a pheasant in some ingenious trap on the land of Lord Delaval and Jessop made a note of their names, then he trailed off into silence.

"Is that all," Jessop barked.

Mennem nodded quickly, and nervously fingered his cap. Jessop sighed deeply. It seemed that there was to be no end to the strike. The miners were not weakening; in fact support for their cause was growing stronger. It was he who seemed to be suffering the most. The Welshmen were an unruly lot. They realized their importance to Lovat and were constantly complaining and arguing about weights and payment and conditions in the pit. They groused about the water. They said they weren't used to working in so much water and three of their mates had a fever from it.

So Jessop's life had become one of constant argument, persuasion and bickering. He wished for nothing more than for things to return to normal, even if it meant succumbing to the outrageous demands of the locals. Outwardly of course, he endorsed every scathing comment his uncle made. Far be it for him to disagree openly with his uncle. Wearily he waved Mennem out, but Mennem stood still with a watery smile on his face and his Adams Apple jumping involuntarily.

"Well what is it?" Jessop wheezed irritably.

"It's Friday."

Jessop's lips thinned and he nodded. He walked over to his bureau and took three shillings from the drawer. He looked hard at Mennem's bright eyes and nervous twitching fingers. "Here!" he shouted, and threw the money down on to the stone floor. The coins jingled and rolled.

Mennem pounced quickly and gathered them up. "Thank you Mr. Jessop sir," he whispered, still on his knees. "I'll keep up the persuasion. I'll do more of it. I promise."

Jessop waved him out again. "Go on—get out," he snarled turning to face the fire, "and keep your eye on those two bastards Simpson and Garrett. I want to know every time they even go for a piss—understood."

Mennem nodded eagerly and let himself out. He peered cautiously through the darkness and sighed with relief when he saw that the gibbous moon was behind a cloud. He worried himself into a frantic state each night in case someone should see him come or go, so he usually approached Jessop's house from the side farthest from the village which meant describing an arc through the fields rather than take the direct path which skirted the pit.

Tonight he felt lazy. The moon looked as though it would be covered by cloud for hours. It was dark, pitch dark. He felt safe and he felt happy with three bright shillings in his pocket. He decided to take the direct route home.

"Evening Alfie, been visiting I see?"

The words came softly but lethally through the darkness.

Alfie let out an agonized yell and made to run, but his arms were immediately grabbed in Daniel's great hands and at the same time Sid pressed his hands from behind, over Alfie's mouth. George, well warned by them, stood back and waited with sickening foreboding for his father's explanation.

"Scream again and I'll break your effin neck—understood?" Sid whispered in Alfie's ear.

There was a pause then a quick nod and Sid relaxed his hold.

"Who is it—Who's got me?" Alfie whimpered through the darkness.

"You'll never guess," Daniel growled.

"It's you Dan, isn't it?—I recognize your voice. You and Sid Garrett—what do you want with me?"

"I want to know what you've been doing at soddin' Jessop's house—that's what I want," Daniel growled, squeezing Mennem's bony arms harder.

He let out a cry of pain. "Nothing—honest—I—I just went to see if the Welshies were going to stay for good."

"You're a lying bastard," Sid spat vehemently. "What's that janglin' in your pocket?"

He pushed his hand into Mennem's coat pocket and withdrew the coins.

"Money!" he breathed fingering them in the palm of his hand. "Shillings I'll bet. You effin Judas!"

George could stand it no longer. He felt a mixture of hate and pity and sorrow boiling up inside him. "Dad, Dad," he sobbed, "what have you done. Eeeh! Dad what have you done?"

Mennem let out a bleating cry as he recognized George's voice. Daniel eased his grip and he slid into a heap on the ground.

"It was Jessop," he wailed. "Jessop and Lovat, they made me do it—they threatened me. They said if I didn't try and persuade you all to go back, I wouldn't get set on after the strike," he lied, "and me with four sons and three lasses and another on the way."

"You stinking lousy bastard," Sid hissed, standing over the crumpled form as he flung the coins far into the night. He spat down hard and loud before Daniel took hold of his arm. There was a silence that spoke more than any words. Slowly Daniel turned away, guiding Sid with him. They walked back toward the village, leaving Mennem sobbing on the ground with his son kneeling beside him. They knew their fate. The villagers would scorn them. They would be "tin-panned" every time they appeared on the street. The children would sling mud at them. They were social outcasts and would be for a long, long time.

George felt shame and degradation as the tears burned his cheeks. He pulled his father from the ground and steered him toward their camp. He felt hate for his father for what he had done, and for the scorn and ridicule he would bring on the whole family, but he felt a far stronger hate for Jessop. It made his fingers twitch and his stomach twist itself as he thought of the evictions, with Jessop arrogantly supervising them with an obvious enjoyment. And now this, Jessop again, taking advantage of his scrawny weak-willed father, who worried himself frantic about anything under the sun. Who took a delight in gossiping and telling tales but who was his father and a father whom he painfully loved. The vision of Jessop's heaving chest and bloated face burned savagely into George's brain that night.

The next day was Saturday and the fortnightly payday for the miners. Lovat had drawn one hundred and fifteen pounds, seven shillings the day before and Jessop had collected it from him in the evening. Lovat had felt a sudden urge not to hand over the money. A wild idea had flashed through his mind that the Welshmen need not be paid—they could wait another week or two—but he dismissed it almost immediately as wishful thinking. But still as Jessop had left, he had felt a strange sensation run through him, as though he were being robbed and he had to fight off the urge to follow Jessop and recover his money.

Now as he rode home in his carriage from his office in Newcastle he sat nervously squirming in the seat, a feeling of panic flooding through him as he looked over the Tyne to the crowded town of South Shields. The distance seemed to take his breath away and he gasped for air. By sheer will power he took hold of himself and convinced his mind that lack of sleep and worry over the strike were getting the better of him. He took a deep jerking breath and settled back in the seat. Suddenly the nagging fear returned as he realized that the two bills that he was fingering in his pocket would see him in the red at the bank. Furiously he calculated and imagined the manager's reaction to his situation during the inevitable meeting on the Monday. He tried to convince himself that all would be well and the bank would understand and await the end of the strike. As soon as he was back in full production all the bills would be paid and the overdraught and the loan.

The carriage pulled up outside his door and he sat for a while before dreamily alighting. He mumbled to the driver to stable the horses and instead of ringing the bell, he walked around the side of the house to where the garden wall ended and the grassy slope toward the river began. It was low tide and he could see the rhythmic swaying seaweed among the rocks below and smell its peculiar salty odour. Away to the left the ruins of the priory stood proudly and persistently against weather and time and over the river, again the crowded town of South Shields, huddled against the east wind and shrunk with the distance. Suddenly he shrank. He felt himself like a blade of grass beneath his feet, with the great world of distance overpowering him. He felt a dizziness and nausea and an overwhelming fear. Quickly he turned and staggered towards the house.

He felt better after he had washed his hands. The warmth of the water and the creaminess of the soap were the ultimate in purification. He looked at his wrinkled, pink fingertips and smiled wanly. He turned his hands over and examined his nails, then over again and gave his palms a minute inspection. He could feel himself calming down as though a gale that had been blowing around his head had abated to a gentle breeze. He sat in his chair and looked out over the river again. It was fine. Just like he usually saw it. Thank God, he thought.

There was a knock at the door and Ellie the maid gave a polite curtsy.

"Mr. Jessop sir," she said then took the bowl of water and bustled out.

Jessop walked right up to the window and stared down at his uncle, his face twisted in a frightened grimace and his mouth gulping air noisily into his lungs.

"What is it?" Lovat asked quickly a worried frown creasing his brow.

"The miners—the Welshmen—they've packed up," he wheezed, putting an arm against the wall for support.

There was no movement from Lovat except that his eyes grew bigger and then seemed to cloud. Slowly he lowered his head and held it between his hands. There was silence other than the muffled whooping of Jessop's chest.

Finally Lovat raised his head. "What happened—where have they gone?" he whispered.

"They took their bloody pay and said they'd had enough. They say the water's too bad and they say they're not getting near the sixteen shillings you promised them. We're weighing light and there's too many coal being laid out."

"Where are they now?"

"I left them packin' their bits and pieces. They'll be away now."

"Get them back!" Lovat screamed. "Get them all back! Promise them anything. Promise them the Earth!" He felt a wild anger burn inside him. How dare they walk out like that. How had they the nerve to scorn his generous gift of honest labour. "Where's all the water coming from anyway? It's in the High Main isn't it. Well, where's it all coming from?"

Jessop shrugged his shoulders. "Don't know. It's always been there. There's porous rock above the High Main. It's always swimmin' with water—but it's been worse lately. Mebbe it's running down from the gut at Seaton. We're getting near the sea you know."

Lovat ran his fingers wearily through his hair. "You surveyed that seam, Mark, what's it like?"

"It runs up—but slowly. I reckon we've ten fathoms of rock above us at the face."

Lovat stood up quickly and grabbed Jessop's lapels. "Then get the pumps working properly—get them pumping water out of that damned pit and get the men back," he croaked hoarsely.

Jessop was afraid. He had never seen his uncle so agitated. "It's no use Uncle," he whispered, "the pumps are working flat out—and the Welshies won't come back—I've begged all flamin' morning. They're sick. They're going home."

Lovat's eyes went wide and wild again. "Then get some more, d'you hear—get some of the Irishmen or the Cornishmen from the other pits—offer them anything."

Jessop shook his head. "We can't manage it Uncle. There's hardly enough in the whole area to run two pits properly. They're all frittin' off home, not changing pits—you know that."

Lovat sank down in his chair. "Get out Mark—get back to Shirehill. I want everyone of those cottages boarded up d'you hear? There's not one Shirehill miner'll get back till the strike's over—D'you hear?" he roared. Jessop nodded quickly and fled.

Lovat swallowed hard and wrung his hands together. He could see his world crumbling about him. He felt desperation chase a strange desire to laugh around in his brain. He rang for the maid. "Ellie," he shouted, "Ellie come quick. Ellie," he pleaded, as her tiny mouselike face appeared around the door. "Soap and water—quickly."

The normal peace and quiet of Sunday was non-existent in Shirehill. Jessop had hurriedly rounded up a dozen or more men, and guarded by the soldiers, they banged and clattered and hammered to the accompaniment of hoots and jeers and laughing by the villagers. The news that the Welshmen had left had sparked off dancing in the streets. One or two fiddles that had been silent of late, scraped out lively jigs. Suddenly in the face of despondency they saw success. As they fought against the idea of inevitable failure, the smell of victory blew strong and hard over their tattered encampment. They didn't really mind about their homes being boarded up. It could only be a matter of time before Lovat and those like him would acknowledge defeat and they would be reinstated in their own private cottages with more pay and better working conditions and a great victory to recount to their grandchildren.

Daniel and Sid had stood watching as Jessop organized his men. They followed him around the lanes, gloating each time he angrily looked towards them and nodding and pointing with mock ridicule as they watched his face become redder and angrier. There was also someone else who watched him intently. It was George Mennem.

Jessop had left the men to their work during the afternoon and with a deep foreboding and reluctance had drawn the galloways, out of the pit. Once again he had initiated the closing of the mine and this time he had the hollow feeling that it might be a long time before it reopened.

It was almost midnight before the horses were stabled and all the equipment secured. Jessop had sent the under-manager and his two hired hands home an hour before and he was making a final check of the pit-head before he made for home himself. He cursed the fact that the boiler would have to be continuously fed to keep up enough steam for the pumps to draw the water from the sump at the bottom of the shaft. Nevertheless, he pottered around, holding his lamp up to the doors of the stores and out-buildings to make sure the locks were fast and bolts were in position. It was a still night and the only sound was a gentle hiss from the boiler and dull slow clatter as the pumps did their job. It felt strange to Jessop standing there in the darkness surrounded by the higgledy-piggledy of a pit-head. There was a peculiar finality in the silence. Usually the place was a hive of activity with men and boys and horses pushing or pulling waggons or tubs, and the winding engine clanking its cage up and down the shaft; shouts and yells of orders and the braying reluctance of horses with the curses of their chargers as they whipped them into action. But in the darkness, accompanied by Jessop's intimate faithful wheeze and a pitiful hint of mechanical sound, the pit was at rest and hushed.

Finally, with a weary look up the stout lattice work to the winding wheel, he turned and set off for home content that the pit was safe at least until the morning. He took only three or four steps before the big wooden pinch bar used to lever the wheels of the big waggons into motion along the tracks, came swinging out of the darkness and caught him squarely across the chest. He gave a loud agonized groan and keeled over backward as the precious air was knocked from his body and his lamp rolled from his hands and went out. Before he could realize what had happened there was a body lying on top of his and hands, warm and clammy gripped him at the throat. Jessop panicked. He strained at the hands and at the same time stared through the darkness at his assailant. He could see the form but it was impossible to make out any features. With an adrenalin effort he managed to prise the fingers from his throat and gulp at the life-giving air. As soon as the hands broke free he lunged upward with a clenched right fist toward the obscure face above him. It found its target and the face, followed by the body, fell to the side of him. Gasping air into his burning lungs, he struggled quickly to his feet, but his attacker was quicker. By the time he was up and balanced, a fist smashed into the bridge of his nose and stars burst in his head. He staggered back, with blood gushing down his throat and down from his nostrils into his mouth. He gave a roar of almost insane rage and lunged forward, but a fist buried itself into his soft flabby stomach and he dropped on to his knees, almost screaming air into his lungs between great gushing bouts of vomiting. His attacker stood over him and finally spoke.

"That's you settled Mr. Jessop. That's us about evens."

"Who is it?" Jessop coughed out.

"If you don't know I'm not tellin'."

"Y've a young voice, I'll remember the voice, ye bastard," he gasped, in little more than a whisper.

"Please yourself. You can do your worst Mr. Jessop. It was worth it. I hate your lousy pox-ridden guts."

Suddenly Jessop lunged at the legs in front of him and the body fell backward. With a gleeful cry he stood up and peered down at the still figure, hatred and anger boiling inside him. It was a bad mistake. A studded boot caught him in the solar plexus and Jessop staggered back one pace, then another, then his arms shot out sideways and described great circles of air. His blood-curdling echoing scream seemed to last for hours before it died away into nothing as he went headfirst and backward down the shaft, turning over and over, bouncing off the side, then off the dividing brattice on his long journey to the sump, where the pumps slowly sucked at the water in their absolute darkness.

George Mennem burst into tears when it happened. Then with a furtive look around him, slunk back into the village, afraid, but strangely elated.

CHAPTER 8

There were gasps of amazement from some of the villagers and mutterings of "good riddance" from others when they heard that the under-manager, assisted by some of the soldiers still encamped at Johnson's farm had fished Jessop's swollen white body out of the sump of the Lovat pit. It had taken only three hours of the following morning, of searching and wondering before one of the soldiers spotted the dried blood and vomit mixed with the coal dust and mud around the shaft. On closer examination it became obvious that a struggle had taken place and it was only a matter of lowering the cage before John Bewick the under-manager caught sight of Jessop's body in the dim light of his lamp. He was floating face upward, his eyes wide open, his limbs snapped and twisted and the agony, of violent death locked on his face. Soon the word "murder" spread like lightning through the village and the people of Shirehill huddled into little groups furtively exchanging rumours that ranged from the unlikely to the ridiculous. Some-one had heard that he had the shape of a crucifix burned into his forehead. Another, that his heart had been cut out and could not be found. Two people who should have been spread-ing the rumours and enjoying every minute of it had not been seen that morning. Alfie and Mary Mennem sat within the bounds of their camp with their children beside them and terror rising in their throats each time footsteps or a voice was heard in their vicinity. George had crept home the night before, making sure he was not seen and determined to act as though nothing had happened. He had slunk into his bed but his muffled sobs that he could not control had wakened his mother. With her first soft enquiring words, George had blurted out the story. Alfie froze in horror. He asked a thousand questions, repeating himself over and over again. He broke out into a cold sweat. He had been worried about all sorts of things in the past, but never like this. Panic and wild ideas ran through his mind, yet he knew that short of fleeing there was nothing to be done. He was now an outcast among the people who were once friends and neighbours—no one would help. No one would speak. He would be ignored except for shouts of derision. In fact if someone found out, they might even report George just out of spite.

When the morning crept up on their tired faces, it was plainly visible that George had been fighting. Jessop's blow had caught him on the mouth and his lip was puffed and discoloured and the knuckles of his right hand were skinned and swollen.

Suddenly a voice called out their name and they held their breath.

"Mennem are you in there? Your mate's been murdered, d'you hear? Some bugger killed your marra—where's your money coming from now?"

There was a loud laugh of ridicule and the faceless voice moved on.

Daniel was angry when he heard the news. He felt no sorrow for the man. He had never treated them like human beings and had never registered any human emotions to them other than anger, so now it was impossible for him to feel any sense of loss other than that his sour bloated face would be missed. Still, he was angry because if indeed it was murder and if it was one of the striking miners who was the murderer, then it could only mean that reports of Jessop's violent end would weaken the growing support for their cause. It was something he had dreaded all during the strike, and now after so many weeks of tolerance and self-control, violence in its worst form had come to Shirehill, of all places. At first Sid was all for going to the pit and getting first-hand news but realized the wisdom of keeping clear after Daniel had told him that everyone in the village would be suspect. So they listened to the rumours and the tales and impatiently waited for developments.

88

The Mennems heard the excited cry with a quiet resigned foreboding.

"They're looking for someone that's been fighting. They say there was a hell of a scrap up there and Jessop got pushed down the effin' shaft."

Alfie looked sadly into the deep quiet eyes of his eldest son, pride welling up inside him and over-powering the nagging, withering fear for a moment. George's lip stood out, black and blue and so swollen that he could not close his mouth. He knew that it would only be a matter of hours before they searched each little camp and finally dragged his son away to hang.

Mary Mennem fought back the urge to cuddle him to her. For the first time she could feel the child in her womb twitch and make its presence felt; but it was an unknown, unseen and as yet unloved. Characterless, faceless, and Mary Mennem would have gladly traded its life for the life of her eldest.

Before they could move, Daniel pulled the sacking to one side and stood among them, his piercing blue eyes radiating amusement. "Y've heard about your mate then Mennem— what have you to say about that. Why aren't you away to tell Lovat and cry on his shoul . . ."

His voice trailed away as he caught sight of George's face.

"Jesus Christ," he whispered. "George Mennem—was it you?"

George bowed his head and nodded. His mother put her arm around his shoulders and lifted her red eyes to Daniel's. "He's only fifteen," she sobbed. "He's only fifteen."

Alfie sagged. "The boy did it for me," he whispered.

Daniel rubbed a hand over the blond stubble on his head. "You stupid young sod. Why did you kill him?" he hissed. "They're hunting the village now. You'll hang for this."

"I didn't mean to kill him Mr. Simpson," George said in his steady confident voice. "I just went to belt him for everything he's done to us and, when we wrestled, I kicked him. He went backward into the shaft. It was worth it Mr. Simpson, for what he's done to us, it was worth it."

Suddenly Daniel snapped his fingers and beckoned urgently to George.

"Take heed of this Alfie. I'm doing this for the good name of the miners and the Union and not for you. You're still a liar, a cheat and a soddin' Judas—remember that. All of you remember that!"

He took George's arm, then beckoned to Tom, his brother. He ushered them to the far end of the enclosure where there was a little more room. "Now," he whispered. "George, hit Tom squarely in the eye with that right fist of yours."

George and Tom looked incredulously at each other.

"Are you mad?" Alfie croaked.

"George—hit Tom in the eye if you don't want to swing," Daniel commanded.

George hesitated, then lashed out, trusting in Daniel's over-powering confidence. Tom reeled backward with a cry of pain, and George's face twisted painfully as he nursed his swollen hand under his opposite arm-pit.

Daniel and Alfie rushed to help Tom. It took a full five minutes to take the dazed look from his face while his mother wailed fussed about him like a mother hen. His face began to puff up around his left eye and Daniel nodded, satisfied that the result would be black and the eye would close.

"Now son," he whispered to Tom. "You want to save your brother's life—don't you?"

Tom nodded, lost as to the reasoning behind the actions but sure of his own feelings.

"Good lad, you've been brave—braver than a lot I know and you've got to be brave again. I want you to punch the side of that chest of drawers with your fist—Hard mind. It'll hurt, but you've got to skin those knuckles good."

Tom squared up to the chest. He was like his eldest brother, broad and muscular and with a quiet resolute manner. He let fly with his fist as hard as he possibly could and it banged against the solid wood. His eyes closed and his mouth opened in a silent scream. Daniel examined his hand. It would do. He then looked at each of them in turn, his ice-blue eyes boring into their souls. "Now," he breathed, "never a word of what's happened here to anyone, or we'll all hang. You were never out last night George, nor you Tom—understand. You had a friendly brotherly scrap yesterday—the pair of you—is that clear. That's the story you'll tell them and if they don't believe you, you've had it—so make them believe you—d'you hear. Now pull yourselves together and for God's sake try and act normally."

Alfie took hold of Daniel's arm. There were grateful tears in his eyes.

"Thanks Dan. Thanks for your help."

Daniel pulled his arm away and his face twisted savagely. "Piss off Alfie. Don't go gettin' any fond ideas. I told you before. It's for the miners who've gone wantin' all these weeks, not for a sod like you."

He pulled back the sacking and strode away.

It was the next day before the Mennems were interviewed. The two boys were questioned longer than most but their explanation seemed a natural one when their ages were known. When the authorities had questioned the whole village and determined that no one had fled, shoulders were shrugged and they departed, assuming that Jessop must have owed one of the Welshmen money, perhaps, and he had crept back seeking revenge. He had pushed Jessop down the shaft and vanished away into the night.

When they were sure they were safe, the Mennems got down on their knees and prayed. Daniel Simpson's name was in each of their silent offerings.

When Percy Lovat heard the news from John Bewick, his mouth began to twitch and he blinked furiously before looking blankly out of the bay window and across the river. Finally, he turned to face Bewick with the little finger of his right hand stuck in the corner of his twitching mouth.

"Mark? Dead?" he said in a quiet singing voice.

Bewick nodded. "He was accosted sir and flung down the shaft."

Lovat shook his head and tutted loudly, his little finger still stuck, baby-like in his mouth. "Who was it?" he asked, "was it one of the miners?"

"They don't know who it was sir, they're still investigating."

Lovat jumped up out of his chair and paced across the floor, his hands clasping firmly behind his back and his shoulders bent forward. He stopped at the wall of gleaming guns and looked up at them, his eyes wide and shining, before turning swiftly to face Bewick. "I promote you Bewick. You are the new viewer of Lovat pit. Come here and be invested." Bewick frowned and walked forward.

Lovat strode quickly to the fireplace and took one of a pair of crossed rapiers from its mount.

"Here Bewick!" he shouted. "Come and be invested."

Bewick shuffled toward him, an embarrassed look crossing his face.

"Eeeh Mr. Lovat sir, there's no need to do anything special."

Lovat ignored him. "Down on one knee, Bewick, while I dub thee viewer of Lovat pit—It's a great honour you know."

Bewick's face broke into a watery blushing smile and he knelt down.

Lovat's voice was triumphant as he tapped Bewick's shoulders. "Arise viewer of Lovat pit," he shouted.

Bewick stood up and glanced nervously toward the door.

"Now John Bewick, now you are viewer of my pit you must use these to keep order," he whispered, pointing to the array of guns.

Bewick made to leave. "I won't need those sir—soon as the strike's over the men'll be like lambs. We won't need guns and what-not."

Lovat stared at him. His words seemed to echo in his head and the echoes of Bewick's former statements reverberated back. Suddenly a wave of sorrow ran through him and he felt tears well up behind his eyes. "My God," he gasped. "Mark, my boy, my viewer. Sarah!" he yelled, striding up to the door and opening it. "Sarah—Mark's dead—The lad's dead."

He leant against the wall and buried his eyes in the crook of his arm and sobbed. When Sarah came he could not rest until he had washed his hands.

After the excitement aroused by Jessop's death, the villagers of Shirehill returned to their silent struggle for justice. The weeks seemed long and were frustratingly negative. Soon July came and passed by without any change, but suddenly at the beginning of August it was rumoured that the miners of Durham had capitulated and returned to work. Counter rumours followed quickly and soon the villages were in a state of confusion. Daniel and Sid were mobbed everywhere they went with desperate cries for truth and reasurance that all the strikers were still united against their masters. With flagging confidence they tried to convince them that the Union was as strong and determined as ever to hold on to the advantage they had accumulated over the weeks. Finally, after waiting in vain for some firm news from Martin Judd, they set off for Newcastle to search him out again. Martin Judd was frantically busy. It was true the Durham miners were returning, but the Union leaders were organizing a meeting on the Town Moor for August 13th. It would show the miners of both counties that the Union was still strong and united and the strike in Northumberland, at least would continue. The meeting was held but only a thousand or so turned up. Gone were the brass bands and the cheers and the banners. The smiles of confidence had evaporated. Hunger had defeated them. It had weakened their spirit and whittled away their determination. All that was left was a handful of the most hardy. Daniel and Sid were among them.

The leaders of the Union then began to tour the collieries in the district. They passed a resolution that "seeing the present state of things, and being compelled to retreat from the field through the over-bearing and cruelty of our employers, the suffering and misery of our families and the treachery of those who have been their tools during the strike, we at the present time deem it advisable to make the best terms we can with our employers"

And so the strike drew to its close and with heavy saddened hearts the miners of Shirehill, along with their thousands of comrades, looked toward a future that would be in no way any different from their thankless, pitiful past.

It was a day thrown straight out of winter on that Monday morning in August. The rain lashed down and the wind blew hard from the north. The caked cracked surface of the summer roads and lanes became a squelching morass of brown clinging mud that weighed down the feet and added lead to the hearts of the queuing miners. They had left their tattered sodden camps that Monday morning and shuffled sadly along the familiar path toward the Lovat pit. They stood silently waiting their turn to put their mark on a piece of paper that would bind them by law to work for Percy Widmore Lovat, for the same wage and under the same conditions as before the strike.

They were defeated men, sullen and brooding, angry but weary and resigned now to their fate. Most of them felt some consolation in the fact that they could at last return to their cottages and have the relative comfort of a roof over their heads and a dry bed and food enough to smother the hunger pangs.

John Bewick was a different man to Mark Jessop. He had been a miner since he was six and knew and understood the moods and likes and dislikes of his fellow miners. His heart went out to them that day as they queued in the rain but he could not, with his new elevated position show them any favours. He was the viewer of Lovat pit and Lovat would take note of his handling of the men as well as the mine. He had to be a good viewer. He had to treat the miners hard and uncompromisingly. But still he felt for them as they, each in turn, appeared at the little open window of the viewer's office and scrawled a shaky cross on the document before them. As each one came into view they glanced up at him with wide unemotional eyes before taking the quill pen and lowering their heads. The rain dripped off the peaks of their caps and ran with the ink, but it didn't matter, the mark was made. They were employed again; they had somewhere to live again.

They all came back. Billy Charlton, his back as strong as ever. Alfie Mennem, with an apologetic smile on his face. His two eldest sons, George and Tom—silent and positive.

Harry Bilston, his one remaining arm only good enough for picking stones out of the coal, but he earned enough to eat and live a sort of life with his wife. Ernie Cowell, almost seventy years old, weary and worn out and all alone. He signed knowing the workhouse was the only alternative—or to continue living in the open. Harry Skinner, a mongol—almost twenty, smiling happily from his tiny watery eyes and making a glad sucking noise with his lips signed with his father Joe. Harry chased dogs and kicked them during his off hours; while he was at work no one could control the galloways better. They were all there, all the men of the village; all except the senile and the very young.

"Right! away back to your house," Bewick said to each after they had signed, and off they went to gather their soaked possessions, their families, and prise the boards from across their doors. For Daniel and Sid, the walk back to Lovat pit was humiliating. After all their efforts to convince their fellow

94

workers that they could not lose; that all their suffering and hardship would be rewarded, they found themselves shuffling along with the queue, waiting to sign a bond that gave them nothing new or improved. Daniel seethed inwardly. Even the prospect of returning to his cottage did nothing to weaken the anger that boiled inside him. They had fought and lost; he could not accept that. He had never allowed the possibility to enter his head. And yet he knew it was a fact and he hated everyone and everything that had defeated them. So now he waited. The pit was his life and he was compelled to accept defeat whether he liked it or not.

To Sid, the prospect of returning to work was mellowed with visions of the comfort of his little cottage and Martha fussing around him. Perhaps when he got some food into him, Robert, his son might improve. The weeping ulcers on his trunk and legs might heal up and he would be fit again. It had pained him to see his children waste away, but at least if nothing else they could be fed and kept warm and dry. Then of course there was always Thursday. It could take on its old meaning. He thought about Elizabeth and then about his wife Martha. How he had missed both of them. Elizabeth for her deep sexual need of him and Martha for the contentment and comfort of family life.

Strange he thought, how she had gone from one extreme to the other. When robbed of her home, the roughness of the of the make-shift camp apalled her and seemed to deaden her instincts. She became slovenly. The children were left to their own devices and Sid began to miss the little traits that had once irritated him.

Daniel got to the window first and Sid, behind him gave a wry smile and put his arm around the bony shoulders of his eldest son, John. Daniel looked toward Bewick. There was no paper pushed forward and no pen.

"Come on!" Daniel shouted angrily, "where's the effin bond then?"

Bewick looked sadly into the ice-blue eyes. "Sorry Dan. Lovat's orders—you and Garrett don't sign. You're not gettin' set on. Nor is Garett's sons."

Daniel's hands shot out and grabbed at the lapels on Bewick's jacket.

"Jesus Christ—is that his game. Is that his effin revenge?"

he shouted.

Bewick could not change his mind. He had argued for almost an hour the night before, but Lovat, despite his bubbling good humour and back-slapping and laughter had been adamant. For their part in prolonging the strike they were barred.

When Lovat had heard the resolution of the Union leaders, he left his sick bed immediately. It was as though a great pressure had been released from his head. Suddenly he felt wonderful. He felt fit and healthy and elated. At last he could make up for lost time. At last the bleating creditors would stop knocking at the door. At last the bank manager would stop crowing and grovelling in a nice way. Now things could return to normal.

He tipped the vile concoction the doctor had given him for his kidneys and liver down the gully that ran into the Tyne and he laughed to himself as the grey-green liquid ran thread-like with the water, away for ever. It had done nothing but give him constipation and if anything, made his headaches worse. But now he felt good. The miners had been whipped like dogs and were crawling back begging for work. Once again a sensation of power came seeping into him and he resolved there and then to buy another ship as soon as his financial position would allow. That would show them, he thought. That would show everyone that Percy Widmore Lovat was still in business, bigger and better than ever. Suddenly he saw himself at the gates of Buckingham Palace and the young Victoria waiting for him at the other side. As the gates opened she rushed forward and curtsied quickly before throwing her arms around his neck.

His mouth twitched as he turned his glazed eyes up toward his house and stumbled up the grassy slope to tell Sarah about his trip to London.

Daniel released his grip on Bewick's lapels as Sid squashed himself forward to get a look at him.

"You're a bastard Bewick—just like the one before you," Sid screamed. "We've got as much right to work as anyone. One striker's the same as another."

Daniel pushed him away. "Don't argue with him Sid, it's Lovat—he's the bastard, Bewick's just got pumped with a bit of his own importance. Sod them all."

96

Sid was frantic as he followed Daniel away, with John running behind them.

"Jesus man, what'll we do," he pleaded. "Where will we live? How the hell will we live?"

Daniel didn't answer. He didn't know. His anger seethed inside him like a brooding volcano and made him, for the moment, unconcerned as to whether he lived or worked or ever saw the inside of his cottage again. They made their way through the wind and rain and mud, around the pit heap and along the path skirting Johnson's field toward the limp soaking rags that was their shelter, to tell their eager waiting wives that they were not moving that day.

Henry Drummond hummed a little tune as he made his way from the house to his shop that Monday evening. The rain had stopped shortly after three and the wind had dropped and the sun had begun to shine, sending wisps of steam snaking up into the sky from the roads and fields. He was relieved that the strike was at an end. His relief manifested itself in a warm smile to Elizabeth and a light hearted sensation as he tramped through the cloying mud toward the shop. He had decided to do a little stocktaking, seeing that the miners were returning to work; he would make sure his shop was full of everything they would need when they got paid for their labours and came hurrying to spend. He decided to check all his fixtures and sacks and array of hardware. He would make sure that he was short of nothing the miners would want. He expected a boom in the next few weeks and the thoughts of it made his thrifty little heart beat faster and the increased blood flow to his brain forced an unrecognizable tune from his thin colourless lips.

He wondered if he had been too frivolous; entirely out of character and blaming it on his joyous mood, he had taken a bottle of port from the cabinet, told Elizabeth not to bother coming to help him—she could sit and enjoy her sewing, and then sneaked out with the bottle tucked under his jacket. He would have a drink while he was working—and why not? It wasn't every day that he was delivered from impending ruin. Elizabeth had seemed in a good mood too. She had said that she would finish her sewing and then take a bath, and to

97

Henry that statement coupled with the quiet demure smile he received as he kissed her goodbye, sent a little tingle down his spine. A sudden flush of desire came over him and he knew that she would be warm and receptive and scenty, when he returned. He could hardly wait.

Soon he was lost among the cluster of hardware and bags of dried peas and flour. He counted his bunches of tallow candles and jotted the numbers in his book. He ran his eye over the pre-weighed packets of tea and allowed himself a little song as he carefully lit a lamp when the daylight began to fade. He took another sip of port from the bottle and smiled as he thought about Elizabeth sitting in the bath, the soapy water gleaming on her breasts as she prepared herself for his return. As the port ran warmly down his gullet he broke into an excited sweat. He felt better than he had done for months; he was happy and he took another drink of the port as he continued his task.

It was completely dark when his eyes began to have difficulty in focusing on his shelves and on the book in which he was writing. This fact crept on him suddenly and he realized that he had to make a conscious effort to read and count. He pulled the lamp closer to his book and saw his writing progressing from the impeccable copperplate to an almost unrecognizable scrawl. He was drunk and he knew it. He gave out a ridiculous titter and stood up. The room began to swim before him, and it was hilarious. He laughed as he thought about being drunk. It was many a year since he had allowed himself such a carefree liberty. Yet here he was drunk and he was enjoying it. Again he thought about Elizabeth and again desire flooded through him. He smiled as he let his mind play little fantasies with her, then decided he had had enough. Elizabeth would be waiting for him. He would go home; there was plenty of time for stocktaking the next day. He was in a worse state than he thought. As he walked through the shop, holding on to the counter for support, the eerie glow from the lamp danced on the door and it split into two and then into three as he attempted to focus on it. "Whoa, whoa there," he shouted before laughing joyously through his nose.

Suddenly his toe was stopped short by the protruding corner of a sack of sugar and all his forward motion was transferred to his shoulders. He went sprawling forward and hit the floor with his outstretched hands. He didn't feel the impact. The only fact that registered was that he hadn't landed on his face, and for that he was grateful. He let out a wild giggle and lowered himself slowly down until his chin rested on the stone floor. You're drunk Henry—you're dead drunk you silly man, he thought as he slowly raised himself from the floor. His face changed immediately from a stupid smile to a look of horror. The lamp he had been holding had been flung as he fell and had landed on a pile of brooms. The bone dry twigs took no time at all to feed the hungry flame. As he lifted his head the flames were already licking and crackling, hot and yellow up toward the ceiling. Henry Drummond sobered at once. He dashed to the door and opened it, a strange gurgling issuing from his throat. He ran as fast as his spindley legs would carry him, screaming "fire" and falling and stumbling through the mud, toward the village of Shirehill. He began knocking on doors and yelling himself hoarse for help. Slowly the sleepy miners realized what was happening. The commotion spread like a chain reaction and soon everyone was out of doors. No one ran to the shop. When they saw Drummond they laughed. His mud covered body was pathetic as he begged them to help him. They walked to their lane ends and watched as the flames licked high into the air, colouring the sky red. The children woke up and danced with glee at the premature bonfire. Drummond begged at the miners' feet, but no one took any notice. They watched the flames and the flames illuminated their smiling faces. Only Sid spoke to Drummond; he had ran from his camp and into the village.

"Where's your wife?" he asked urgently.

"Home," was the only coherent word Sid could understand as Drummond grovelled at his feet. Sid relaxed and watched the blaze.

The fire burned for two days and the glowing embers lasted a week. The children of the village enjoyed themselves pulling potatoes from Johnson's field and roasting them among the hot ashes.

CHAPTER 9

Daniel and Sid watched with a predictable envy as the men who they had coaxed, persuaded, laughed with, and suffered with returned to work; a grim reluctance silencing their chatter to the barest necessities. Within a week the routine got back to some semblance of normality and the only signs of almost five months of misery was the remains of the camps; the odd piece of wood, the bundle of discarded rags or a broken pot. Separated by forty yards or so were the two remaining camps of the Simpsons and the Garretts. One small comfort they had was the quiet journeying of almost every family in the village to sympathize with them and promise them food and help when they received their first pay. There were offers of shelter from some with a little more room than most, but they refused it, part from pride, part from the fact that both men knew Lovat's reaction if he should find out. It could create more trouble than enough for the offerer.

Dorothy Simpson took the news surprisingly well. She had become conditioned to her way of life. She had grown an invisible shell over the long months into which she kept ensnared her natural desires and feelings for Daniel, matching his cold unemotional manner and managing to control any outward signs that she wanted to be his wife, his proper wife and for the two of them to raise their daughter with love and normality. Into this shell she had crammed the sickening hopelessness of living like a tramp and now this latest news had simply bounced off her shell and fermented before it finally filtered through to her. They had survived for nearly five months; they would survive another five. That was her first thought as Daniel noisily breathed out the news. She had said so, quietly, without looking at him as she tried to protect Margaret's cot from the dripping rain with a piece of tarred sacking. Margaret had survived too; she was thin and small, but alive and relatively healthy. At least she could say that much for her husband; he had fished all day at Seaton to bring perhaps only two "poddlers", or he had scoured the neighbouring woodland for berries and rabbits and anything else edible. He had given it all to her. Sometimes he had gone two days without a bite himself. He had fed her and she had fed Margaret and they had all survived.

A little flurry of regret ran through her as she thought of the others going back to their homes but she dismissed it. She dismissed everything from her mind except that the three of them were together.

She had lain awake in bed that night, her mind streaming with ideas and imaginings of how they would make the best of their predicament. She wondered if Daniel would decide to move on to some other village—to somewhere where he was not known; but then she knew he would not. She knew he would not accept defeat.

The commotion started and became louder. Daniel leapt out of bed and Dorothy followed him. Drummond's shop was blazing fiercely and lighting up the whole village. She could see the Garretts standing transfixed further up the lane, then she saw Sid scurry away. She listened to the children of the village laugh and clap and dance. Daniel stood, hands on hips, his strange gloating smile lit up in the glare from Drummond's. No one ran to put out the fire. She turned reluctantly to tend to the crying Margaret.

Martha had also taken the news without undue panic. She was already numbed. This new development shook her to her very roots but she absorbed it all deep within her. She looked into the wondering faces of her children and felt nothing; no joy, no pride, no sadness, no despair. Her once clean, tidy, exact little empire had been reduced to a few tattered, soaked possessions. Inwardly she was dead.

At the end of the first week, Billy Charlton respectfully shouted through Daniel's makeshift door and Dorothy pulled back the cloth to let him in. Billy was a short bow-legged man who walked with a rolling sway, his rump pushed backward and his neck held stiff, typical of the miners who had spent years crouched in low passages. His once black hair was now grey and his hands and rough face were marked with numerous blue scars—the random tatoos from a lifetime of cuts and bruises, coaxing the coal from far below. He had inherited his mother's bright alert eyes, which seemed to smile irrespective of his mood, but he had not taken after her for her boundless energy or quick decisive movements. He was a slow deliberate man, long-armed and thick-necked. He took his time. He thought before he spoke. Even when he was lying on his side, swinging at the coal face it appeared that he was working in slow motion, but he was not. He would study the grain of the coal and swing his pick slow but hard and he hewed more than enough to keep the putters busy.

"Yes Billy," Dorothy said, more as a question.

He mumbled some unintelligible apology as he passed her and stood shyly blinking at Daniel.

Daniel rose from his stool. "How Billy? Fit?"

Billy nodded. "Aye, all right. Stiff after the long layoff." He looked around to determine Dorothy's whereabouts then looked at the cot. "Bairn all right?" Daniel gave an expressionless nod then sat down again. He sensed the visit was not entirely social but decided to let him take his own time. Dorothy moved expectantly to the side of the bed and folded her arms. Billy took the offered stool and gave a painful grunt as he lowered himself down. He seemed to think hard for a while before he opened his mouth, and even then the words took time to come. "I've some news for ye and Sid, Dan. Thought y'might like to know. Bewick mentioned it when we came t'bank. He says that Johnson's lookin' for a couple of men."

Daniel leant forward. "A couple of men? Johnson the farmer?"

"Aye."

"What's that got to do with us. Does he want us to work for Johnson?"

Billy shrugged. "The way I figure it Dan, he's not to blame for you and Sid not gettin' set on and he's trying to help out. There's cottages wi' the job."

Dorothy kept a respectful silence, but her heart leapt. She

102

gazed at Daniel's furrowed brow and tried telepathically to make him be interested.

"But we're not bliddy farmers, Sid an' me—we're miners. What do we know about planting tetties and whatnot and feeding stupid sheep and cows," Daniel said, beginning to receive Dorothy's silent message.

"Johnson'll keep you right man—anyway the work'll be manual at this time of year. There's the harvest to bring in, and it might only be for a bit. Lovat might have the pair of you back. There's not many as can chop coal like you two. The way things are mind, y'll be best up top. Man, the water's bad in the High Main. Pissin' in it is. No wonder the Welshies left." He gave a broad grin, "We'll all have webbed feet afore long."

Daniel frowned. "Is the pumps takin' it?"

"Seem to be, but hell it's twice as bad as before the strike. Bewick says it's running from the Gut at Seaton." He winced as he rose from the stool. "Man, I'm as stiff as a plank. What with the water and soft muscle I feel as rough as hell. Mebbe I should get a job wi' Johnson." He walked slowly backward toward the doorway. "Ye'll try the job, will you Dan?"

"I'll see what Sid's got to say," he whispered.

Dorothy had to grip the large ornate bedpost to stop herself running to hug him. She knew somehow that he would go for the job. She knew that he would get the job. For the first time in a long time she knew happiness.

A horse and cart arrived that day from Sunderland. Drummond and his brother loaded the cart with his possessions and Elizabeth gave a hand. The three of them worked in silence, moving slowly up and down the path with a piece of furniture or a carpet or a bundle of clothes. Elizabeth carried heavier things than her husband because she was big boned and had muscles from years of humping sacks and boxes around in the shop. Her husband and his brother staggered out with the grandfather clock and she stood watching while they fumbled it on to the cart, its chimes ringing out an undefinable little tune as it came to rest against the large mirror. Suddenly Elizabeth felt a choking desperation well up inside her. She felt afraid and at the same time sickened at what the future held for them. The pathetic ending to their livelihood, the pathetic way in which her husband was now collecting together their worldly goods, the pathetic pile of ash that was the remains of their shop, the pathetic grubby collection of hovels that had supplied them with a living—all this suddenly revolted her. She wished she could run a million miles away. Away from her husband who had cried and wailed constantly for a week, and away from the colourless drab scene of industry, to India perhaps or the lush green jungles of Africa, where exciting, mysterious men would look upon her and admire and she would look back and lust. But with a feeling of impending doom she visualized her new life. Back to Sunderland, to a dull existence of servitude working for her snivelling brother-in-law who had so unhesitatingly offered them assistance while at the same time leaving them in no doubt as to his unbounding generosity. He was a thin, drawn, wormy looking man, against whom her husband was just a pale imitation of a miser.

Finally the house was empty and the cart loaded. There was just enough room for the three of them at the front. Silently they climbed up. Henry's brother made a clicking noise with his mouth and flicked the reins. The cart moved slowly forward. Henry Drummond gazed forlornly at the pile of black ash as they passed the remains of the shop, and he gave out a little groan. Elizabeth did not look, nor did she look back. She was deep in thought about Sidney Garrett and livid that even he had not gone to help.

As Daniel and Sid walked up the wide deeply rutted track toward the big white farmhouse, Sid was bubbling over with childish enthusiasm. He was overwhelmed that out of the blue, a job and a cottage could be theirs. Never in his wildest dreams had he thought they would work anywhere but the pit, yet here they were, and the prospect of money to spend and a roof over their heads again, filled him with excitement. Daniel was his usual solemn self, throwing out the occasional doubt or drawback in answer to Sid's interminable chatter, but inside him he was relieved that this possibility had presented itself. It was not what he would have chosen, but it was something from where they could regain their strength and confidence to continue the struggle.

Soon they arrived at the farmyard and approached the long low byre. They could hear an occasional bovine grunt and the swish of a tail. As they walked alongside it the large head of a cow appeared over the low wooden door. Its eyes were big and wide, its nose running and its mouth frothing from chewing cud. The two men kept at a respectful distance.

Ebenezer Johnson was at the far end of the yard. He was squatting down, filling his clay pipe as they approached but he stood up as they got nearer. He put his pipe into his mouth and stood expectantly waiting for them to get within talking distance. He was a tall man, almost as tall as Daniel. He had close cropped white hair with long bushy sideburns and matching eyebrows that hung over doleful puffy eyes. His face was craggy and brown and withered from exposure to a multitude of seasons. He wore a roughly woven waistcoat over a grubby white shirt and a pair of baggy pants tied at the ankles with bits of rag. "We've come about the job," Sid said eagerly.

Johnson nodded his head and scrutinized both of them silently, his bushy eyebrows coming together. "Aye, you're the lads that John Bewick mentioned, eh?" he said at last.

Both men nodded. Johnson took out his pipe and spat on the cobbled yardstones, rubbing the spittle under his mud-covered boot. "I'm looking for a couple of strong men. I've no axe to grind about your not gettin' set on at the pit. Do your work and y'll get paid and you and your families have a cottage a piece over thonder," he said pointing a finger down past the byre. "There'll be work for two, mebbe three months if you keep out of trouble and work hard. D'yous want the job?'

Sid nodded eagerly and looked to see if Daniel was doing the same.

"What's the pay?" Daniel asked coldly.

"Y'll get five shillings a week each and a dozen eggs and sixpence of the pay will come off for rent on the cottage—all right?"

Sid nodded again.

"What's the work?" Daniel asked.

"Harvest's comin' up—there'll be the barley to cut and there's the tetties to pick. Can you use a scythe?"

"No, but we can learn—eh Dan?" Sid said quickly.

Johnson's face broke into a smile, showing a sparse set of

crooked brown teeth.

"Ye'll either learn or chop each other's bliddy legs off. Well, do you want the job?—Oh, that's another thing. What about horses? Do you know anything about them?"

Daniel's face paled. "Horses? Why?"

"'Cos that's another job. Ye's can muck out the stables and see to the horses."

"Y've got horses," Daniel said downheartedly.

"Aye. I've the two big ploughin' horses in the stable there, and I keep eight of Delaval's hunters; sort of room and board y'might say. I look after them and use the shite for the land."

Sid's heart fell into his boots. He looked anxiously into Dan's face convinced he would refuse the job, but Daniel saw his worried look and the refusal stuck in his throat. He knew that if he refused, Sid would refuse. He saw the anguish in his eyes, like a child with the threat of his favourite toy being deliberately broken. Somehow he couldn't refuse; for that reason and for another. Five shillings a week and a dozen eggs would be luxury. They could be fed and dry and warm. All of them, Dorothy, Margaret, Martha and Sid's four children. He gave a sickly sort of grin, "We'll take the job Mr. Johnson," he whispered.

Johnson nodded and Sid grinned from ear to ear.

"You look like you could do with a feed now," Johnson said. "Tell you what. I'll give you a week's pay in advance. That means if you pack in you've got to work a week past your last pay and you get nowt when you leave—understand?"

"Eeeh that's good on you," Sid almost shouted. "Isn't that good Dan?"

Daniel nodded. "Champion," he said.

"All right lads, start at five in the morning. Yous can move in as soon as you like."

"Can we borrow a cart and we'll shift now?" Daniel asked.

Johnson turned and waved up the yard. Y'll find some up there. Help yourselves, and don't forget to come for the money."

Daniel and Sid made their way back to the village. Sid was more excited than ever. Even Daniel allowed himself the luxury of an inward smile but he was still not completely

106

happy. He was a pitman and despite all the drawbacks of working in the pit, he wanted to be there. It was like a drug. His mind and body had known the feel of the pit and the smell of it and the taste of coal dust for so many years. He could not do without it.

They loaded most of their belongings on to the big low cart and both families pushed it slowly toward the farm. Dorothy was overjoyed and as they got nearer her eyes gleamed and she pushed harder so that the cart might get there sooner. Martha was silent. Her face was dirty and her hair unwashed and matted. She pushed at the side of the cart while Sid babbled encouragement in her ear, but she did not care where they were going. Her mind was numbed. A little voice inside her said she should be happy and relieved that things were returning to normal. She tried but she could not. Another little voice said it was a dream, a joke, an hallucination that would vanish as soon as she allowed herself to believe, but still she pushed.

The two cottages were joined and had been painted white unremembered years ago. They were similar to the pit cottages. One room, a scullery, one door and an earth closet and as they entered they realized it was also unremembered years since they had been lived in. The air smelt of decay and stagnation. The stone paved floors had long spindly yellowed grass and dandelions growing from the cracks, striving to reach the sunlight. The walls had obscenities chalked all over them, probably the work of a bored soldier lately left for other parts. Yet they were dry and represented so much more security than their last homes. Dorothy looked at Daniel for his reaction. It was the usual. She carried Margaret in and put her in her cot. Then the tears of relief began to flow.

Martha looked around her, bewildered. Her children brought in little bits and pieces from the cart and set them down in readiness for the furniture. Sid smiled and put his arm around her shoulders and gave her a reassuring squeeze. She looked at the floor then at the walls and at the cobwebbed rafters. She cried in sheer desperation.

When everything was offloaded the two men returned to pick up their few remaining possessions, leaving the rest to make the cottages as habitable as possible. As they trundled the cart down the path toward the road, they saw a horse-drawn cart, piled high with furniture but they took no notice. They were preoccupied with their new life and what they would do and how they would do it. By the time they reached the hawthorn boundary to the farm, the horse-drawn cart was out of sight behind it. Unaware, they pushed their cart out into the road. There was a frightened neighing and the horse reared up in front of them. Henry Drummond cursed loudly while his brother grappled with the reins. Daniel shouted out before retreating out of the way behind the hedge. Sid stood awkwardly looking at Elizabeth as she held on to her bonnet amid the noise and movement and arm waving.

The horse calmed itself. Elizabeth looked startled as she recognized Sid, then she smiled an apologetic smile almost automatically, then silently cursed herself for doing it. She remembered how angry she was with him. Somehow he looked ridiculous standing there, thin and drawn behind his red beard. He was the one excitement she had known in Shirehill; he was the one who had made each week bearable as she waited for his next visit, and yet now he looked ridiculous. For a second Sid felt a flutter of pleasure and warmth as he gazed into the deepness of her eyes. She sat there, erect and lovely, her skin clean and clear and her lips red and inviting. Suddenly he realized what was happening. The loaded cart took his gaze for a moment and he knew almost instinctively that he would never see her again. He made to speak, to say something nice; a thank you perhaps or a little word that only she would recognize for its real meaning, but he could not. She lowered her eyes and Sid swallowed hard.

The cart moved on. Elizabeth did not look at him as she passed, nor did she look behind her. Sid watched the cart creak and groan on its journey down the road. He felt a sadness within him. He felt as though his life would never be quite so complete again.

Billy Charlton could bear it no longer. It was almost a fortnight since he had returned to the Blue Whins face in the High Main and if the water had troubled him then, it was ten times worse now. He lay on his right side, trying to swing at the coal with his pick but the water was lying at least three inches deep and running down from the roof in torrents. His candles kept going out and the water ran into his eyes, making them red and sore. He was chilled and aching from lying wet for hours on end but above all he was worried. He had worked in wet seams before, but never like this. Never so much water spraying out from the roof, seeping up out of the floor, running down the coal face.

"Eff this," he shouted in anger. "Let me out-bye. Bewick's ganna see this."

He rode up the shaft with some tubs and found John Bewick in his little cabin adjoining the winding house. Within half an hour they were back at the face.

"Jesus, it's bad." Bewick gasped.

"Taste it man," Billy growled.

Bewick rolled off his stomach on to his side and opened his mouth to one of the sprays. He retched and spat out the offending liquid. "Salt be buggered," he gasped, "could have picked it up from the rocks?"

"Like hell it did, Mr. Bewick," Billy shouted, "that's sea water—I can tell the effin' difference."

Bewick wiped the water from his eyes and looked at Billy through the temporary flicker of a spluttering candle wedged above the water level. He knew Billy Charlton. He knew he would not speak, let alone protest unless he was sure—very sure. "What do you think Billy. Do you think it's the Gut or the sea proper?" Before Billy could answer there was a low rumble, faint but definite and the pillar supports groaned ominously. Bewick looked up and around him. Again the low rumble with a vibration that was delicate but penetrated even the air around them. The supports creaked again.

"Right! everybody to bank," Bewick shouted. "Quickly now—pass the word. Every bugger out. Low Main first then the Yard seam, then us!"

Billy slithered out after Bewick and the startled face of the putter spoke volumes when he was told. The message was passed from one to the other and within the hour everyone was at bank and being counted. When Bewick was satisfied that no one was still below he strode grimly past the sea of murmuring black faces to his cabin. On the way he glanced at the tall boiler chimney. The thick smoke was sliced away from the chimney top by a strong easterly wind. He blew a low worried whistle from his lips and slammed the cabin door behind him.

109

He had never doubted Jessop's surveying, so he had had no cause to check his charts—but now he did! Urgently, as though the men were still below, he pulled the charts from the drawer and unrolled them. He measured with his rule and spaced off with his dividers. He scribbled on a piece of paper. He multiplied mentally then checked his calculations on the paper. Then he double checked. Then he looked up and out of the window at the miners sitting or squatting or standing, dirty and wet, waiting for news from him. He felt shaky and his face paled. He licked at his dry lips. Jessop's calculations had been wrong—entirely wrong. The High Main did not lie under ten fathom of rock at the face, nor was it under the Gut. There was only two fathom of rock above the face and they were working a hundred yards beyond the low water mark! Bewick swallowed nervously. The wind was strong from the east. The rumble was the noise of the waves crashing on the rocks at Seaton.

Sarah Lovat was pleased with her husband's progress. Ever since the strike had finished he had become his old self. A little stooped perhaps; a line or two more on his face, but exuberant and jolly, boastful and overpowering once again. She was relieved that his release from worry had had this effect. She had been more than a little frightened when he came to her with his fantastic stories and she had not known whether he was joking or serious. But now that was in the past—some unpleasantness that would soon be forgotten.

When John Bewick entered the house she was in the drawing-room and she only saw him as he passed the open door behind the scurrying Ellie, but she saw the grim hard set features of his face and she knew that something was again wrong.

"Drawn out the men and horses—why? In God's name why?" Lovat shouted, jumping out of his chair near the window. His mouth began to twitch and he felt a tingle of pins and needles behind his knees.

Bewick had expected his reaction and nervously moved his weight from one foot to the other. "The pit is in dire danger of flooding, Mr. Lovat. The High Main is only two fathom from the sea bed."

"Rubbish!—Bloody rubbish. Jessop said it was wet, but there's a god deal more rock than that above. Jessop said so!"

"Mr. Jessop was wrong sir," Bewick said softly, "Mr Jessop's calculations were all wrong."

Lovat's face flushed with anger. His brow tightened. He made to speak but his tongue felt locked in his mouth and his mouth twitched violently. He swung away from Bewick and paced quickly over the floor. "Every time you come—or when Jessop came, it is bad news," he breathed at last, looking into the dead fireplace, his hands gripped firmly behind him. "You, Mr. Bewick, you are not fit to be my viewer."

"But Mr. Lovat, the men . . ."

"Silence!" Lovat screamed, still looking at the fireplace. "You are not fit to be my viewer Mr. Bewick. You have drawn out the men and the horses because of a trickle of water and a cock and bull story about the position of the High Main. You are a traitor. You are in league with those who wish to destroy me—are you not?"

"Mr. Lovat you're wrong—come and see for yourself." Bewick protested.

The lounge door opened and Sarah appeared, tutting and fussing across the floor toward her husband. Lovat turned. His eyes were wide and his pupils dilated. His face drained to a chalky white. "Get out—get out woman!" he screamed, his voice high pitched and frantic.

Bewick could take no more. He ushered Mrs. Lovat toward the door and her husband stared wildly after them. When the door closed he felt a withering rage well up inside him. His head pounded painfully and his hands felt clammy and filthy. He tried to fight off the feeling but he could not. He reeled toward the window but the view swam before his eyes. The terrible fearful distance tore at his soul. He heard his wife cry out his name from behind the door. Suddenly in a fit of anguished frustration, he threw himself on the floor, his legs flaying wildly in the air and his teeth sinking satisfyingly into the edge of the carpet.

Ignoring the protests of his wife and the family doctor, Lovat visited his pit the following morning. When he arrived Bewick was there, silently standing near the shaft with

111

a few doleful looking miners. As he stepped from his carriage he decided to show them how much of a needless fuss they were making.

"Now Bewick my boy," he said pleasantly, "about this water in the pit, the pumps'll have cleared it by now—eh?"

Bewick smiled dryly and folded his arms. "Come with me Mr. Lovat and I'll show you something."

Lovat followed him past the staring miners and stood near the shaft as Bewick stooped and picked up a large piece of coal. With a look of almost amused supremacy Bewick heaved the coal down the shaft. He counted slowly to three then the sound of a dull splash stopped him. He nodded grimly. "Your pit Mr. Lovat sir, is flooded to within twenty-four fathoms of the top. The sea broke in. The pumps cannot pump the sea dry. The pit is finished."

Lovat winced as though dust had been thrown into his eyes. He blinked stupidly and his mouth began to twitch. He turned and strode stiffly away. Without a word he climbed into his carriage and it moved off.

It seemed no time at all until he was home. He had not been aware of his journey back. His mind had been elsewhere. Where? he couldn't remember. Sarah was anxiously waiting for him but he gently chided her for being worried. He felt calm now, strangely calm and settled. He convinced her that he was all right and with a glazed watery smile, walked to his beloved lounge. He slumped down in his chair and gazed out of the window. He stared for a long time. The distance did not bother him. He could see the river and the ships and South Shields and the seagulls. The river was blue and rolling with the turn of the tide. Out at sea he could see a ship, heeled over in the wind and heading for the Tyne. South Shields was smoky and industrious. The seagulls still hung in the wind and cried their eerie forlorn cries. The view was as always, but it never failed to please him. He felt nice now. Calm, deeply rested, almost elated. The solution came to him suddenly and he wondered why he had not thought of it sooner. It was so easy and so simple and so foolproof. Steadily he stood up and walked to the wall of guns. He let his eyes play over them for a minute before choosing one. He chose a beautiful twin-barrelled Prussian pistol. The barrels were set one above the other and the butt was ebony with exquisite inlaid mother-ofpearl. He looked at it in his hand and rubbed it lovingly, feeling the weight and the balance. A gun was to him, the supreme power. Invincible, uncompromising, it could not be defeated. No one was quick enough to dodge its speeding bullet. No one was strong enough to withstand its power when it struck. He loved guns. He loved to look at them and touch them and be in command of them.

He took the gun to his bureau and unlocked the bottom drawer. Slowly and calmly he took out two caps, then a small leather powder bag with a bright brass measure. He opened a box marked "0.33" calibre, and selected two round lead balls. Finally, with two pieces of wadding in his hand, he wandered almost lazily back to his chair at the window. As though he had all the time in the world he measured the gunpowder into each of the barrels and tamped it down. Then followed the balls and then the wadding. Finally he cocked the two percussion locks and placed the caps in position. Now the gun was loaded. Now it was transformed from an innocent ornament into a lethal weapon. Lovat's eyes gleamed as he held it up in front of him. Slowly, almost erotically, he ran his lips along the shining octagonal barrels until he felt the muzzle. Then in complete contrast to his former pace, as though he hadn't a second to lose, he opened his mouth and pressed the twin barrels hard against the back of his palate. The absolute finality of his action never occurred to him. What he was doing seemed to him as innocent as taking medicine. It would cure him of all his problems and release him from the griping nagging irritation that ate at his soul. He pulled both triggers simultaneously. The hammers flew down and the caps exploded sending tiny sparks into each barrel. Suddenly the gunpowder was transformed into hot violent gas, anxious to expand, striving to show its power. The two lead balls began their journey. They arrived at the muzzle. The gas, now free to expand further, vented its fury by blowing out Lovat's eardrums. Even before that the two bullets had entered the flesh of his palate and tore up through the Pons Varolii, before slicing a pathway through the Cerebellum and then the Cerebrum. After just a split second they arrived at the relatively hard skull, but that was no obstacle to the ever-powerful bullets. They flattened slightly before breaking through and then journeyed on.

The view that Percy Widmore Lovat enjoyed from the window of his lounge was suddenly obscured with a mass of blood and hair and skin and bone.

They buried Lovat in the grounds of the ruined priory at Tynemouth and Bewick attended the funeral. He was unsure of the future and attended to show respect and in the hope that Lovat's son might mention something about arrangements. Yet he would have gladly stayed at Shirehill that morning. His respect was false and Lovat's son struck him as a younger version of his late father. At least at Shirehill he would have been among his own kind. The village in fact was almost as quiet as a graveyard with the miners hushed and shocked at the prospect of again having no work. The mine was finished. Already the honeycomb of workings would have collapsed. It was not their employer they were fighting this time. It was not a human being who could be persuaded or forced into changing his mind. The action of the sea was irrevocable. It had flooded their pit and drowned their livelihood completely.

Daniel and Sid could not believe their luck. The tables were completely turned. Now they were the only ones in the village who were working. The flooding of the Lovat pit had brought gasps of surprise from their lips and praise for Bewick for drawing the men and horses out. Now Lovat was dead and the pit was no more and both men felt a sadness. The job at the farm was not satisfying to them. They were pitmen, born and bred to hew coal and although they were thankful for their present position, the prospect of joining their mates and returning to their old job was eliminated.

It was barely a week after the funeral of Lovat and Daniel and Sid were cleaning out the stable. Sid knew the agony that Daniel was going through. He had asked, then almost begged him to stay out of the stable, but he would not. Daniel was like that; he had accepted the job, now he would not shirk any of it. Sid watched him among the pile of stinking straw, the sweat running down his face not from exertion but from determination not to run or vomit as the acrid stench reached up and gripped him.

Sid turned when he heard Daniel's name shouted out by someone a long way off. It came again, closer this time and both men moved to the stable door. They recognized Billy Charlton moving unusually quickly up the track toward the farm. Soon he staggered breathlessly up to them. He put a strong hand on each of their shoulders. His eyes shone as he gulped the air. "We're saved lads—we're saved," he gasped.

"How's that Billy?" Sid said incredulously. "What the hell's happened?"

"Pack in—pack in," Billy urged excitedly. "We've just got the news."

"What bliddy news?" Daniel growled, before Billy had a chance to explain further.

"That's what I'm trying to tell yous man. They're sinkin' a new shaft down the road at Hartley. They want all the men they can get!"

Daniel threw down his pitchfork and got hold of Billy's arms. "Are you sure?" he shouted.

"Sure?—of course I'm sure. Everybody's going. Come on lads, make sharp. Let's get signed on; they're building houses for everybody."

A great excitement gripped the two men. A new pit, a new house, a chance to return to their proper occupation. Hartley, only a couple of miles down the road. Hartley, a village they must have all mentioned in their conversations a million times. Hartley suddenly became another word for salvation.

Book Two

HARTLEY

CHAPTER 1

February 1852

> Two, four, six, eight
> Mary at the cottage gate,
> Eating cherries off a plate
> Two, four, six, eight.

Joseph Mennem heard the dull monotoned chant even before he reached the bottom of the row and with a growing fear gripping at his stomach he cautiously eased his blackened face a little way out from the first earth closet and watched the four girls skipping and chanting only ten yards from his cottage door. In normal circumstances a seven-year-old boy could have faced four girls of eight or nine and held his own, but this confrontation would be different; Joseph Mennem didn't quite understand why, he only knew with a bewildering certainty that the girls, once they spotted him, would call him names and throw stones at him. He also knew that if he retaliated, he would be punished by his father and that would make his mother cry. So whenever possible, he kept well out of the way of the other children of the village. He had been told it was something to do with his father, during the big strike, before he was even born, and he couldn't in his seven-year-old brain understand what—or why he was scorned. Even his fellow tally-boys at the pit made his life a misery, playing tricks on him and ganging up on him. Joseph Mennem was a puzzled, frightened lad, whose lonely mind told him everyone outside his family was an enemy.

He watched the girls skipping, his eyes wide with apprehension. He could see Margaret Simpson, her blonde ringlets

119

bobbing and glinting in the weak winter sun as she skipped and chanted. He watched her and he watched Daisy Finch and Mona Chapman and Alice Cairns. He looked towards his brown cottage door and wondered whether to make a run for it or wait for his father and brothers. They were the only friends he had. They spoke to him and played with him and comforted him. He looked down at the poorly looking bunch of snowdrops he had picked for his mother from the hedgerow. He had seen them and picked them and dashed excitedly ahead of his father and brothers. The fore-shift had come to bank and they were heading wearily home for sleep and food, but Joseph, in his excitement, had found energy to run with the flowers; now his excitement had changed to caution and he decided to wait for his protectors.

Soon they caught up with him, Alfie and his four other sons, George and Tom and Bill and Fred. George saw him peering around the closet wall and up the back lane. With a grim smile he realized why he had not continued home. Alfie shook his head sadly and muttered something as George put his arm around Joseph's frail shoulders. He was a thin boy, lanky and deep, with big, sad searching eyes. They all walked up the lane and he felt safe. He even chanced a brave smile at the four girls. All five Mennems filed into their cottage. Joseph glanced over his shoulder. Four feminine tongues poked from four twisted girlish faces. Joseph's heart sank. For once he would have liked them just to ignore him.

The four girls resumed their skipping. They were pleased that they had managed to stick out their tongues at Joseph Mennem. It was their favourite pastime and besides, he never ever retaliated. They heard their parents treat the Mennems with derision and they copied. It was right and proper that they should do so, because everyone did it and no one ever got into trouble for it. They skipped and chanted and the other miners from the fore-shift, black and hunched and tired, walked past them. Some smiled, some spoke, others ignored them. Soon George Finch appeared around the corner and Daisy stopped her skipping and ran to him. Mona Chapman and Alice Cairns did the same when they recognized their fathers. Margaret Simpson skipped on. She wondered why her father was late, he was usually among the first batch. She decided to skip down the back lane and look along the road toward the pit. When she reached the bottom of the row, she saw them. Her father was staggering along the road, supported on each side by Sid Garrett and Billy Charlton.

Daniel's head was hung forward and his feet felt like lead. A swirling nausea reached down his throat and his head swam as though he had drunk a gallon of ale. Margaret panicked. She had never seen her father like this. She dropped her skipping rope and ran toward him.

"Da'—da'," she yelled as her small legs flew across the ground.

"Easy bonny lass," Billy said gently. "He's all right. He's had a bit stythe that's all. He'll be as right as rain the morn. Run home and tell your mam to make some nice hot tea."

Margaret walked alongside them for a minute. She stared at her father's fluttering eyes and longed to hug him to her. Perhaps this time, when he's not well, he might not mind she thought. She wondered if she dare hold on to his jacket or say something comforting to him. She had never dared in the past because for as long as she could remember he had treated her coldly with impatient tolerance and with no outward appearance of love. He had never sat her on his knee and told her a story or tickled her or played with her or tucked her in when she went to bed. She had puzzled over this—wondered and puzzled. She had asked her mother a dozen times why he didn't love her and she could remember her mother lifting her on to her knee, eyes bright with the hint of tears and telling her that he surely loved her—sure as sure, but that he wasn't a man to show it. He kept his love deep inside him and that was the best kind. Margaret wasn't so sure it was the best kind. She would have gladly settled for a story and a hug and kiss.

She plucked up her courage and tugged at his jacket.

"Da'—are you all right?" she whispered.

Daniel lifted his head. "Wha's matter? Wha's wrong?"

She tugged harder. "It's me da'."

"It's the bairn Dan. It's your Maggie." Sid shouted into his ear.

Daniel's face twisted. The great dome of his shaven head seemed to come down to examine her as he tried to focus his eyes.

"Gerraway," he shouted drunkenly. "Gerraway home to your bliddy mother."

Margaret let go of his jacket as though it had burned her fingers.

"Come on now Dan—that's no way to talk to the bairn," Billy said reproachfully.

"Shuddup—jus' get her away from me. She's a bliddy nuisance."

Billy saw her sad wondering look. His face broke into a tight knowing smile and his head nodded up and down. "Go on pet. Get your mam to make some tea."

Margaret ran half-heartedly up the back lane. She felt as though she was crying but there were no tears. Her mother's remembered words rang around in her befuddled head. "The best kind of love."

Dorothy was already at the door when they arrived. She took Daniel's jacket while Sid and Billy supported him, then as they eased him on to the bed she got down on her knees and unlaced his big soaking boots.

"What happened?" she asked without looking up.

"He caught a whiff of stythe, Doss," Bill whispered. "He's a bit woozy, that's all. He'll be all right the morn."

"A whiff of bliddy stythe—tha's right," Daniel mumbled. "Stythe and soddin' water—just like the Lovat—one shaft, no air and plenty of effin water." Dorothy tutted loudly.

Billy flushed and coughed to cover his embarrassment.

"Sorry about that Doss," Sid said with a sickly grin, "he's drunk wi' the stythe he doesn't know where he is."

He bent down and shouted in Daniel's ear. "Stop your swearing Dan, you're home—understand? You're home."

"One shaft—only one shaft—no air," he continued mumbling. "Hester pit—jus' like a bliddy woman."

He gave a cynical laugh through his nose. "Hester pit—what a laugh. Jus' like a bliddy woman."

Dorothy frowned, then nodded knowingly. She lifted her tired, lined face and looked at the two men. The years of strain were ageing her quickly. Her eyes were dull and a sort of forlorn acceptance dominated her every action. "All right lads," she said, "he'll be all right now. I'll see to him." The two men moved to the door. Margaret watched the proceedings from the scullery. She watched through the knot hole in the scullery door, as though her restricted secret view would render the scene imaginary. She was afraid that her father might die,

122

and she wanted to run and ask her mother for reassurance that he wouldn't; but she was afraid she would say the opposite. Silently she watched her mother slowly undress him. She heard her grunt as she manoeuvred him into the bed. Suddenly she was sure that her father must be dying. It was the first time she had ever seen her mother touch him.

When Sid got home, his two sons were already there. In one glance he weighed up the situation. The boys were at the table and their sisters were spooning the broth from the big black pot and into their bowls. Martha was in bed. Sid sighed angrily. The cottage was reasonably clean and tidy, but Sid knew it was the girls' doing. His two sweet girls cleaned and dusted and cooked while his wife sat ordering them here and there, or she took herself to bed sometimes for days and left the running of their home to his two willing daughters.

He walked across to the bed after he had taken off his jacket and hung it behind the door. Martha sensed he was there. She turned off her side and opened her eyes. Gone was the plumpness of satisfaction and contentment. Her face was thin and haunted and the ingrained dirt of years, coloured it a sickly yellow colour. He hair, once smooth and shining brown, was coarse and threaded with grey. She looked up at Sid and her mouth opened to give him an apologetic explanation but his youngest daughter spoke first.

"She's sick da'. She's been really sick this morning."

Sid turned. His four children sat observing him, their faces wondering what his reaction would be. Martha had never completely recovered from the shock of the evictions. When they settled at Hartley it had not been as Sid had thought. His once exact and loving wife took a long time to even begin to be the woman she once was. She began by taking an interest in the girls. She guided them and told them and showed them but she did little or nothing herself. As their daughters came into their teens they worked all day cleaning and cooking and sewing and Martha sat brooding and unkempt, content that some-one—anyone, was at hand to work for her. Sid did not understand. He was angry that she put on to them so. Why was she so lazy? Why couldn't she be bothered? Where was the pride in her house and family that she exuded at one time? Sid was worried . What would happen when the girls married? How would Martha cope? He saw them alone, his sons and daughters married and away and just he and Martha together. He could only imagine the stink of slothfulness and his body shuddered.

"What's wrong with her?" he asked flatly.

"She's been sick—twice," his eldest daughter said quickly.

Sid looked down again at Martha. She nodded endorsing her daughter's statement.

"I feel bad Sid, sort of sick and dizzy," she croaked.

Sid's lips thinned. "Get some sleep," he said and turned toward the table.

The broth and dumplings were good and hot and strengthened him. He lifted his spoon to his lips slowly, savouring the flavour and wiping his arm across his bearded face in between spoonfuls.

His sons were at their usual pastime. They talked incessantly about being rich. They rambled on about searching for hidden treasure. They imagined finding the secret formula for changing base metal into gold. And all the time Sid listened, amused by their youthful keenness and fantastic dreams and remembering his own youth. Dreams and hopes and imaginings had come easy to him. He had craved for importance and standing. He had had a sniff of it during the big strike, but that was long ago. He had dreamed of riches and luxury just like his boys, then one day he realized that it would never come. It would be the pit, day in—day out, only the pit. But it was good that the boys dreamed such dreams, he thought. It kept their boundless spirits high. It was fodder for their agile inventive minds. If they realized that their inevitable fate was only the pit, it would be frightening for them.

He ate and listened and watched. He was proud of his family. The boys were growing up strong and true and the girls were like their mother was years ago. Florence the eldest, was huffy and easily hurt but soft hearted and intelligent. May was different, true she was only eighteen months younger but she was still a baby at heart, giggling and silly but loving and nice. He watched them; both had different faces but still, both looked as Martha had been. He suddenly felt sorry for his wife. She looked ill for once. He left the table and went to the bed. He took hold of her hand and she again opened her eyes. He smiled down at her, trying to tell her that he was not angry.

"Are you all right hinny?" he asked softly, "you do look a bit pelchy. D'you fancy some of the broth or a piece of warm stotty?"

She shook her head. "I was sick this morning Sid—really sick."

"I know, I know, try to rest now—you'll be up in no time."

She turned her head to the side and stared dreamily at the wall. After a while she whispered. "I was going to bake the stotty you know. But I was sick to my stomach, so the girls baked it."

She turned her head back. Sid was again at the table with their children. "I was going to bake it," she repeated.

But they didn't hear her.

The headgear around the Hester pit stood high above the rows of cottages. It stood out black and stark and seemed to watch over all and sundry and remind them that they owed allegiance to it and to the men that owned it. Daniel looked up at the large pulley wheel on the morning he returned to work and for the first time it seemed to mock him. He felt a revulsion at the conglomeration of wood and metal and brick that clustered around the shaft. He could smell the sulphurous smoke from the furnace far below that displaced the foul air and to some measure allowed fresh air to take its place, and it sickened him. His chest still pained from the effects of the gas and his anger at having once again been overcome by it was given vent among his fellow workers. He had been dragged from the pit unconscious. He had lost three days pay; it was the fault of the pit—the pit and its owner. Now it was right that they should be reminded of it.

"One shaft divided down the bliddy middle with a brattice —and a furnace to displace the soddin' air. What sort of ventilation is that!" he shouted deliberately loudly as they waited to descend.

Sid shushed him, anxiously looking around to make sure none of the officials had heard.

"There's no difference to the Lovat—water pissin' in everywhere and stythe lurkin' behind every swing of the pick," Daniel continued.

125

There were murmurings of agreement from the miners.

"For Christ sake. Shut up Dan," Sid hissed. "You'll get yourself sacked and that'll be the end of you."

Daniel gave a derisive grunt and shuffled forward with the queue. "What kind of improvements have they made for pits," he argued to the men.

"None—not a bliddy bit. Two men almost killed last month —I get gassed for the umpteenth time. It's money, that's all that it boils down to—money. They'll not spend a farthing more than they should. They dig a hole in the ground and as long as men'll go down and work they're content."

Sid spotted the under viewer approaching from behind a set of waggons. He tugged urgently at Daniel's sleeve then looked casually down at his boots. Daniel saw him approach and smiled sarcastically at him as he passed, but much to Sid's relief, didn't attempt to antagonize him.

Daniel seemed to calm down after he had said his piece and Sid was glad when it was their turn to descend. At least down below, among the myriad of workings, his audience, if he started again, would be safely limited to a putter or two.

Daniel crawled back to the Dyke face in the Yard Seam where he had been working four days before. He smiled grimly as he stuck his tallow candle in the cleft of a rock and looked at the gleaming black seam of coal, speckled with blue and gold and yellow. The air was dank but clear now and the dripping water was no worse. He couldn't remember the moment he had blacked out. He had felt himself going dizzy then the next thing he knew he was at bank. Today it was much colder and the water made him shiver. Quickly he sorted his picks and chose one. He swung with practised ease and the coal fell away. Soon he was sweating.

It seemed like only an hour or so but he later found it was nearer four. The frantic message was shouted urgently to him. "Quick lads—outbye and away t'bank! Everybody's to get to bank!"

Daniel threw down his pick and squirmed along the two and a half foot high passage way. He didn't argue. They didn't lowse the pit for nothing. There was trouble somewhere. He met up with Sid coming off another part of the face. George Finch was behind him and Alfie Mennem behind him with his two eldest sons.

126

"What's up Dan," Sid asked anxiously.

Daniel shook his head. "Dunno," he barked as they scuffled along toward the main way.

"But what about little Billy and Fred," Alfie whined at his two sons. "They're in the Low Main. D'you think they're all right? They're not trapped d'you think? And where's Joe—little Joe—where's he?"

George spoke to him gently, reassuring him, because he knew no one else would.

As they reached the main way their numbers had grown. There were putters and rolleyway men, hewers and doorboys. Sons looking for fathers, brothers shouting for brothers and all wondering with fear prickling at their stomachs, what was so wrong that they were all called to bank.

Eventually after an agonizing wait at the shaft they all arrived at the pit-head and stood exchanging theories and rumours until the viewer appeared from his cabin and silenced them.

"Men, you have all been called to bank because there is every possibility of a bad flooding of the pit. We have hit an immense feeder of water in the High Main and there is but a few hours grace to draw out the galloways and important equipment."

A loud groan rippled across the crowd and there were shouts of "not again—for hell's sake not again."

The viewer held up his hands for silence but Daniel took no notice.

"And what does that mean to us. Does it mean we're out of work again because the owner of the pit will not spend money on proper surveying gear?" he shouted angrily.

The viewer looked sourly toward Daniel. "There we are—already people are jumping to conclusions. Will you let me have my say and then you can have yours!"

There were murmurings then silent nods.

"We have had an idea of this feeder for sometime and remembering the fate of the Lovat we have been very careful with our surveying. This feeder can be controlled and will be controlled. Already work is in hand to build a giant new condensing engine—here at Hester pit. This will work equally giant pumps and these will keep the pit dry and safe from inundation. What have you to say to that?"

There were few cheers but most sighed with relief. At least they were still in work and that was a Godsend.

"If you knew of this, why did you not tell us before. Why risk our lives?" Daniel shouted. The viewer flushed slightly and the way he breathed through his mouth signified his anger. Sid gave out a groan.

"My dear sir," the viewer said coldly. "We have kept you working as long as was possible and in our opinion, safe. We have drawn you out because it is no longer safe. You have worked for almost two months, since the problem was first envisaged. If we had laid you off then you would all have been two months pay the poorer."

The miners muttered their agreement to the viewer's statement. Still Daniel persisted.

"How long will we be laid off, until this giant pump is erected then," he yelled sarcastically.

The viewer shrugged, "Four, perhaps six weeks."

"Will you pay us in the meantime?"

Sid tugged violently at Daniel's jacket. He was expecting him to be sacked on the spot.

The viewer gazed intently at the uncompromising face of Daniel Simpson, then he smiled. "You jest," he said quietly before turning back to his cabin.

The miners turned and drifted away to tell their families the news. Daniel stood silently weighing up the implications of the viewer's statement. Just a few short hours before he had been complaining that no money was spent improving the pit, now this. Now a giant pumping engine! It was certainly a step in the right direction he thought, perhaps they had in mind a second shaft to ventilate the pit, as well. Perhaps that was the next thing they would do. He wondered if he had misjudged them; maybe he was becoming too cynical and suspicious. He turned, Sid and the rest of the miners had gone home. He started a slow, stooped stroll toward the village. He was still puzzled but he was a lot happier leaving the pit that day, than he was when he approached it, even if it meant a month or more without pay.

By the time he reached the bottom of the row Daniel felt himself stiffening up after his three-day lay-off. The wind was biting and already the sun was setting over the Cheviots far off in the distance. His wet clothes chilled him to the bone and he still felt a little weak from his gassing. It was a night to be in front of the fire, he resolved, and provided his wife and daughter kept quiet and out of his way he knew he would enjoy it. His mind was a whirl of how they would manage for the next few weeks and his memory brought back the long months of the big strike and he knew it would be difficult but he had managed to save a few shillings and he knew for certain that Dorothy had a pile of silver wrapped up in a pair of her drawers in the big press.

It was the voices of children that brought him out of his daydream. The voices were raised and angry and unusually harsh for children. Perhaps it was Margaret's voice that sub-consciously triggered off the desire to stop and listen and as the sound came from around the side of Chapman's closet he crept up close to the closet door and kept out of sight.

"It's a lie—you're always tellin' lies," he heard Margaret say in a voice that now sounded on the brink of tears.

"Yah, it's true, my mam says so. Your da' hates you and your mam—he hates all women. He's crackers."

Daniel recognized Alice Cairn's unusually high-pitched voice and he fought back the urge to bring the argument to a premature halt.

"It's not true, my da' does love us. He's got a special kind of love. He doesn't need to kiss us and whatnot. My da's the best da' in the world," Margaret countered.

Daniel opened his mouth ready to shout and chase Margaret's tormentors, but something held him back. He was fascinated by this encounter. His daughter's defence of him again brought lines of puzzlement to his face. Why didn't she agree—why didn't she tell them the truth—why did she say she loved him.

This time Mona Chapman started. "My mam says your da's a beast. He whips you and your mam and keeps you locked in a cage."

Margaret retorted quickly. "That's all lies as well Mona Chapman. You're all jealous 'cos my da's nice. Anyway my mam says there's something the matter with you 'cos you're always picking your nose or scratchin' your bum."

Daniel heard the shocked "ooh" from Mona and the hint of a smile crept on to his lips. He found himself mentally cheering his daughter on against the unfair odds.

Margaret's two adversaries began a chant in retaliation. "Simple Simpson, Simple Simpson," they shouted, and Daniel felt the anger in his daughter's voice when she shouted. "I'll show you. You'll see. My da's promised me that big doll in Stell's shop for my birthday. That'll show you how nice he is."

The two girls threw out a few more shouts of "liar" then ran off well pleased with themselves. Still Daniel did not move. There was silence from around the closet wall. Then he heard a deep jerky in-rush of breath, then a sob, then another, then quiet sorrowful crying as though the end of the world had come. Margaret came into his view but she did not see him. Her little hands were screwed up to her eyes and she walked almost instinctively up the lane, towards her house. Daniel followed her with his eyes. There was still no feeling for her, still only a vacuum of tolerance, yet as he saw the bowed head of blond ringlets and sensed the deep, deep hurt in her tears he somehow felt detached from his body and that it was he, as he was over thirty years before.

When Sid arrived home prematurely, Martha sat bolt upright in bed and held her hand to her throat in shock. Sid closed the door behind him and looked silently around the room; it was empty except for his wife.

"Oh, Sid, what a fright. What are you doing home so soon?" she bleated in a voice that was cringing and full of self pity. "The boys—is it the boys?"

Sid looked at her contemptuously. The lazy bitch, he thought. In bed again. She didn't expect us back so soon. Caught her lying rotten in bed, the lazy bitch.

He walked slowly up to the bed, his top lip twitching into a snarl and pulled the blankets savagely off her.

"Get up!" he yelled. "Get your bliddy self up and do some work!"

Martha cringed. "No, Sid please! I've been sick again since you went out to work—honest I have."

Sid took hold of her wrists and heaved her to the side of the bed.

"Get up woman. There's nothing wrong with you that a bit of housework won't cure."

Martha yelled out in pain. "Oh, my wrists. Sid you're hurt-

130

ing my wrists. Please, oh, please Sid let me be."

Sid heaved harder and she tumbled into a heap on the floor.

"Now get yourself up and clean this pig-sty out. Waiting for the lasses to come in to do it eh? I know your flamin' tricks," Sid hissed as he turned toward the fireplace, his breath coming quickly and the pulse in his temple pounding with the anger he felt.

Slowly Martha pulled herself to a kneeling position and then stood shakily on her feet. Her matted hair hung over her face and she pushed it back with her hands as she stood giving out little high-pitched gasps in between loud sniffs.

Sid turned to her again. "You're a lazy bitch Martha— there's no two ways about it. Just think of what you were like at Shirehill. You had some pride then. You were somebody to be proud of. Now you're a slut."

Martha sniffed loudly and shuffled over to a stool. She sat down and stared into the fire for a moment, then looked up at her husband. Her voice was calm and cold and her eyes were red and puffy. "I have been sick Sid. I've been sick every day this week, and I've been reckoning up. I haven't shown for near six weeks. I reckon you've bairned me again Sid."

Sid froze on the spot. He had heard the words but he felt he must have dreamed them.

"No," he whispered. "No, Martha—it canna be, man— surely not—not at our bliddy age!"

Martha nodded unhappily. "It looks like it."

Sid sat down at the table still cluttered with the breakfast dishes. He held his head between his hands. He imagined dirty, slovenly Martha pregnant. Then he imagined her with a neglected baby, lying unchanged in its crib all day crying for food and attention.

"My God no!" he spluttered. "It's all wrong. It canna be true."

131

CHAPTER 2

March 1852

Work on installing the new pumping engine at the Hester Pit proceeded surprisingly quickly. Within a few weeks the boilers, big and round and knobbly with their rivets, were positioned in line and stood silently broadcasting their potential power. The great square chimneys began to rise above them, squat and awful, ready to suck the smoke away when the boilers began their task of making steam to move the giant engine.

The Hartley miners watched the progress of the work with an urgent interest. The sooner it was completed, the sooner they could return to the pit and earn money to live, and there were daily crowds at the pit-head to watch and mark the advancement. The women and children came too, to see the gigantic undertaking and for their husbands to point out some of the strange items of equipment not yet installed and wonder at the ingenuity of engineering science. They were all well pleased at the size of the project. To their minds, the size related to the safety and the safety meant more peace of mind. The pumping engine would be big. They were sure the pit would be safe from flooding. That was one of the haunting dangers they could forget about.

Alfie Mennem and his sons took the rest of the family to the pit-head. They all went together; that way they were not so conscious of the other villagers turning their backs or giving them furtive looks or whispered asides. As a family they could speak to each other, pretend to be light-hearted and happy and show everyone that they didn't care. Everyone pretended except Alfie. He exuded misery as ever and ambled slowly behind his two eldest sons while his other children followed behind him. Mary Mennem waddled alongside her husband, her double chin pulled sternly down on to the massive shapeless roll of her chest, trying hard to ignore the glances of her neighbours. There was a derisive cry of "Lovat's boys" from someone among the other groups but all the Mennems ignored it .They had had years of practice in building up the thickness of their skin, but inside it still hurt.

George enjoyed showing his mother and sisters around the pit-head. He pointed to this and that and proudly explained the workings of the winding engine and showed them step by step, the progress of the coal from when it appeared at bank to when it was loaded into the big waggons for its journey to the drops at the Tyne or Seaton. The rest of the Mennems followed like sheep, pretending to be oblivious to the way the other villagers moved out of their path as though they had leprosy. They looked and listened to George as he bubbled with enthusiasm about the new pumping engine. George was one of the old school—a pitman to his roots. Tom was the only one not listening. Tom had noticed Victoria Taylor. He had noticed her many times over the past few years; he had undressed her a thousand times in his mind and he had made love to her over and over again, in his dreams.

Victoria Taylor with the big brown eyes had never so much as spoken to him. She had looked at him with those big talkative eyes; she had looked at him as none of the other girls had ever looked at him. Whenever she saw him her head went slightly askew and her lips parted ever so discreetly and to Tom's stimulated mind her big brown eyes invited him, teased him, implored him to touch her. She was standing at the far side of her father, Matthew Taylor an onsetter at the pit and had gently moved her shoulders back just a fraction and turned her head toward him. Her glistening lips parted slightly and those big inviting eyes seemed to devour him. Tom felt his heart pound and a warm gush of excitement rise to his head. In all his twenty-two years he had never had a woman. He had never spoken to a girl since the incident with Jessop had branded the whole family as outcasts. He had had his imaginings, but how he longed for a girlfriend, someone whom he could love and impress and marry; but now Tom felt afraid. Questions and doubts raced through his brain. Why did she flirt with him so, with those eyes of hers, when the others ignored him? Should he speak to her?—No—he couldn't do it. He was terrified of a rebuff. He would have to make his fantasies with her an acceptable substitution. Yet she looked at him so imploringly. He had overheard the other young men at the pit talk about her many times. She was easy and willing. Victoria Taylor liked men—any man—he had heard them say it—so she must like him. She must! He gulped stupidly when he realized his bottom jaw was sagging as he day-dreamed about her, but still she radiated a warm amused look before she decided to take an interest in what her father was saying.

Tom sighed deeply. Sometimes the weight of the cross they had to bear for their father was a little too heavy. He had wished they would move away to some other village, in Durham perhaps, where no one knew and they would be treated as normal, but Alfie and George would not hear of it. They had both done wrong and it was as though they were prolonging their own punishment. They were their own jailers; only they would know when they had paid their debt. He looked again toward Victoria Taylor as she moved off with her parents. Someday he thought, someday Victoria Taylor I'll have you, so help me I will.

Even before he opened the door, Daniel heard a whispered urgent command and a quick scuffling movement, but when he entered, everything looked normal to him. Dorothy looked up from her sewing, then down again, muttering "Your supper's on the hob," as he warmed his hands at the fire. Daniel grunted an acknowledgement and peered into the deep black pan. He was hungry and he was in a relatively good mood. Work was progressing well at the pit and he had heard from the under-viewer that another three or four weeks would see them all back at work. On top of that he and Sid had drunk four pints of ale at the Hastings Arms and he was mellowed, hungry and sleepy all at the same time.

"What was that noise?" he growled, still standing at the fire.

"What noise?"

"That bliddy whispering and scuffing about."

"Dunno."

He turned to face her. "Ye must know woman. I heard it as

134

I passed the window."

Dorothy looked hard at him for a moment, then put down her sewing, a mirthless smile thinning her lips. "Do you know what day it is tomorrow?" she asked him quietly.

"What the hell's that got to do with it?" he said irritably.

"It's got everything to do with it. It's Margaret's birthday Dan. You didn't know that did you? She's eight years old. Soon she'll be a woman Dan. Soon it'll be too late for you to give her any happy childhood memories of you."

Daniel's face twisted into a derisive snarl then he turned and spooned himself some stew. He carried the bowl to the table and began to eat. Dorothy sat stiffly upright watching him intently. "She's having some friends for bread and jam and a bit of cake," she said at last, rushing the words out in the hope he may not have heard them.

Daniel continued eating. He put the stew noisily into his mouth, sucking it off the spoon, keeping his eyes focused on his bowl. He said nothing until he had scraped it out and Dorothy hoped he had forgotten his original question.

"You've money to spend on others have you?" he asked with a menacing softness.

"You still find money for beer," she countered indignantly. "A few pence on the bairn's birthday'll not make us starve."

He sucked pensively at his bottom lip. "I'll ask again—what was the bliddy noise?"

With a loud sigh of resignation, she stood up. "It was a surprise for the morn, but it'll not matter if you see it now," she whispered flatly. "Y'can come out hinny—it's all right," she continued, raising her voice.

Slowly the scullery door opened and Daniel watched wide-eyed, his spoon still gripped in his hand as Margaret shyly moved out of the darkness and into the yellowed light of the room. Dorothy's eyes glowed proudly as she followed the movement of her daughter.

"Here pet," she whispered, "come and let your da' see your beautiful birthday dress."

Margaret moved toward her father. Her blond ringlets hung down like twirls of gold and her face searched his for some smattering of approval. With a burst of bravado she gasped, "D'you like it da'—isn't it lovely?" Daniel sat almost hypnotized. Suddenly he began to struggle for his breath. The smell of

135

horse dung reached up his nostrils and tugged savagely at his stomach. The dress filled the whole of his vision. All that whiteness. All those bows and frills and the nerve-shattering rustle it made with each slight movement. His fingers began to tremble and the strange tingling ran up his arms and down his body. A searing pain burned its way from his brow, across the stubble of his head to the nape of his neck.

"That dress—get that soddin' dress off," he whispered in an agonized sort of croak.

Margaret paled and glanced quickly to her mother. Dorothy jumped up and held her daughter's shoulders. "For Christ's sake Daniel, have you no sense at all," she shrieked desperately. "Tell the bairn she looks nice will you—God Almighty, tell her she looks nice."

Daniel's face twisted into a tortured grimace. "The dress!" he yelled, standing up. "The dress—get it off!" He lunged toward them. Dorothy tried to move her daughter behind her, but it was too late. With two simultaneous and opposing swings with his great arms, Dorothy fell one way and Margaret spun across the room and landed in a heap in the corner. She lay there sobbing, her head wrapped by her smooth little arms as she tried to hide away from the reality of the nightmare around her.

Dorothy was on her feet in an instant and with the blind animal instinct of a mother protecting her young, she sunk her nails into the thick, stiff neck of her husband, with an almost insane scream. Daniel did not move. He felt something at his neck, but no pain. He stood rooted to the spot, his body numb and his mind grappling with the scene in front of him. He could see a figure, a form in a white dress lying sobbing in a corner. He could see the mass of blond hair and hear the desperate sorrow that emanated from beneath it. He could see himself. He knew exactly the horror, the fear, the desperation. It was him and he was his mother, his wretched, evil mother. With a deep shuddering groan he pushed Dorothy away and moved toward Margaret. He was suddenly, miraculously, flooded with the compassion that he himself had longed for as a child. As he stood over her he felt a deep, deep love gush up out of the depths of his soul and it was so strange to him he did not know how to handle it. He bent down and touched her shoulder. She screamed, but he did not hear her. Slowly

136

he put his arms under her and lifted her up.

Dorothy made to attack him again but she stopped in her tracks. Her husband's face was ecstatic, triumphant and his eyes, for the first time since the birth of their daughter were soft and warm and at peace.

Margaret hid her face from him in her abject terror. He laid her gently on the bed, then turned. He looked toward his wife but the ice blue eyes stared straight through her. He moved slowly to the door.

"God forgive me," he whispered as he took hold of the latch.

He opened the door and stood for a moment looking out and heaving the cold air into his lungs. He turned his head and looked back toward the bed. There was a terrified wonderment in his face. "God forgive me," he whispered again as he stumbled out and let the darkness envelop him.

Tom Mennem recognized Daniel's great form as he wandered resolutely down the back lane but there was no exchange of greetings. As he passed him he noticed his hunched shoulders and his bowed, shaven head in the brief illumination of a cottage window and he wondered where he was going with such positiveness at that time of night. As for Tom, the shroud of night time gave him a freedom he couldn't experience during the day. He could wander alone and at ease and be himself and think his own thoughts without having to worry about the stares and sniggers and scowls of the rest of the village. Funny, he thought how it never affected George that way. It was as though George enjoyed all the antagonism. Sometimes he even boasted about it. He never seemed to miss female company. All he ever talked of was the pit and the taking of coal was an exciting challenge to him. It devoured all of his energy and thought. It was a private contest between himself and nature and he enjoyed every soul-sapping minute of it.

The air was cold that night and there was already a skin of ice on the water in the rain barrels as Tom ambled slowly on down the lane. His ears were nipped with the frost and his nose end was numb but it did not bother him. He enjoyed the sanctuary of solitude and as he passed each little cottage, the muffled conversations of the inhabitants came sneaking through the air to him. Sometimes the words were harsh and

137

voices raised, other times slow and loving, other times happy and gay. The occasional baby cried, sometimes a fiddle scraped out a tune. He could smell the fresh stotties Mrs. Chapman always baked and the pickling spices from the Finches. A dog barked from inside as he passed the door, then he heard it yelp as it got a foot in its ribs. Tom drank in each noise, smell, sensation. In his mind he lived in each of the cottages. He was friends with them all. He imagined himself knocking on each door and being greeted and asked in.

Then he saw her. Victoria Taylor was standing against the closed door of her cottage, hands behind her back, her head gently elevated, looking up with those big brown eyes into the twinkling eternity. She was bathed in the faint yellow light from the window and her breath billowed slowly up into the frosty night. Tom stopped in his tracks. He swallowed nervously as his mind fought itself for the decision of what to do next. Even as he thought, she turned her head toward him and her eyes immediately began to dance and sparkle in the weak yellow light. They beckoned him, they toyed with him and he could not resist. Cautiously he walked the few paces toward her and stood with his heart pounding wildly, only a scant three feet away from her glistening lips. Her hands slowly appeared from behind her back and she lifted them up and placed one on each of his cheeks. They were warm and soft and Tom felt his knees begin to tremble. He gazed into her hypnotic eyes as they silently implored him to love her. He took hold of her hands and kissed each warm intimate palm in turn, then moved his lips towards hers.

"No, not here," she whispered. "Not here."

Tom could hardly control himself. His body ached with his want of her.

"Where? tell me where? Victoria," he breathed.

"Behind Stell's warehouse," she said as she ducked deftly under his arms, "follow me."

She lifted her skirts and flew silently down the lane. Tom followed, his whole body trembling with anticipation. She did like him, he thought, at last beautiful Victoria likes me, and wants me. His feet didn't seem as though they were touching the ground as he made his way a few paces behind her. His mind was flooded with the intimate delights to follow and his heart thumped the hot flush of desire around his body.

At the bottom of the lane they turned from the pit and along the path toward Stell's shop. The warehouse, long and low and made of blackened timber adjoined Stell's house proper and backed out over the fields toward Seaton. Victoria had gained on him along the path and he sensed she stopped and made sure he was still following before she disappeared completely into the inkiness of the night behind the buildings. Tom stopped when he reached the corner. He could not see her. His eyes strained through the darkness but he could not see her. "Victoria," he whispered hoarsely. There was complete silence.

"Victoria," he said again.

He sensed the rustle of a dress and the hint of a suppressed giggle. He breathed cautiously.

"Victoria, I'm here," he said again.

"This way Tom," said a voice in the darkness. "Come to me Tom."

Tom smiled broadly and moved forward.

"Beyond the wall Tom—I'm here."

He could just make out the low solidity of the stone wall bounding the field and with his hands outstretched, moved slowly toward it. As soon as he touched it he vaulted eagerly over. The sudden animal noise almost made his heart stop. The screeching and squealing and movement of the animal as he landed beside it terrorized him. Then he heard it grunt and squeal again. Then he heard the loud mocking laughter and the giggling amusement. There was a crowd of them; black shapes in the night. Men and women, laughing, mocking, ridiculing him. And there was the pig. The great heaving mud-covered sow snorting and screeching beside him where he expected Victoria Taylor to be. His heart sank into his boots. He picked himself up and ran as fast as his legs could carry him out and away across the field. Away from the mocking laughter and the pointing fingers to somewhere where he could again be alone to lick his wounds in the solitude he could trust.

When Dorothy woke the next morning, Daniel was still not back. She had slept fitfully with Margaret in her arms and as she stirred, so Margaret gave a bleating little sigh and woke as well. As she realized where she was, the fear returned to her face but a quick glance at her mother reassured her.

"Happy birthday little lass," she said, giving her a big squeeze.

"You're eight today. You're a big girl now aren't you."

Margaret nodded. "Where's da?" she whispered.

"Dunno pet. Forget about him. Let's have a nice birthday for you eh?"

"Are we going to bake the cake?" she asked eagerly.

"Shortly. Come on help me tidy the place up and put the fire on."

Both of them set to with an excitement that blotted out the memories of the night before.

By three o'clock the cake was baked and collared with some red cloth and eight little candles placed nicely on the top. Dorothy was washed and dressed and her hair combed neatly into a bun. Maragret was in her new dress, her ringlets cascading over her shoulders and her face scrubbed to a glowing red at her cheeks. Soon her guests arrived. There was Daisy Finch and Mona Chapman and Alice Cairns. They entered with beaming faces and Sunday best and with the excited anticipation of an occasion. Soon there were games and the cottage rang with the unusual sound of laughter. They chased each other. They played hide and seek. They recited nursery rhymes. They enjoyed themselves. When tea-time came they sat down and ate their stotty lashed with home-made crab apple jam and finally it was time to light the candles on the cake. Dorothy lit a spill at the fire and then lit each candle. The eight little flames danced in eight little eyes and Dorothy stood back as they sang "Happy birthday". It sounded so good to her to hear four innocent bell-like voices fill the room with their purity, for Margaret joined in and sang as well. She watched her daughter's happy face and prayed that she was supplying enough love for two people.

Suddenly the door opened and Daniel walked in. Dorothy and the four children watched him in awed silence as he stood observing them.

"Come here Maggie," he said coldly.

Margaret looked toward her mother but she gave no hint of what she had to do. She sat still. Daniel nodded. "Will you come for this then," he said, turning at the open door and pulling an object out of the lane. He held it up above his head, a smile creasing his face. It was the doll. It was the big doll from Stell's shop. Margaret ran to him and he scooped her up like a feather. He buried his face into her neck and he could smell the sweet innocence of her skin. He gave her the doll and she hugged it and he hugged her.

"Oh da'," she whimpered, "it's the doll. It's my doll. Thanks da'." Daniel laughed and held her to him again. Daisy Finch and Mona Chapman and Alice Cairns sat dumbfounded in their seats. Dorothy moved to his side and could not help herself putting a hand on his arm. She did not mind when he removed it gently but firmly. The tears were not for that, they were because her husband had at last found his daughter.

CHAPTER 3

April 1854

The four men squatted in the top section of the iron cage as it rose ponderously up the shaft toward daylight and fresh air. The fore-shift was over and Daniel and Sid and Sid's two eldest sons gazed through unseeing eyes, awaiting the luxury of being able to stretch their aching muscles and wash away the black grime and staleness of the pit. They had had a hard shift. They had hit coal that was like granite and their picks had blunted early, so their efforts had been doubled to hew their usual quota and fill the expected number of tubs to keep the putters happy.

They were sore and tired as they crouched in the moving darkness and none of them spoke. None of them had the energy to speak let alone the inclination to put their thoughts into words. As they slowly rose toward the surface the air got colder and purer and sweeter and their lungs seemed to grasp at it to rejuvenate their deadened bodies. The noise of the great pumping engine also got louder. Its low thunderous roar as the piston returned for another working stroke, then the slow, slow whoop, gradually rising in pitch as it sucked at the water and drew it from the sump up to the Yard Seam and then to the High Main and finally through a small connecting shaft up to the surface, to gush away, brown and black and grey and clayey, to find itself a new resting place.

It was almost two years to the day that the monster had been completed and when the roof finally went on the pumping house, the miners agreed it was even bigger than they had ever expected. The main pumping beam was thirty-seven feet long and eight feet deep at the central pivot point and it was made of forty-two tons of finest cast iron. One end was connected to the great condensing engine within the pumping house. It was pivoted near the outer wall and the working end protruded out of the building, over the up-cast section of the shaft so that the connecting pump rods were vertically down the shaft. The pumps worked well. They kept the water at a safe level. It was almost two years to the day, since the noise of their power joined in dominating the village of Hartley. Day and night; constantly working; ever roaring and whooping, slowly and steadily at four strokes a minute. At first the people of the village were irritated by it. They could hear it all day and all through the night, but soon the noise became part of them. They became unconscious of it, yet it was always with them, calming their subconscious fears and reassuring them of its constant efficiency.

Sid remembered well the day the pumps first started up. He and Daniel had walked eagerly to the pit to witness the testing of the new equipment and as the great beam reluctantly moved to the four-hundred horsepower of the engine, a great cheer went up from all who were present. A pleasant satisfaction ran through them. They worked. The pumps worked. Now the men could return to work. But Sid's pleasure was short lived, that day. He heard the voice of his youngest daughter shout his name and in an instant he could tell from the tone of it that there was something wrong. He turned and saw Mary running up the path toward them.

He ran to meet her.

"Da'—come quick," she gasped. "It's mam—she's awful sick—she's bleedin'."

Sid's brow tightened and he ran without further question down the path toward the cottages. When he got to his door he burst in and stood gulping air as he observed the scene. Martha was ashen grey and in bed. Florence lifted her tear stained face and looked helplessly toward him then at Dorothy Simpson who worked at his wife with an urgent grimness.

"What happened," Sid whispered as he gingerly approached the bed.

"She's bleedin'. She's ganna lose the bairn," Dorothy said matter-of-factly without looking up.

"How did that happen for hell's sake."

"Dunno, Florence here just found her on the floor."

Sid looked at his daughter who nodded a solemn confirmation, then he cautiously peered over Dorothy's shoulder. He swallowed hard and closed his eyes as he turned away.

"Will she be all right?" he asked, frantically.

"She should be. Mebbe for the best anyway," Dorothy said with a sigh.

"What's for the best?"

"Losin' the bairn. She doesn't want lumbering with a young'un, not the way she is."

Sid nodded silently. He moved around Dorothy and tapped his wife's cheek.

"Martha," he whispered. "Martha hinny, it's me, Sid. What happened?"

Martha slowly opened her glazed eyes. Her mouth moved slowly to say words and as her lips parted the thickened saliva stretched between them. She smiled a weak apologetic smile. "That's it Sid. I did it didn't I. Are you pleased Sid?"

"What are you talking about," Sid growled as a prickle of fear ran up his neck. He looked up at Dorothy and Florence.

"What's she talking about?"

Martha continued before they could answer.

"I did it. It's gone. I got rid of it Sid."

Suddenly the realization came to him. "My God," he breathed. "Oh, my God."

"What the hell did she use?" Dorothy shouted, looking frantically around her. "What did you use Martha?"

There was no answer, only a stupid wan smile.

Sid stalked quickly around the room, looking here and there and finally he threw himself down on his hands and knees and groped under the bed. Dorothy and Florence drew their breath in a quick noisy grunt as he retrieved the long wooden knitting needle, blood covered and evil looking from its hiding-place.

"You stupid bitch," he screamed as he threw it dramatically on to the fire, on his way to the door. He ran all the way to Seaton and rode behind Doctor Jenkins as he galloped back on his big brown hunter.

It took almost three hours before the doctor pronounced his verdict. "She'll live," he snapped, "and she's still got the bairn—but don't ask me if it'll live or what it'll be like. She could have deformed it or anything, the silly bugger."

Sid thanked him profusely, then a serious look clouded his

face. It was only the second time in his life that a doctor had been called to his family. It was a luxury the miners could ill afford and in the majority of cases the old fashioned household concoctions had to be relied on. But Sid in his fright and eagerness had forgotten that doctors came expensive and that he was not in work at the moment.

"Can I pay when I get back t'the pit," he asked humbly.

Doctor Jenkins stood for a moment with pensive pursed lips, then he nodded positively, "D'you think I didn't know I wouldn't get paid. All right. It'll be fifteen shillings—and I'll put it down in the book so I'll not forget," he added reproachfully.

Sid sighed with relief. He thanked him again and again as he saw him to the door and watched him, mounted on his horse, trot slowly up the lane.

Sid smiled in the darkness of the shaft. He couldn't in his wildest dreams have imagined the outcome. As Martha regained her strength and became swollen and the child within her started to move, so she returned to her old self. She once again began to take a pride in her appearance and in the appearance of her home. She returned to her specific and exacting ways. In her later months she glowed with health and it gladdened the hearts of all her family. When the baby was born it was a boy and their dread evaporated instantly when he was pronounced perfect. They called him Jacob and he had Sid's curling red hair. It was not long before they realized that Jacob was something special. He was bright and alert and a joy to his mother and father.

Daniel was thinking about the two young men who had been badly gassed the week before and silently calling himself names for even thinking that a ventilation shaft would be sunk to help improve their working condition. He realized that the great pumps had not been installed to keep the men safe from drowning. No—the fortune had not been spent with the welfare of the miners in mind. He wondered how he could have been so foolish as to even think it was so. The pump was there to keep the water low because there was a thousand times the fortune in coal, lying there silent and black. As long as the coal was accessible, it could be brought to the surface and sold and the fortune would then be in money.

He reflected on his forty years. He tried to compare the conditions of the pitmen when he started at six years old to now, in his forty-first year. The changes were few and slight. Boys had now to be ten before they could work below ground. That was something, but not much. Ten was a tender age to be thrust into the frightening black chasm of a mine, among swearing naked men who recounted their tales of prowess at drinking or seduction with avid and unashamed clarity. "Tommy" shops had been abolished which was a good thing. No longer did the few shillings that they earned go straight back into the owners' pockets. But there again, some of the private owners were just as bad; tight fisted and ruthless—like Drummond at Shirehill. He felt a tingle of frustration run through him. There was so much that could be done if only they had the power. If only they could unite. If only they would listen. He had seen men die. He had seen men maimed for life. Needlessly, they altered the course of their lives and the lives of their families for a few shillings and a torn back and aching tortured muscles. He wished he could do more. His thoughts turned to home and food and a hot bath. He thought of Margaret who would be at the pit-head to meet him as she always had been for two years. How much he had missed of her in those first eight years. Just the feel of her small, warm, delicate hand in his, as she skipped along beside him was a whole new experience each day. He had tried to make up for those eight lost years. Almost every minute of his spare time they were together. He told her stories, he took her to the whippet racing on a Sunday morning; he took her to the sparrow shooting competitions and laughed at her love of being afraid of the banging guns. They were friends, great friends and Dorothy was happy for them even if a twinge of jealousy did sometimes creep through her at their new-found relationship. Daniel still only tolerated her. She was nothing to him except a housekeeper and although Margaret loved them both, the void between them seemed eternal. The miracle that had occurred on Margaret's birthday would not it seemed, repeat itself for Dorothy.

Suddenly the grey, wet stone, that lined the shaft became visible and rapidly the brightness increased. Sid could see Daniel's blue eyes blinking as he accustomed them to the daylight. He looked to his right then to Daniel's left. His sons' blackened faces, streaked with dried sweat and coal dust, were slumped forward. They were dozing. The cage jerked to a halt and the sunlight and activity of the pit-head enveloped them. The boys woke up and with painful grunts the four of them crawled unsteadily out into the world again. They nodded an insincere greeting to the banks-man and with their blunted picks slung over their stooped shoulders they wandered unconcerned past the bee-hive of the pit.

Daniel glanced around him. Margaret was nowhere to be seen. He swivelled his head this way and that and shielding his eyes with his free hand he gazed far down the path for some sight of her. He could see no one except for early fore-shift miners, dark and sluggish, wending their way home ahead of them. Down near the first of the cottages he could also make out a crowd of people gathered in a circle. He quickened his pace and Sid noticed his concern as he and his sons kept up with him.

"Howay Dan, slow down man," he said with mock annoyance. "She'll be down among that crowd I'll bet. It'll be gipsies or a tinker sellin' wares."

Daniel nodded, his features grim. He said nothing and did not slacken his pace. Before they reached the crowd they realized it couldn't possibly be gipsies. There were four sleek black horses nibbling at the wayside grass. They were big and well fed and groomed expertly. The curiosity of the four men grew as they pushed their way through to viewing distance. Margaret ran to Daniel's side and he subconsciously put an arm around her shoulders, as he gazed spellbound with the others. The four cavalry men stood straight and proud in their immaculate uniforms of blue jacket and red pants and black gleaming boots. Their faces were scrubbed and handsome and radiated health. One was speaking, his helmet off and held under an arm, while the others nodded in agreement with his words or smiled broad white teeth at the fluttering eyebrows and coy glances of wives and daughters.

"It's the chance of a lifetime men," the soldier shouted. "How many of you have been farther than Newcastle? Join the Queen's army and see the world men. You don't want to work in a coal pit all your lives—do you?"

147

He threw a quick amused glance at his companions. "The Queen herself requested her cavalry to recruit her loyal miners to fight in this war. She's relying on you lads. She knows you won't let her down. You'll get pay and three grand meals a day and you'll be kitted out in a fine uniform like this. What about it lads—you can't fail with the girls dressed like this."

"What's happening in the war?" somebody shouted.

"The war?—why the war's a doddle lads," the soldier shouted with an unconcerned wave of his arm. "Those Russians sank the poor little Turkish fleet last November—now we wouldn't want our Turkish mates to go without help—would we? All we've got to do is show ourselves and the Russians'll turn and run like hell—it's true! They've no stomach for scrapping with the British—or the French. The Frenchies are enlisting in their thousands and we want more of our lads to scare those Russian devils once and for all. What do you say lads—who's for joining the Queen's army. It's the chance of a lifetime."

Robert Garrett brought the muttering of the crowd to a premature halt.

"What's it like in Turkey?" he asked.

"How do you mean son."

"Well," Robert said cautiously, "can a man find fortune out there?"

The soldier laughed a great belly laugh and winked at his smiling companions. He bent forward as though to tell a secret. The crowd was hushed.

"I've heard it said—by more than one—mark you, that the hills outside Constantinople are filled with gold," he said in a hoarse whisper.

"You lads are miners—but you wouldn't have to dig—not in Turkey. You can pick those great big nuggets straight off the ground."

He knelt down and mimed the action, while the crowd oohed.

Robert looked at his brother. They stared at each other for a moment each weighing the excited glint in the other's eyes. The soldier got up and dusted his knees.

"If there's any among you," he continued a little flatly, "who are man enough to see the delights of the world as a soldier of the Queen, you can sign on tonight at the Hastings

Arms or tomorrow morning at the barracks in Newcastle."

The crowd began to break up. Daniel wandered home with his daughter. Sid followed his smiling sons up the back lane. Alfie Mennem and George guided Billy and Fred and Joseph up to their door. Tom stood where he was. When the crowd dispersed he stood watching the soldiers chatting among themselves. He also saw Victoria Taylor speak to them before her father bawled her name. She left them with obvious reluctance and began to walk away. As she passed him she smiled a thin mocking smile. A few moments later Tom turned and with a deep sigh he kicked a stone out of the way and made for home.

The soldier turned to his companions. He smiled broadly.

"Christ, they don't seem very enthusiastic this lot—and I gave them the whole effin' story."

They walked to their horses.

"It'll be all right Charlie, don't worry—you'll get your quota. The reason you're such a good recruiting officer is because you're also the best bastard liar in the flaming army."

They all laughed. They mounted their horses and cantered leisurely along the road toward the Hastings Arms which was their camp for the night.

John and Robert Garrett sat gulping down their food while Sid bounced Jacob on his knee and tried in vain to get his spoon past the waving arms of his youngest son and into his mouth. In between his attempts he recounted the story of the soldiers to Martha, oblivious to the unusual silence from his eldest boys.

Martha listened to the tale as she busied herself and smiled inwardly as Sid loudly lamented his age and what he would have done if he were twenty-five years younger. The two boys listened as well. There was an excitement that gripped at their stomachs as they finished off their meal. Even when they dashed out straight afterward Sid thought nothing of it. He tutted as the door banged loudly but that was not unusual. They were always rumbustious and he always tutted. It was no more than half an hour and they were back, still-black faces split with wide grins and sparkling eyes. John in his excitement could hardly give them the news. Sid was in the bath in front of the fire. Martha and May were clearing the table while Jacob played at their feet. They didn't have Florence to help them now. She had been married three months earlier and lived with her husband in Earsdon.

"Da'—we've got some news—some great news," John blurted.

"Shut the bliddy door," Sid yelled.

Robert slammed the door, then joined his brother in front of the bath.

"We've been to see the viewer da'," Robert said gleefully.

For the first time that day Sid took full notice of his sons. "The viewer? what for?"

Martha turned and wiped her hands on her pinafore, her look asking the same question as her husband. There was a sudden stillness in the house. The two lads became serious. "We've asked him if we can join the army?" John said quietly.

Sid blinked furiously for a few seconds, then stood up.

"The army," Martha whispered in a cracked voice.

"Aye—the cavalry—like the men we saw today," Robert yelled, his excitement returning.

"We're going to Turkey and get rich—we're sick of the pit— eh John?"

John nodded.

There was a profound sadness in Martha's face as she passed her husband the towel. She stared at her sons. She wanted to clout them around the ears and tell them not to be stupid but she knew she could not. For the first time she saw them as men and not boys.

"Why—why did you go to the viewer," Sid mumbled.

"We heard that he had to have the say. There's got to be some young'uns left at the pit or the women get hoyed out of the cottages. That's what he said."

"He's let you both go?"

"Aye—because there's you da' and there's little Jacob coming up in case . . ."

Robert's voice trailed away.

His mother's words were hard and piercing. "In case what Robbie?"

Robert smiled weakly. "In case we don't come back," he gabbled quickly—"but we will mam—the soldier says the war's safe as anything. The Russians'll not fight. They just run

150

—eh John?"

Again John nodded. "We'll be back Ma, and we'll be rich and have a big house built down near the dene."

Sid smiled as he dried himself. How he envied them. They were doing the right thing. They had a chance to get away and see some of the world. There was the chance of adventure and the possibility that they'd come back rich. How much he envied them. He couldn't argue as a tightness gripped his throat.

"When will you go?" Martha asked.

Robert looked at his brother. "We'll sleep on it just to make sure and go to Newcastle in the morning."

Sid nodded his approval. His boys were wise. He was proud of them. That night it took them a long time to drop off to sleep. They heard their mother quietly padding around the room gathering their few bits and pieces together until well after midnight and the next morning she found that her work had not been in vain.

Tom Mennem broke the news at the table. Alfie's jaw sagged and a piece of potato dropped out of his mouth.

"Get away man," George shouted. "You're bliddy mad—you're a pit-man not a soldier."

Tom gave his brother a mirthless smile. "I've made up my mind—I'm going."

"But what do you want to join the army for?" Alfie bleated. "Hell's bells y'll get killed Tom—y'll get blown to smithereens."

"Take no notice man da'," George said derisively, "he'll not join up—he's having us on."

Tom stood up and walked to the fireplace. He stared down at the flames for a minute. "I'm not kiddin'," he said at last. "There's nowt here for me—for any of us. I'm sick of being shunned as though I was some kind of monster."

"There's the pit. That's what we know. That's our life so be content," George shouted angrily.

Tom turned to face his brother. His eyes gleamed as he sucked his breath through his clenched teeth. He opened his mouth to speak and the words came with measured deliberation. "I'm sick of the soddin' pit and I'm sick of having to suffer for what he did. For God's sake, George, do you never want to have a girl and get married and settle down and live a

151

normal life."

He pointed to his father. His face was now twisted and red with anger.

"Why should we have to suffer all our lives for his mistakes. If he wanted to get one up on his workmates that his fault not ours."

George leapt to his feet and grabbed his brother. He pulled him by the shirt until their noses almost touched. "You sod," he hissed. "He did it for us you ungrateful bugger. He's paid all these years for keeping us from starvin'."

Tom gripped his brother's wrists and tried to prise them from his shirt. Alfie jumped up and tried to get between them while Billy and Fred cheered and Joe joined his sisters in bawling loudly. Only Mary Mennem was unaffected by the rumpus. She sat in a glazed silence her mind far away and on other things.

"You're as bad," Tom yelled into his brother's face. "There's summat wrong with you. You enjoy being an outcast. —Well you can have it all to yourselves—I'm going to join the army."

"Can we join da'?" Billy and Fred shouted together. "Can we go with our Tom?"

Alfie ignored them. He concentrated on his two eldest. "Eeeh lads come apart now—come apart or you'll hurt each other, you're not just lads now y'know."

Slowly Tom released his grip, then George did the same. They continued their wild staring.

"It's a long time since I hit you Tom Mennem," George whispered vehemently, "but you nearly got it there."

A smile came to Tom's face, a wide sarcastic smile, "and the last time I hit you it was to save your bacon—have you forgotten that, 'cos I haven't."

George sagged. He stood for a few more seconds then turned exasperated and sat down at the table.

His mother spoke for the first time. Her voice was soft but firm and they listened to her. "He's right—Tom's right. He's the only one with any sense. We should have all left here long ago, and it's about time something was done about it. Me and da's too old to move now, but seeing that Tom's going off, perhaps it's time the lasses found somewhere where they'll have a chance to get married. They can get away to Newcastle or somewhere and find work—they're old enough now. Billy and Fred and Joe'll go as soon as they get a few more years on them—and you George—you should go now—tonight, if you've any damned sense."

George swung around to his mother. His voice carried a pitch of surprise and amazement. "I'm not going anywhere. I'm staying here. I'm next in line for deputy overman—the viewer says so."

Alfie nodded sadly. "You're a funny lad George—you're already married aren't you son?—to the flamin' pit."

Tom walked around the table and put his hands on his mother's shoulders. He looked at the staring faces of his family.

"Can we come wi' you Tom?" Billy piped up as he ran to his side. "Me an' Fred want to go wi' you."

Tom tousled his hair. "There'll be another turn for you's later. I'll bet. If George isn't coming, I'll go myself. I'll go in the mornin'."

He turned and walked out. It was still early afternoon but he didn't care. He walked up the lane, past the playing children and wives possing their washing. He walked and walked. He came to Johnson's farm, only Johnson was long dead and a man called Swinney had it. Then there was the vast meadow that finished at the Tyne. All afternoon he trundled through the grass that was speckled with early dandelions and clover. Eventually he came to the river. He could smell the salt air, that smacked of far off places and he could see the sailing ships huddled to the banks like leafless forests. He felt a freedom within himself that made the butterflies move in his stomach and a happiness that made his heart sing. He knew he was doing the right thing.

The next morning was a tearful one in Hartley. About fifty men set off to walk to Newcastle. They left in twos and threes and the handkerchiefs were used for waving and drying eyes. Robert and John Garrett yelled and waved their goodbyes until they were well down the road. The whole village turned out to see them all off. Tom Mennem kissed his crying mother and his sisters and little Joe, then shook hands with Billy and Fred. George stood stiff and grim but he gripped his brother's shoulders and the good wishes flowed through to him. Finally Tom turned to his father. He noticed the brightness of his eyes and Adam's apple jumping in his scrawny neck. He embraced him. "I'm sorry da'," he whispered.

"So am I son—so am I," Alfie croaked in his ear. "Come back to us son—for God's sake come back."

Tom looked back only once. His solitary silhouette stood out against the morning sun and his family waved hard trying to convince themselves that he was sure to return unscathed. The rest of the villagers ignored him as he passed. There were no cries of "Good Luck" or "Well Done". Only one person felt a twinge of sadness at his leaving. She watched him as he walked by, solemn and stooped with his small bag of personal belongings slung over his shoulder.

It was Victoria Taylor.

The men of the village never got to join the cavalry. Before they realized it, they had signed on for the infantry. Within a month they had learned to march together and use a rifle, and with the newness of their boots still pinching their feet they were shipped to Constantinople. From there they moved to Varna where they waited in vain for the enemy.

Robert and John Garrett found, to their bitter disappointment that there was no gold, no fortune, no riches—only the army. Finally in September they sailed for Calamita bay in the Crimea.

CHAPTER 4

John Garrett glanced quickly at his brother then surveyed the scene in front of them. Robert's eyes were cemented on the hoard of black moving dots across the snow covered valley and his muscles were locked and primed, cat-like, ready to pounce when the time was right—and that time was fast approaching. The grimness of Robert's features gave some smattering of comfort to John. He knew he was afraid; they were all afraid and as he swallowed to clear his tightened throat he stopped the tremor in his hands by gripping his rifle harder.

It was cold, intensely cold and the crisp new snow had smoothed the contours of the valley and turned it into a vast pure arena where one would expect the happy laughter of tobogganing and snowball throwing, rather than the sizzling of cannon-balls and the quick lethal swish of sabres.

John looked again to his right; he looked past his brother and along the line of infantrymen that thinned into the distance. Behind them he could see the artillery and the cavalry—the dashing handsome cavalry. Everyone was waiting. Everyone was silent as the prayers fought their way upward. Suddenly John realized that his hands had gone numb and he blew on them furiously to bring back the circulation. He couldn't hold his rifle properly, let alone fire it with deadened fingers and that was one disadvantage he did not relish. Behind him he heard a hoarse muffled cry then the heavy thump of a cannon whose noise reverberated through to one's innards. A second or two later the snow across the valley erupted into little plumes that made the black dots move here and there quicker than before and when each plume settled, a few of the black dots stayed where they were.

There was a line of flashes from the other side, followed by a string of dull explosions and the missiles flew in retaliation. On and on the cannon roared and finally the order was barked down the line. John and Robert scrambled up and ran clumsily through the snow toward the enemy. Back on the ridge they had seemed to be miles away—in another world perhaps, but now in just a few short minutes the black dots had turned into men and their bullets whistled past their ears. Soon the smooth blanket beneath their feet was churned and trampled and littered with the bodies of men and horses shivering in their death throes. There was a pandemonium of screams and flying blood and exploding guns. The smell of sulphur hung heavy in the air and wisps of grey-blue smoke swirled around the milling seething bodies. A slow choking sound came from between John's clenched teeth as he swung his rifle as a club one minute, then rammed its gleaming bayonet home between someone's ribs the next. He would have liked to look around for his brother but there was no time; as soon as one fell there was another to take his place.

Robert concentrated with all his might on the giant of a man running toward him and he set himself for yet another struggle for his life. The Russian had his mouth wide open and a blood curdling scream came out with a cloud of billowing vapour. His beard was matted with snow and ice and his eyes were wide and wild with the frenzy of killing. He was big but he was clumsy. He thrust at Robert with his bayonet but the blade hit only air. Before he could turn Robert brought the butt of his rifle around and hit the man on the back of the head. He issued a quick grunt and fell face forward into the snow. Robert stood over him, the adrenalin of triumph pounding through his body. He raised his rifle vertically until the bayonet was almost level with his chest as the Russian groaned and turned over. His eyes opened and he blinked himself back to reality. He tried to lift his head but he could not. His eyes filled with terror—with the abject fear of death to come. Robert hesitated as he squirmed his last few seconds of life, a feeling of pity running through him at the degradation one man could bring upon another. Then he thought, you bastard—you bastard! You wanted to kill me; you did you great woolly sod. You wanted to actually kill me—me Robert Garrett!

The long blade sunk smoothly through the uniform and

through the heavy winter underclothes of the Russian soldier and into his soft flesh. The man uttered no sound. A look of disbelief crossed his face. A hand clawed uselessly at the air and his eyes stayed open as his head turned to the side. Robert retrieved his rifle and turned for the next encounter but it never came. There was a blinding flash of orange light and a tremendous heat that prickled at his face. At the same time an uncompromising force bundled him head over heels for what seemed like an eternity.

Tom Mennem almost fell over him as he ran toward an intense skirmish a few hundred yards away. He looked down and recognized who it was and with the blank unemotional acceptance that is bred in war, made to carry on. But something held him back. What or why he didn't know. The very fact of the discrimination at Hartley should have been enough to make him ignore Robert Garrett—but he could not. He was not the enemy. He was friend and he was lying there seemingly untouched and breathing, but very vulnerable. Quickly Tom looked around him for a medical orderly but there was none—only men locked in battle. Without another thought Tom threw down his rifle and hoisted him over his shoulder. Unsteadily he staggered through the hell that surrounded them and managed by some miracle to lower him to the ground well away from the scene of sudden death and gore. The exertion of battle and the carrying of Robert Garrett had made him sweat under his uniform, but as soon as he relaxed the cold crept through his clothes and chilled him to the bone. Quickly he fished in his pocket for his woollen helmet to try to take some of the sting from his ears then he concentrated on Robert. He rubbed at his hands and face then he found his helmet and pulled it over his head. He looked up and over the top of their shell hole to see how the battle was progressing but could make nothing from the confused scene. He pondered on whether to leave Robert in the relative safety of the shell hole and find help for him. Then he realized that the vast white canvas that surrounded them was deceiving. He had lost his bearings in the featureless valley. He was unsure of the direction of their lines and as the snow again began to fall he realized that their position was becoming more serious by the minute. All he could do was to wait and hope that help would come as the coldness silently and stealthily penetrated their bodies. He waited a

157

long, long time. It was the next morning before they were found huddled together in the snow. They were barely alive. Somewhere in the dim chasms of his mind, Tom heard voices but he could not move or open his eyes or lips. It was as though he was a soul without a body. He sensed he was being picked up and he felt the uneven juggling as the cart in which he had been laid moved off. Then mercifully he sank into sweet unconsciousness.

"Robbie—Robbie."

The voice was soft and blew through his mind like a gentle zephyr. He opened his eyes but there was darkness. He could hear a low muffled backcloth of echoing coughs and groans and smell the strange odour of unrecognizable chemicals. Then the voice came to him again out of the darkness. It was louder this time and he could recognize it. It was John his brother.

"John—where are you?" he croaked.

He felt a hand get hold of his and squeeze it. "Here sonna— I'm here beside you."

Robert panicked and tried to raise himself on his elbows but a myriad of stars burst in his head and a pain shot across his brow. "What's happened—where am I. Are we in Heaven?"

He heard his brother laugh through his nose. "No bonny lad—we're still in the land of the living. You got yourself blown up, but you're still in one piece. You're in hospital."

Robert exhaled noisily. He felt weak and sleepy. "Is it night time? I can't see you John."

John squeezed his hand again. "No it's not night time. You've got a bandage on your face. That's why you can't see."

"Oh—oh," Robert said cautiously, as though unconvinced. "Can I take it off?" he added, feeling the thick padding and bandage around his head.

"No, not just now. In a few days the doctor says. In a few days it should be all right."

"Oh—how long have I been here?"

"A week. You got some metal splinters in your face. It looks like a shell exploded right in front of you and instead of blowing your nut off, it just booled you along the ground. You should be dead but you're not. Somebody picked you up and

158

bliddy well carried you away. I always knew you were a lucky bugger. He wrapped you up and kept you warm all night until help came. You were as stiff as a board when they found you. Man, you had me worried. I'd almost given you up for lost."

Robert smiled, "I told you I was the lucky one. I'll bet I find gold before you do."

John laughed. It was a dry almost sickly laugh with a thin veneer of jollity around it. Robert heard a voice saying that that would do for today and a prickle of fear ran through him when his brother let go of his hand.

"No John don't go. It's funny not being able to see where I am or who I'm with. What's all that coughing and groaning?"

He felt John pat his head. "Easy sonna—you're in good hands here and besides I've got to get away to the front. I wish I could stay but they'll not let me. I'll be back Robbie—soon as I can. Take it easy and get well."

"Then we'll make our fortune after it's all over. We're bound to with my luck—eh John?"

"Aye Robbie we're bound to. So long Robbie. Wish me luck."

There was a quick fierce clasp of hands and he was gone. The background hubbub again invaded his ears. "John!" he yelled. more to convince himself that he wasn't dreaming. He heard a soft feminine voice approaching from his left and it gently chided him. "Come on now soldier, you're all right. Try to sleep. You'll feel better when you wake up."

Robert turned his head toward the voice and felt the sheets on the bed being smoothed across his chest. "Are you a nurse?" he asked.

"Yes, I'm a nurse—well sort of one. I'm here to help you and all the other men. But there's an awful lot of you and I haven't time to sit and hold all of your hands all of the time; so be a good boy and be quiet now."

Robert groped with his hand and took hold of her arm, then found her hand. It was a strong hand but he could somehow tell she was gentle. She tutted with mock annoyance and removed it.

"I said I haven't time to molly-coddle you all. I've work to do."

Robert sighed. "I'm sorry. It's strange being in the dark. It's different from down the pit. What sort of day is it?"

159

There was a pause. "It's not bad," she said quickly. "Tell me mister, where are you from? Do you come from the North?"

Robert nodded.

"What's your name?"

"Robert Garrett."

There was another pause—longer this time.

"Nurse—are you still here?"

The voice was sad now and had a strange catch to it. "Yes soldier, I'm still here. I'll be here for as long as you need me."

Tom Mennem woke up and focused his eyes on the dull glow from the lamp above his bed. He could see the dark cold arches of stone and hear the cries of pain and smell the chemicals. He knew it wasn't a dream, a nightmare; it was starkly real and the sudden acceptance of his predicament brought a mirthless smile to his face and bitter tears to his eyes. The last few days had sped by unbelievably quickly and now as the doctor had told him, the worst would be over. But to Tom's mind the worst was yet to come. Years and years of the worst —endless days of struggle and discontent. And yet he tried to convince himself that he had been used to discontent and he would be strong enough to accept his fate as just another facet of his misbegotten life.

He could remember everything. He remembered the seemingly endless journey on the cart after he had regained consciousness. Then the blazing heat from the giant fire and the merciless pummelling to restart his almost stagnant circulation. Then the journey to the hospital and the solemn faces of the doctors and nurses as they examined him.

"Will I live?" he managed to whisper to a nurse.

The nurse's face broke into an automatic smile. "Of course you will. You'll be fine—it's just your legs that are giving a bit of trouble."

"How?"

"Well, it's a little early to say but it looks like a touch of frostbite. You've some nasty blisters on those feet of yours."

Tom nodded, blankly accepting the verdict.

A bearded doctor with tired eyes and sallow features bent over him. "Did you feel anything?" he asked.

"When?"

"Just this minute. Did you feel this—in your feet?" He held up a gleaming needle.

Tom shook his head. The doctor breathed in deeply and moved to the foot of the bed. Another doctor joined him there with the nurse and they muttered annoyingly quietly and lifted the blankets more than once.

The doctor returned to his side. "You've got frostbite son, in your feet. We'll have to watch them carefully for a few days."

He patted Tom's shoulder and left him. He examined him twice a day for almost a week. There were many tests with the needle and many muttered consultations. Finally he came to his bedside and Tom knew from his forced smile and reassuring manner that there was bad news.

"Well Tom, I'm afraid that those feet of yours are still giving us some concern."

He waited a minute, perhaps hoping that Tom would pronounce the verdict himself but there was no reply. The doctor rolled his tongue around in his mouth then nodded. "Your feet are useless Tom—they're dead. There's gangrene in them. They'll have to be removed."

The shock stunned Tom into speechlessness. His brow furrowed and his eyes closed. The words had registered in his head but his subconscious had rejected them as fantasy.

The doctor continued. "Be brave son—the worst will soon be over and you'll be on your way home."

Home! Visions of Shirehill flooded through Tom's mind, then Hartley and the faces of his family. He grunted as he forced himself up on to his elbows. He looked down the bed. No, he definitely hadn't been dreaming. He could see the shape of his legs under the blankets—and where they came to an abrupt halt where his feet had been.

At the other side of the hospital in a similar ward, Robert Garrett had also struggled with his mind in an attempt to convince himself that life was still worth living. On the morning that he learned the truth about himself; a truth that had sneaked into his thinking on several occasions, but which he had forced out again, his nurse had comforted him. The doctor said he would never see again. Tiny splinters of iron had severed the optic nerves. The doctor had thought so the first day he examined him. John had known it when he visited him. Now Robert had to accept it; he would never see the sun or the sky or the green meadows of home. The pit would be only a noise, his friends and family voices. His life would be restricted to touch and sound and smell and taste, just as it was at that moment. He had the strong but gentle hand of the nurse held in his. He could hear her voice, soft and clear as she read to him and he could smell the delicate perfume from her skin that surmounted the reek of coarse soap and dying men. Perhaps life could still be worthwhile he thought. The calm cool entity that had hovered around him all these impressionable days had instilled into him an enjoyment—a pleasure that had almost made him forget he could not see her. He had touched her face—a not too young face, then her hair and formed a vision in his mind —a face to suit the sound and the feel and the smell. They had talked and laughed together during the days that he tried to hide the truth from himself. He had rambled on about Shirehill and Hartley and the pit and what he and his brother would do when the war ended. Someone had told them that there was gold in Canada and they had resolved to go there and find it and come home with a fortune. That was their plan. That was what they wanted to do; but now that was all changed. Robert could only go home and stagnate. Yet his nurse would not hear of it. She encouraged him, she rekindled his flagging confidence in all sorts of possibilities. She became almost part of him and he could recognize even the rustle of her skirt. One day as they walked in the garden and his nurse guided him by the hand, he knew he could not face life without her. She had become everything to him. He could exist without eyes but not without her; she was more important than sight and as he swamped himself in the intimacy of her faceless being, that became the worst of his torments.

The dreaded day that he knew would come, finally came. He sat stiff and sombre on the edge of the bed as she buttoned his tunic and brushed his hair.

"There," she said in a satisfied voice. "You'll do Robbie. You look good."

He didn't answer.

"What's the matter. Cat got your tongue? Come on now—you're going home Robbie you should be all smiles."

He stood up. "Take me outside for a minute will you?" he asked flatly.

She hesitated for a moment, then said, "Surely Robbie—come on."

She led him by the hand and the echoed sounds of coughs and moans and hard, quick steps were left behind. He felt the warmth of the sun on his face and the soothing rustle of the trees in the breeze. He gripped the hand tighter and felt the fingers interlace themselves around his.

"I don't want to go," he blurted. "I want to stay with you. Please let me stay with you."

The voice was soft and sad. "Oh, Robbie don't be silly. Of course you do. The war's almost over and your brother will be going home as well. Then you can plan to do all the things you've wanted."

"I don't want to do anything but be with you."

She stopped walking and he knew she was looking at him. "Robbie—oh Robbie, you don't mean that. I'm—I'm old enough to be your mother."

He put out his hands and placed them on her cheeks, then on her eyes.

"I'm not crying," she whispered.

Robert hung his head. "You must have some feeling for me. You've been with me for so long. You couldn't do that without feeling something for me," he said desperately.

She tried to answer him, but the words stuck in her throat. Finally she whispered, "I've a job to do here Robbie. There's lots of lads like you to look after. They need me as well."

Robert's heart sank to his boots. He was silent on the way to the harbour and did not answer her light hearted chatter. He left her at the quayside amid the hubbub of a loading ship. A strange masculine voice said, "Come on chap, I'll see to you now."

Suddenly he felt the warmth of her lips on his. "Goodbye Robbie—and good luck." Robert felt himself being led away. He stopped and turned to where he sensed she was. "Will you come and see me—will you? Will you let me know where you are?" he shouted.

"Yes Robbie, I promise," he heard among the thousands of

other voices.

He turned again and let himself be led up the gangplank. "Please," he begged to his new keeper, "let me stay on the deck until we sail."

The man laughed. "Surely soldier, you're the boss."

They stood for almost half an hour. His nurse stood on the quay watching him.

"Is that your girl," said a new voice in an accent he recognized.

Robert turned his head. He sighed. "It should have been—it is—I mean, yes that's my girl. You're a Geordie. I can tell."

"Yes that's right."

"What happened to you?"

"Lost a couple of feet."

"What? You mean you're a midget now. Your voice is coming from low down."

He laughed. "No—I lost the feet I walk on—Frostbite. I'm in a chair."

"Oh, I'm sorry. I'm blind you know."

"Yes I know. Your girl's waving down there. Wave back."

Robert waved.

"What's her name?"

Robbie suddenly stopped waving. He swallowed hard. "Isn't that funny, I don't know. I never even asked her. Come to think of it, with me not being able to see her it's as though she didn't need a name."

"If you knew my name you'd not be very pleased."

"What do you mean? Robert snapped irritably. "Why should I not be pleased?"

"Because it's Tom Mennem."

There was a long silence, then Robert said quietly, "Tom Mennem of all people. War changes a lot of things Tom—Petty squabbles at home seem so bliddy ridiculous when you think of what we've been through. I'm sorry you lost your feet. How did it happen?"

"Oh, just in the winter you know. The winters are bad here."

"I know. I nearly froze to death myself. Is she still on the quay?"

"Yes she's still there. Wave—she's still waving."

Robert waved. "Oh, my God I wish I was staying," he

164

whispered.

He heard the gangplank scrape up over the gunnels and the hoarse orders yelled to the crew. He heard the splash of the mooring ropes into the water and the flap of unfurled sails. The ship moved gently beneath him.

"Come and see me. Please don't forget," he shouted.

"She's still waving. She's stopped now. She's going," Tom murmured.

Robert bit at his bottom lip. A frightening, sickening desperation welled up inside him. He somehow knew he would never meet her again and he knew he would never be the same without her.

On the quayside, Elizabeth Drummond turned and allowed all the pent up emotion of the last few days to have full and uninhibited vent.

Sid Garrett gazed at his reflection in the shining barrel of his trumpet. The reflection was twisted and distorted and made his brow look ridiculously foreshortened while his face and beard were drawn out so that he looked like some kind of comic Methuselah. But even the distortions of his reflection could not disguise the sadness in his face. As he looked, then polished, then looked again his mind tumbled with the thoughts of his two eldest sons. He had almost got used to the idea that Robert was coming home blind, but at least alive. That was some consolation; but John—he couldn't understand John. Why had he decided to stay away? Why couldn't he have come home and seen them first before going off across the world again. Sid had a frightening feeling that he would never come home to them again.

He tried to forget his own sadness and concentrate on the reason for making the trumpet look its best. Jacob was at his side, asking his endless questions while his bright eyes took in anything that was new or unusual.

"What's that for da'?" he asked pointing to the valves.

Sid smiled sadly and tousled his hair. "Valves son," he said.

"What's valves?"

"Well, valves are for making notes."

"How?"

Sid sighed. He thought for a moment, then gave up. "I don't

know son. They just make notes different when you press them."

Jacob's small round face poured over the trumpet. "But you must know da'—please tell me."

Sid tutted in mock annoyance. "You're too young to understand. I'll tell you when you can understand." He looked up to where his wife was brushing her hair at the cracked mirror on the mantelpiece. "Martha d'you hear this little bugger—there's no satisfying him."

Martha turned and her lips thinned. She nodded silently.

"When Robbie gets home he'll tell me," Jacob said with a pet lip.

Sid shot a quick look at his wife then back at his son. He put down his trumpet and pulled Jacob toward him. He stared into the wide inquisitive eyes. "Eeh what a little bugger—y'll not be beat. Three years old and you're like a little old man. Listen now son, I've told you before, Robbie'll want peace and quiet. He's got a lot to learn now he—he can't see. Don't ask him questions Jacob and don't ask him why he can't see—understand?"

Jacob nodded solemnly. Sid pulled him to his chest. He remembered John and Robert when they were his age and it seemed only a few short weeks ago. Now they were men—veterans of the Crimean war and Robert at least, along with others, was due home that afternoon. He remembered that day in September when the news that the war had ended had reached them. There had never been scenes like it. Sid was down the pit at the time and word spread among the workings like wildfire. The war was over. Husbands, sons and brothers were coming home. Yells of delight echoed along the ways and songs and cheers tumbled over the coal and stone and mud. In the restriction of the low seams they hugged each other. In the higher roadways they danced and jigged and whooped. That night the village seethed with noise and merriment. Bonfires were lit at the end of each lane and from the top of the head-gear of Hester pit it was as though everyone in the country was of the same mind. Fires speckled across the darkened country-side in every direction.

And now the day had arrived. Joyful for some and sad for others. A few of the smiling exuberant faces that had left the village were no longer smiling. They were grey and dead and left in a strange far off land.

The pit was still working—the viewer had made sure of that, but the recently finished fore shift, with sleep farthest from their minds were making sure that the soldiers were welcomed home in style. The colliery band had been rehearsing for weeks. The womenfolk had baked cakes and stotties. Barrels of beer had been brought from the Hastings Arms and a large notice chalked along the side of Stell's warehouse by Septimus Stell himself. It said "Welcome home to the brave lads of our village." And the village meant it; they were in a carnival mood the like of which they had never had the excuse or the inclination to feel before.

It was almost four o'clock when the first cart was seen lurching up the rough, uneven road. The band, who had blown themselves prematurely out of wind an hour earlier, got their instruments poised and the mugs of beer were suddenly left alone and frothing at the tables. The villagers lined the lane ends and hearts began to beat faster as the cart drew nearer. The band blasted out its first notes and the dogs began howling again. Sid blew with all his might, eyes swivelled hard to the right, forcing his vision to pick out his son. Martha was farther down the lane, Jacob clutched in front of her, anxiously bobbing her head this way and that for some sight of him. Cheers rang out among the crotchets and quavers and barking, then there were cries of "George" and "Joe" and "Bill" as people ran to greet their loved ones. But as the cart, followed by the others creaked into the village, the cheers and shouting died away to nothing. The tune from the band petered out with a watery, hesitating, off-key note and the shocked silence seemed even louder than the noise before. The men were thin and haunted. Some were still bandaged and most bore the signs of bitter conflict. There were sobs of grief mixed with joy as the dazed soldiers were reunited with their families. Sid left his trumpet and ran past the first cart, then the next. Martha was by his side. Then they saw him. He was at the front of the third cart, staring sightlessly around him.

"Robbie—Robbie," his mother bleated, more as a question.

But Robert seemed not to hear. Sid leapt up on to the cart.

"Robbie," he breathed reverently. "It's me, son—It's your da'."

Robert slowly held out a hand. It cautiously explored the

thick-fingered one in front of him, then the dense, curling beard. He forced a smile to his face yet he didn't want to smile. Returning to the village was almost as traumatic to him as it was when he left his nurse. He felt a mixture of bitterness at his affliction and desperation at the finale of his experience of the outside world. That chapter of his life was now closed. There was no hope for him to be with his nurse again. He had forced himself to accept that; and yet all during the voyage home the very fact that he was still out of the confines of Hartley made him cling to the glimmer that he might meet her somehow, somewhere. But now he was home and the only thing he had left was John. Perhaps his nurse had been right. Perhaps he and John could still do things together.

"Oh, Robbie lad, what have they done to you?" Sid wailed. "Come on—come on home."

"Where's Tom?" Robert asked flatly as he stood up.

"Tom who, son?"

"Tom Mennem—where's Tom?"

Sid guided him down to the waiting arms of his mother, muttering some puzzled unintelligible excuse, but Robert was adamant.

"Where's Tom—where's Tom Mennem?" he yelled.

Sid looked frantically around him. He could see George Mennem and Alfie solemnly lifting Tom from the cart. He winced when he saw the loose flapping legs of his trousers.

Tom had heard him. "I'm here Robbie—don't worry I'm just here."

Sid gazed poker-faced at the incredulous glances of George and Alfie. "What do you want with him?" he whimpered to Robert, but Tom's voice made him forget an answer.

"It's just like you said it would be Robbie," Tom said with a touch of sarcasm, "their faces are a bliddy caution. They really are."

A young voice from the crowd shouted, "Look at Tom Mennem's legs," but a stern faced mother silenced any further comment with a swift crack to the ear.

Robert smiled. "D'you hear that Tom? Nowt's changed here—I can tell you. Can you hear the pump? It's still suckin' and whistlin'."

Tom looked up past the lane ends to the headgear of Hester pit. The wheel was still spinning, the great beam of the pump-

168

ing engine still swinging up and down. "Aye," he said sadly. "It's still there, Nothing's changed—only us."

For the first time Tom regretted his action in saving Robert that day. Not because it was Robert Garrett, but because of the consequences that both of them now had to face. Years of uselessness, with nothing to look forward to except the stifling charity of their families. It suddenly came to him that it would have been better if they had perished in the far off snow.

Robert nodded grimly as his parents guided him slowly away. "I'm coming to visit you Tom—d'you hear. You do the same—all right?' he shouted over his shoulder.

"You're on Robbie—sure as anything."

And so the carnival ended as suddenly as it began. The food and beer were forgotten; limp Union Jacks were dropped and trampled underfoot. Everyone made their way to the privacy of their cottages. Hartley became silent again except for the dull clank of the pit and the omnipresent whoop and thump of the pump.

Jacob Garrett was disappointed at the sudden end to the festivities. He was glad his brother was home and he felt that the laughing and cheering should go on. It made him feel good, yet now, all of a sudden he found himself trotting alongside his brother gazing puzzled and unashamedly at his dead fluttering eyes.

For the returned soldiers that evening was a time for reminiscences, for forced laughter, for reacquaintance with familiar scenes and smells. But in the Garrett cottage Robert's world was sent crashing into further ruin when he learned about his brother.

"When will our John be home—have you heard?" he asked eagerly.

The silence frightened him for a moment. "What's wrong—he's all right isn't he?"

"He's all right Robbie," his mother whispered, "but he's not coming back just now."

"Not coming back—where's he gone?"

"He's gone off to Canada. With some bloke he met in the army. They've gone huntin' for gold."

Robert's stomach twisted itself into a tight knot. His voice carried the high pitch of disbelief. "He was going to take me ma—she said he would. She said we would still go together. Why didn't he come home and take me?"

Sid patted him on the shoulder. "Easy bonny lad. He probably thought you'd want a rest at home first. He'll come back for you."

Robert stood up. "No—no, she said he would take me. She said I could still help."

"Who's she?" his mother asked.

"The nurse—my nurse—she said it was going to be that way. He couldn't go without me—not our John."

Sid guided him back to his seat. "Come on son," he whispered sadly, "he'll come for you. Just be patient."

"No he won't. He won't come. I'm useless. He doesn't need me any more." He sank forward and clasped his head between his hands. "He won't come," he whispered.

"I'll go huntin' for gold with you Robbie," Jacob piped.

Robert held out a hand and tousled his hair, but he did not answer him.

Farther down the row Tom Mennem sat among the embarrassed molly-coddling of his family and it began to irritate him. Alfie wailed out his laments at regular intervals while George brought him up to date with his promotion at the pit. He slapped him on the back and asked him endless questions about the war in a shallow attempt to cover his feeling of pity for him. Billy and Fred and Joe crowded around him and begged for details and numbers of the Russians he had killed. Only his mother was quiet. She seemed to sense his irritation. She knew that his future was even less promising than before he went away; she realized that he didn't need to be fussed over. He wanted to be normal—only the same as everyone else. But she knew that was impossible. He could do no work. He would have to sit or be wheeled or carried. People would gaze at him and point him out as never before, and her heart poured out its silent sorrow for him.

Suddenly there was a knock at the door. George jumped up and stared around at the wondering faces of his family.

"Eeh—who can that be?" Alfie croaked, "no bugger ever calls here."

170

Tom smiled. "It'll be Robbie. Let him in. I told you he'd come. I looked after him all the way home."

George cautiously opened the door. Tom strained his neck to see the figure behind the broad shoulders of his brother. George stepped to one side, his jaw sagging and mouth stupidly agape. Tom's eyes widened. He couldn't believe what they saw. It wasn't the lifeless eyes of Robert Garrett as he expected. It was the big brown eyes of Victoria Taylor.

CHAPTER 5

June 1861

Septimus Stell was a satisfied man. Not in the sense that was altogether happy—far from it; but considering that his wife had been dead for almost three years and that he had no children or relatives to visit him or afford him family comforts and friendship, he was satisfied with the way he had adapted to the new routine of living without a partner. He missed his wife—he missed her every day that God sent; that in the main was the cause of his unhappiness, because she had been more than a wife. She had been a friend—a wonderful friend. Their friendship had enriched their lives. It caused them to derive pleasure from making their partner happy and it hastened the making up of any rare quarrel. The rapport and understanding between them was amazing; they were as one person, so much so that when his wife just dropped down dead in the shop, Septimus Stell could not understand why he had not done the same. He even contemplated suicide so they could be together again, but being the philosophical man he was, he decided against it. Time would again join them, he resolved, and while time was being metered out, he knew he must adapt and change and adjust to suit his circumstances.

He was a thin man of medium height and his skin was white and waxy-looking and almost transparent. He was getting on for sixty-three and the rheumatics in his legs had slowed him down noticeably these last few years, and had often cost him a sale because of his slowness in getting from the small back room of his shop to the counter when the bell rang. He often blamed his pains on the accident he had as a boy. He had fallen from a tree in his father's orchard when he was five and had injured his spine. It caused his shoulders to go prematurely round and a slight hump to form on his back. His neck was permanently stiff and he held his head forward at such an angle that he appeared to be gazing at his feet; only he wasn't. His eyes were swivelled upward in their sockets over the top of his little round spectacles and sparkled inquisitively through the gloom of his shop.

He heard the bell jangle and the noise of young voices. Painfully he stood up and walked as quickly as he could into the shop. He forced himself to move quicker on that occasion because it was Friday and Friday was pay-day at the pit. He knew it would be the keen young lads and their sisters anxious to spend their few coppers pocket-money on sweets and spanish root and all the other rubbish that made his stomach squirm when he thought about eating such things. Resolutely he walked from the doorway to where the brass scales stood on the counter, with slow, jerky movements from his feet. A half a dozen young faces watched in silence as his crooked body gradually progressed, seemingly without legs, along the length of the counter. As he reached the scales the hullabaloo broke out.

"Ounce of sherbet Mr. Stell."

"It's me first. I want a ha'p'ny lolly."

Septimus Stell tutted loudly. "One at a time—one at a time," he said in a gentle, delicate voice. "Who's first?"

"It's me."

"No it's me—it's me."

He gave up with a wistful little smile and served the nearest outstretched hand with money in it. Soon there was only one left. His face was still black from the pit and his hair was shades darker than usual.

Septimus Stell smiled at him as he gazed over the top of his glasses. "You're a keen one, young man. Can't you wait until you've been scrubbed?"

Jacob Garrett's face broke into a wide grin. "No Mr. Stell," he said.

Stell gave a quick little cackle. "Well son, what do you want?"

"I don't know."

Stell raised his eyebrows. "You don't know. Can't you make your mind up?"

Jacob shook his head.

"Well, I've some nice bullets here—Minty flavour. Or there's sherbet, pink or yellow, or . . ."

Jacob cut him short. "I know what there is Mr. Stell, I'm just making up my mind, whether to buy that kite in the window or buy some bullets. How much is the kite?"

"Oh, that's a lot of money bonny lad. It's tuppence."

Jacob looked disappointed.

"How much have you got?"

"Ha'p'ny."

Stell nodded. "Sorry son, you far better have some bullets. How old are you?"

"Nine nearly."

"Well, when you're ten and get down the pit instead of at bank you'll be able to have more pocket-money, then you can buy yourself a kite."

"I'm not going down the pit, Mr. Stell. I'm going to be a doctor."

Stell's mouth formed a neat oval. "Oh, are you now, and what in Heaven's possessed a pit lad like you to want to be a doctor?"

Jacob shrugged. "Don't know. I just do that's all. I want to cure people—like my brother Robbie—an'—an' you!"

Stell's face went cold and stern for a moment as he weighed the boy up. At first he thought it was a more subtle attempt at ridicule but then he realized that this black faced young lad was genuine. There was no hint of a smirk on his face, no derisive laughter in his eyes, only honesty.

"Well now, that's commendable—er what's your name?"

"Jacob Garrett."

"Ah yes Garrett. You've the blind brother haven't you. Yes —very commendable thought son—and how are you going to be a doctor?"

Jacob shrugged again. "I think I'll have the sherbet Mr. Stell The pink sherbet."

Stell almost automatically weighed out a halfpennyworth and thrust it into the eager hand.

Jacob thanked him and turned to go.

"No don't go son. Bide a bit."

174

Jacob stopped. He watched the shopkeeper move painfully to the window and remove the bright red kite. He turned and shuffled back until he stood only a foot from the boy. He looked down at him and his face broke into a toothless smile. He pushed forward the kite. "Here boy—take it for wanting to be a good samaritan."

Jacob took the kite. "Eeh, Mr. Stell, you're a pal. You're not kiddin' are you?"

"No—it's yours. But y'll not fly it today—there's no wind."

Jacob's face took on a quizzical look. "I know. Why does it need the wind to fly."

Stell's smile broadened. "My—you are an inquisitive one for a pit lad. Tell me son have you any schoolin'—can you read and write?"

Jacob shook his head

Stell nodded knowingly. He sighed, his face still radiating an amused interest "Aye, it's a pity son. Y'll need to do that before y'can be a doctor you know. Perhaps you better stick to learnin' to be a pitman."

Jacob frowned. "No," he said positively, "I don't want to spend every day in the pit. I want to learn about things. About why things happen and how things work."

Stell shook his head in quiet amazement. He stood for a moment, blinking at the incongruous youngster. A wild idea ran through his mind which at first reckoning seemed preposterous, then it germinated instantly and suddenly became not only acceptable but almost natural. The lad standing in front of him had something special. He could tell intuitively by the way he spoke and the way his bright eyes drank in each situation. He remembered other occasions when he had visited his shop; always mannerly, always radiating alertness. He turned toward the counter, "Come with me Jacob. I've something to show you." Jacob followed him, walking deliberately slowly so as not to overtake his reluctant jerking body. Stell took him to the small back room that was dark and untidy and littered with papers and boxes and through an adjoining door into the passage of his house. He opened a door opposite and turned his stooped body around so he could watch Jacob's face. The room was unfurnished except for a long unpolished table and a carpet that was flattened and threadbare in places. But it was the far wall that took Jacob's eye. The whole of that wall was stacked with books; from floor to ceiling. Some were brown, some were green and some red. The smell of leather mixed with dank unuse invaded Jacob's nostrils. The books were lying at all angles untidy and undusted but to Jacob's eager mind it could have been a cave of gold that his brothers had dreamed of discovering.

"Well?" Stell said softly. "What do you think of that Jacob. There's all the knowledge of the world over there if you've a mind to take it in."

Jacob looked up at the waxy smiling face, then back at the books.

"Do you know everything Mr. Stell?"

Stell gave another nervous little cackle. "There's no man that knows everything son, but a man can try."

Jacob moved forward, past the old man until he was close to the books.

"Can I look at the pictures?" he asked.

"Surely son—but would you like to read them?"

"I can't read."

"I know, but if you could, would you read them?"

"I'd read every one if you'd let me."

Septimus Stell nodded. He moved to the boy's side and put a hand gently on his shoulder. "Would you let me teach you Jacob? If you're so keen on knowledge, I'll give you the means to learn."

"What—you mean you'll teach me to read?"

"I'll try. If you're as bright as you seem, I'll succeed I think. Then I might be able to teach you the principles of mathematics—you know—sums. Then there's a book or two there on biology and chemistry."

"You *do* know everything Mr. Stell," Jacob said reverently.

Stell was flattered and amused. "No—no, Jacob, I've told you, no man knows everything and my little knowledge accumulated at great mental effort over the years is only the tiniest drop in an ocean. Make no mistake boy, it'll be hard work for you, and it'll take most of your spare time. On sunny days like this y'might want to play—or fly that kite if there's wind enough."

Jacob felt his heart beat faster as the excitement permeated through his body. He held out the kite. "Please Mr. Stell, put it back in the window."

Her fate was not what she expected. Billy wrapped his arms around her waist and his lips easily found hers, but then he increased the pressure and Margaret heard his breath increase in tempo through his nostrils. She opened her eyes in surprise when he started a series of low painful sounding sighs, then in an instant she was off balance and lying down. Billy did not lose a second. With a little cry of delight, he was beside her kissing her passionately, his hands wandering up her skirt one second and then over the mound of her breasts the next. Margaret struggled to stop him, but his hands seemed everywhere at once.

"Oh, don't stop me Meggie," Billy groaned. "I love you Meggie—honest I do."

Margaret managed to push him off her and while he tried to regain his ground she smacked him hard over the right ear. "You filthy little beast," she yelled, "oh, you are Billy Turnbull, you're a dirty little devil."

She stood up, while Billy tried to rub the ringing out of his ear. He raised himself to a kneeling position and looked up at her with a hangdog expression. "Don't say that Meggie. I do love you, and that's what lovers are supposed to do—the big lads at the pit told me."

"Well the lads at the pit are wrong," she yelled, stamping her foot with anger. "Tell them they're wrong, do you hear— and don't you ever speak to me again."

She turned and ran back to the path. Billy stood up. "You won't tell your old man Meggie—will you?" he shouted.

She ignored him. Daisy and Jacky were standing sheepishly making polite conversation. Margaret swept past them with her head high and without a word. Daisy looked quizzically across at Billy, still rubbing his ear, then dashed after Margaret.

"What did he do?—what did he do?—tell me Meg did he squeeze your busties?"

"He did more than that," Margaret snapped.

"More?" Daisy said in a quavering voice. "Oh, Meg, you lucky thing—why are you mad? Wasn't it nice? All the girls say it's nice."

"Well it's not!" snapped Margaret hotly. "I hate him."

Daisy stopped and let her walk on. "Don't be daft Meg," she shouted after her. "Come on back and play. I'll tell Jacky to chase you this time and I'll have Billy."

Margaret didn't stop or look back. She shook her head vehemently and continued along the path. Her mind was in a turmoil. She had been quite satisfied with Billy Turnbull's tightly pursed lips pressed against her; that in itself had been exciting to her and yet when his hands started their fumbling exploration of her body she became aware of a strange new excitement that brought with it a mixture of fear and revulsion. How dare Billy Turnbull presume he could invade the sanctity of her body. It was wrong, yet deep down inside her she felt it was right.

She wrestled with her adolescent feelings as she walked slowly back to the village. Behind her she could still hear the odd persuasive shout from Daisy but she ignored her. The daylight was beginning to fade and the midges swarmed in their frenzied mid-air dance. The onset of twilight in the warm summer air and the gentle silence it brings to the countryside seemed to pacify her. She didn't really hate Billy Turnbull she resolved. She still liked him. In fact the incident now seemed almost funny. Perhaps next time she would be more co-operative even if it meant forcing herself.

Out of the stillness of the evening the thump and whoop of the Hester pumping engine came to her ears. As she made the top of a grassy rise she could see the village and the pit away in front of her and beyond, the blue glass of the sea. The only sound was the pit. The whole world seemed poised on the brink of sleep. Only the pit continued its endless activity.

The rustle in the grass to the left gave her a sudden fright and her breath stopped for a moment as she saw the figure stand up. At first he didn't notice her but as he turned to join the path, his hands stopped the dusting of his shoulders and legs and he stood awkwardly, almost to attention when he saw her. Margaret felt her face flush with embarrassment. She had never been so close to Joseph Mennem on her own, and she suddenly longed for the relative anonymity she had enjoyed when there was a crowd. But this time there was no one to confuse their silent confrontation.

He had grown into a tall, gangling youth with long arms and big hands. He neck was thin and scrawny and a prominent Adam's apple bobbed nervously inside it. His face was pale and hollow and sheltered under a mass of unkempt black hair and it was sad, always sad and apologetic. His large dark eyes seemed to search at Margaret's face for some word of recognition or kindness but he knew there would be none. Even now, after all the years, the Mennems were still outcasts, still objects of derision and scorn, or silent contempt. The fact that Victoria Taylor had married Tom Mennem had done nothing to alleviate their persecution. The village had buzzed with surprise at the news, then Victoria Taylor became a Mennem and joined them in their insularity. She was shunned even by her irate parents.

He blinked for a moment as he stared at her, then hung his head and ambled slowly toward the path leading down to the village. He mumbled some words of apology as she stood rooted to the spot, not knowing whether to run forward or turn and go back to her friends. He glanced quickly at her before starting his leggy walk home.

Margaret suddenly started to laugh. She couldn't help herself. As much as she knew she shouldn't, she laughed out loud and tried to hide it with an arm across her mouth. Joseph's hand-me-down clothes had obviously come from his shorter brothers. His trousers were baggy and riding half-way up the calves of his legs and his shirt was tight, with the sleeves finishing almost at his elbows. Her laughing didn't last long. Joseph Mennem stopped and turned around. For the first time in her life she saw anger burning in the usually humble eyes.

"You mock me Miss Margaret—why?" he whispered in a voice that was cold but softly understanding.

She opened her mouth to answer him; to cut him short with some icy remark that would be befitting someone of his ilk, but she shut it again. She felt conspicuous and still embarrassed. Her self-consciousness was magnified a thousandfold without the company of her friends. His lips thinned as he waited for an answer, then his eyes returned to their usual sad composure when there was none. His head nodded a silent understanding as he turned back toward the village. Margaret bit at her bottom lip. She felt a wave of sympathy run through her. There was something tragic about him. His shoulders were drooped, his comic outfit not funny any more, and in the clinical light of being alone with him she saw his loneliness cry out for appeasement.

On an impulse, yet with the consequences of her rebellious act firmly weighed up in her adolescent mind she shouted, "I wasn't laughing at you. I was laughing at something else."

Joseph didn't hear, or if he did he ignored her.

"Joseph Mennem—did you hear me?" she yelled.

Joseph stopped and turned again, this time his face radiated a mixture of surprise and caution.

"Wait Joe Mennem—wait for me," she whispered as she ran the few yards that separated them, and when she was by his side her action seemed like a dream. She swallowed hard as she tried to convince herself it was really her and she was standing within touching distance of Joseph Mennem of all people.

It seemed like an eternity before he spoke. His eyes blinked in disbelief and then his face clouded.

"You laugh at me for no reason," he mumbled.

"I know. I—I'm sorry," she said feeling her face blush again.

"Why are you sorry?"

Margaret thought for a moment.

"I don't know—but I am."

Joe shook his head.

"Nobody says sorry to a Mennem. It's not done. Is this some trick?"

"No—no honest. I—I just wanted to walk to the village with you."

Joe looked furtively around, sensing instinctively that there was some mischief at the bottom of this encounter.

"Why?" he said softly, "why now—all of a sudden?" as he began his walk again.

Margaret walked beside him. She felt foolish and silently cursed herself for ever instigating the conversation.

Finally she said, "I just do that's all. I just feel like it."

Joe nodded. He felt equally embarrassed but he was enjoying her closeness and sudden interest. He remained silent for a few minutes then he said "You'll get belted off your da' if he sees you with me—you know that?"

Margaret turned her head and looked at the solemn face that exuded a mysterious attractiveness. She knew he was right but she didn't care. Perhaps it was the excitement of Billy's act earlier on that had sparked off her desire to be daring or it might have been the warm exhilarating night, but whatever it was, a strange satisfaction ran through her. She had dared to associate with Joseph Mennem. She was cavorting with the devil and the devil was not harming her.

"He can please himself," she whispered.

And Joe smiled.

By the time Margaret reached the lane end, darkness was catching up fast on the drowsy village. As she looked up the long row of cottages there was one which stood out among the rest. It was her own and even in the failing light she could see her father standing at the doorway, his face stern and his arm resting dramatically against the wall. She ran and smiled as she neared him, but it did no good. Daniel turned and entered the cottage and by the time she got to the open door he already had taken up an authoritative position with his back to the fireplace. Dorothy sat on the edge of the bed and put down her sewing. Her face was a little frightened and Margaret knew she was in for trouble.

"Where have you been 'til this time of night?" Daniel barked.

Margaret waved casually toward the window—"just out—across the fields with Daisy. It was such a nice night we thought . . ."

Daniel cut her short. "Who else?"

Margaret hesitated. "What's wrong?" she countered.

"Y've had me worried sick—that's what's wrong," Daniel snapped.

"Who else was with you?"

"Billy Turnbull and Jacky Stobbs."

Daniel nodded grimly. "It's a bliddy good job y'didn't lie, our Meggie, 'cos y'were seen."

"We didn't . . ."

She wasn't allowed to finish her explanation. Daniel turned his back to her and splayed out his great arms above the fireplace.

"So it's goin' out with lads now is it," he said icily as a twinge of jealousy ran through him. "You're too young for that sort of thing, so cut it out."

"Oh, give over Dan," Dorothy said hotly. "She's seventeen, she'll be thinkin' of marriage shortly."

183

Daniel's blue eyes blazed at his wife. "This is my house and that's my daughter and she'll do as I say. I'll teach her right from wrong. You never knew the bliddy difference. She's too young for courtin', so shut your mouth."

Margaret felt a hot surge of anger rise within her. All too often she had heard him speak to her mother as though she was a dog.

"That's not all da'—do you know who I walked back with from Swinney's fields. It was Joe Mennem. What do you think of that?"

Daniel turned and moved toward her. His massive work-scarred hands gripped at her shoulders and his face twisted into an angry snarl.

"Y'll have nothing to do with them—d'you hear?" he hissed. "Mennem are scum!—rubbish! and y'll go nowhere near them—is that understood?"

Margaret winced under the pressure of his hands and finally she had to nod her submission as her mother yelled abuse to his deaf ears. As he released his hands she wrenched herself away and the tears that had been burning for freedom finally came. She slumped down on the bed beside her mother and buried her head into the pillows. Again she felt his great hand on her shoulder. It was gentle this time and his voice was soft and almost whining.

"Don't cry Meggie—please don't cry. I'm just tellin' you for your own good—and besides you don't want to be courtin' and gettin' married and leavin' your old da'—now do you?"

Margaret forced herself to shake her head, but now, with independence maturing quickly within her, her father's actions had made her all the more determined to be with Joseph Mennem whenever she wanted to.

CHAPTER 6

Wednesday 15th January 1862

Matthew Taylor pulled on the signal rope and the cage containing eight black and huddled figures lifted and disappeared up the shaft from the Low Main. As it did, he turned and smiled at the horde of queueing miners and flapped his arms in an effort to keep warm.

"It's all right for you sods," he shouted jovially at the clouds of exhaled vapour blown from dry and panting mouths, "you're done for th'day—muggin's here's got to stand in the freezing bliddy downcast until me penkers drop off."

"Then your lass'll run up the flag," a voice shouted from way back, "and she'll have time for some sewin' then."

Taylor's face twisted in mock anger. "Who said that?" he yelled, peering through the eerie yellow light.

The queue laughed.

"It's true man—it must be," the voice continued, "your britchy arse has been hanging out for weeks."

The crowd erupted into more laughter as he twisted his head over his shoulder and felt at his pants at the same time.

"Come on Matty, where's the effin' cage?" shouted someone else. "The sweat's freezin' to me bliddy brow."

"Your brow's never seen a drop of sweat in its life," Taylor retorted.

Again they all laughed and the banter went to and fro until the cage dropped for another human cargo. They all pushed forward, eager to be away but Taylor sorted them quickly into line.

"Howay now lads," he yelled, "there's all effin' day—y'll all get there—take your time."

185

He pulled on the signal rope. The chains at the four corners of the cage lifted and tightened and it rose up once more. He turned, enjoying the good natured ribbing that was flying between them all, but his face changed from a smile to a scowl when he saw Joseph Mennem waiting his turn to ride. It took only a second for him to survey the crowd around, and he could see that for once he was not in the company of his father or brothers. His face changed instantly back to a broad smile and he continued his chatter until the cage returned and the miners surged forward. Joe was second in the queue.

"Take your effin' time," Taylor bawled as he stepped among them. The first one got through but as Joe made to pass, Taylor turned and punched his elbow backward into Joe's solar plexus. His cry of pain was drowned among the general melee and by the time he regained his balance the cage was full and moving upward.

"I was next. You pushed me aside," Joe shouted.

Taylor took on a look of mock astonishment. "You talkin' to me sonny?" he asked sarcastically.

Joe's eyes searched for his brothers but they were not there. Something must have held them up at the face, he thought. He clutched nervously at his bait bag. Taylor was waiting for an answer.

"Yes," he said flatly.

Taylor smiled. "Well now, d'you hear this lads—it's a runt of a Mennem tellin' me, me job. Am I right in thinking that?" he enquired of Joe, narrowing his eyes.

Joe swallowed hard. Taylor was a big tough man, renowned for his constant laughing and joviality but when he was angry his fists flew and there weren't many who walked away from them. "I was next and you elbowed me," he said quickly, more to impress the audience.

Taylor planted his feet firmly apart, his hands clenched at his sides. "You're just like that soddin' brother of yours," he hissed. "Cocky little bastard. D'you know he's bairned the daughter—and him earning only coppers as a tally boy." He sneered. "A kid of seven does the same job. He can't afford to keep a wife never mind a bairn."

"Is that what's got you mad," Joe said in a voice that was toned to sudden understanding. "So what if he is a tally boy. He earns his pay. They've got a cottage and they're happy."

Taylor took a step forward. "T'hell with that. My lassy was brought up for better things than a soddin' Mennem."

Joe was quick to retaliate, his anger overpowering the consequences. "She's lucky to have a Mennem Mr. Taylor—She's lucky to have anybody."

The crowd, already amused by the exchange, laughed out loud. Taylor was livid. Never had a Mennem had the audacity to answer him back in such a manner—especially the youngest of the brood. He let out a roar and leapt toward Joe, but the cage suddenly appeared and rattled to a halt. The miners surged forward. Joe saw his chance. He ducked under Taylor's outstretched arms and squeezed himself into the bottom section.

"Rap her away Matty," someone bawled.

Taylor pulled on the rapper. He bent down and gazed into the cage at Joe.

"I'll get you—you little bastard—see if I don't. You'll be sorry you tangled with me," he snarled.

Joe managed to smile at him. Somehow he didn't care. He would make sure he stuck close to his father and brothers. They would guard him as always—let Taylor do his worst.

Soon he was at bank and waiting for his protectors. He walked slowly over the small wooden bridge that spanned the moat-like gully between the pit-head buildings and the path toward the village. The morning was bitterly cold. A strong wind gusted from the sea and whistled forlornly through the headgear. He sheltered behind the viewer's cabin as he waited for them and watched some of the women of the village queueing to draw hot water from the condenser of the pumping engine. Some were already on their way back, staggering with the heavy buckets, heads bowed against the wind to fill their husband's bath. The miners streamed past him, mostly silent now, but some muttering about the weather. Still there was no sign of his family but he didn't worry—sometimes it took almost an hour to crawl and walk from the face to the shaft.

He heard the door of the viewer's cabin open, then slam shut in the wind. The under viewer turned the corner.

"Aye-aye—Joe Mennem isn't it?" he asked, looking hard through the layer of mud and coal dust.

Joe nodded.

"You'll do. Save me walking to the village and finding some-

187

one. Lie idle on the foreshift the morn. I'm switching you to the back shift till the weekend—Jenkin's putter is in a bad way from that fall of stone the s'mornin'."

Joe felt a sudden panic run through him. "Me—why me? I always work the shift with my brothers."

The under viewer wasn't in the mood to argue. "Y'll work the back shift till I tell you to stop," he snapped and stalked off across the bridge, holding his cap against the wind.

Joe sighed and silently swore at the man. He regretted now his encounter with Taylor. He had felt safe enough because he knew that his brothers would constantly be there to protect him. They always worked the same shift. When they were at home, he was at home and likewise at the pit. But now the shifts were different and if Taylor knew that, there would be trouble for sure.

He looked out over the bridge and forgot his worries for the time being. He could see George's broad white smile and his father's ageing stooped roll as they walked with Bill and Fred. He waved and they waved back as they approached him.

Septimus Stell's old and stiffened rheumaticky legs were put to a real test that evening. It was hard enough for him to walk when the ground was dry and level, but with the icy wind trying to unbalance him and the frost covered lanes causing everyone to slip and slither, it was an ordeal he could have gratefully avoided. The object of his mission however had a tingle of excitement running through him that made the long and arduous journey from his shop to the home of the Garretts seem not only necessary, but enjoyable. He cursed his frailty though and his ever running nose as he wiped away the droplets with the sleeve of his overcoat. His severely bowed head was for once a blessing as he could observe and place his feet with relative ease and his balance was also helped to a degree by the small but steady hand of Jacob Garrett clasped firmly in his.

Jacob was bubbling with curiosity. He had gone as always to Stell's home for his nightly lesson but instead of finding pen and paper and books and ink, Septimus Stell had greeted him with a hug and a broad smile and ushered him in front of an unusually big fire while he dithered excitedly as he struggled into his heavy overcoat.

"I've a surprise for you boy," he said. "Come on—I must see your da'."

"What's the surprise Mr. Stell?" Jacob asked as some of the excitement passed over to him.

"Y'll see son, but I must see your da' first. Come on let's go."

Now as they moved painfully slowly up the lane toward Sid Garrett's cottage Jacob could hardly wait. He knew it was something good—it had to be something good for the old man to be so happy and excited.

Eventually they reached the door and Jacob rattled the sneck and opened it. Sid was relaxing after his evening meal. His stool was pushed back against the wall and his stockinged feet rested comfortably on the table. Martha, unaware of her husband's position, hummed gently to herself in the scullery as the dishes clanked in the bowl. Robert on the other hand was waiting for the door to open. He had heard Jacob's voice coming down the lane and he knew there was someone with him. As it did he turned his sightless eyes toward the noise.

"Da'—I've brought someone," Jacob gasped, stepping to one side.

Sid came to his senses and yanked his feet down from the table a split second before his wife poked her head into the room. Stell's eyes swivelled far up above the little round glasses that perched on his nose. He gripped at the door frame with his waxy, gnarled hands and pulled himself over the step and into the room.

Sid jumped up. "Eeh—it's Mr. Stell. Martha it's Mr. Stell. Come and sit by the fire. What's wrong? Jacob here hasn't been bothering you, has he?"

Stell shook his head quickly. "No it's nowt like that." He peered from Sid to Robert and then to Martha as she emerged from the scullery. "Is it all right to come?" he asked.

"Of course it is. Please come by the fire," Robert said as his mother ran her pinafore over a stool.

He muttered a thank you and loosened the buttons on his overcoat. Sid moved behind him and helped it off. With a sigh of relief he lowered himself down on to the stool and warmed his hands at the fire. The sudden silence was unbearable.

"It's terrible weather just now," Sid said casually, hoping to spark off the old man into conversation.

"Aye," he mumbled as though he couldn't really care. He squinted across at the stiff wondering face of Robert. "You're Robbie aren't you?"

Robert nodded.

He looked around at Sid and Martha and then at Jacob. His face was puzzled as though he was hunting for the right words. At last he said, "You know I've been schoolin' the boy a bit?"

Sid smiled. "Yes, and you've done a grand job Mr. Stell—and we're grateful, aren't we Martha?"

"Is that what you want to see us for?" Martha asked, her curiosity overcoming her patience.

"It is. Let me tell you something. You may not have realized this, but the boy's not normal."

Sid glanced a quick worried look toward his wife as memories of the doctor's words from years ago came hurtling back through his mind. "Eeh, surely he can't be that bad," he said weakly, "he seems bright—always did—and he can read and write, thanks to you. That's more than most of this village can do."

Stell smiled. "That's what I mean. I mean he's not ordinary —he's extra ordinary. The lad's got intelligence—lots of it."

Sid's chest swelled with pride. He patted Jacob's head. "Well what do you know? Our Jacob—you're a good lad. I always knew you had something more than the rest of us. Y'll not stick at a pitman son. You might get to be an overman or something."

Jacob opened his mouth to protest but the old man beat him to it.

"Mr. Garrett," he said sternly, "I came through that hell-in-reverse out there for a special purpose. I began to tutor your son partly for selfish reasons I think, and partly because I recognized his unusual alertness. You see, the boy had some fond ambitions and I being lonely, decided it would be good for me and an interesting experiment, to spend some time teaching him. He's a mannerly boy and was willing to learn—it gave me something to—to occupy my mind. It also gave me something to achieve. Let me tell you Mr. Garrett, I achieved something all right and so, by God, did your son. He has

190

drained me of everything I know. He is little short of a genius Mr. Garrett. He has a phenomenal appetite for knowledge and a brain that can absorb all it finds. But he has frightened me sir; an aptitude like his needs careful handling. It is like clay in the hands of a sculptor. It must be moulded with infinite care and skill and the outcome will be greatness—I promise you that." He fumbled in his jacket pocket and produced a letter. He held it up. "I know of such a man. I wrote to him and he has replied. He has a school in London. He will take the boy."

There was a full minute of silence. Both Sid and Martha stared at their youngest son in amazement and Robert's face was split with a broad grin as he squeezed at Jacob's shoulder.

"I always knew he had a bright streak," Sid whispered at last.

"Canna go da'?—please say I can go," Jacob yelled, hugging at his father's waist on tip-toe.

"But what about money?—he'll need money," Sid said desperately.

Stell nodded again. "I was coming to that. I have no wife, no children, few friends and no relatives. I have a shop and I have some money—not a lot mark you—but enough. I am old and I am sick. It would please me greatly to think that I had launched this boy into a distinguished career of doctor, lawyer, politician or whatever he may finally decide to be. I know you are proud and independent, you miners, but for once do not look on this as charity. You will be giving an old man a great deal of satisfaction if you will allow me to pay for his education and the necessary monies it will take to keep him in reasonable comfort."

"Oh, da'—canna go?—please, please say yes." Jacob gasped.

Sid looked to his wife. His mind reeled with the grandiose professions that the old man imagined for his son. How could he refuse such a chance. How he wished he could have had the opportunity when he was a boy. He would have loved to have been a man that was looked up to and respected for his position in life. His wife looked sad, but she nodded.

"Yes son, y'can go," he whispered.

Jacob gave a whoop of delight and leapt up around his father's neck. Sid felt a lump grow in his throat as he hugged the boy. To think that some day he would be a great man.

"Y'll need to see the viewer."

Robert's words brought the celebrations to a premature halt.

"The viewer?—why?" Sid queried.

"Remember when me and John went off to the war. The viewer had to have his say as to who left the pit."

Sid stroked his beard. "You're right son—so he did. But it's different now, surely he'll not say nowt."

"Better see him first just in case."

Sid grabbed at his jacket. "Stay a while Mr. Stell. Have a cup of tea—I'm just away to tell the viewer the news."

He opened the door with a flourish, then smiled and winked at Jacob before the black and freezing night enveloped him.

He was back within half an hour. The door opened slowly and his pale wrinkled face was long and sad under his mop of greying red hair. Robert sensed the bad news from the silence.

"It's no good son," he whispered.

Jacob ran to him. "What do you mean da'—how's it no good?"

"He wouldn't hear of it. Says there's hardly enough at the pit now. Labour shortage he says. He needs all he can get."

"Pity for him," Martha snapped as Jacob turned imploringly to her. "Take no notice son, y'll still be going."

Sid shook his head. "He can't bonny lass—I told him that." He shrugged and slapped hopelessly at his thighs. "If Jacob leaves, we get thrown out. That's his last word—he said so."

Again there was a silence. They all knew it was useless to pursue the matter further. The viewer was all powerful; he could and would do what he threatened. With a loud sigh old man Stell finally staggered to his feet and struggled into his overcoat. He moved jerkily across the room touching the table for support. He came to Jacob whose head was bowed as he gently sobbed into his mother's apron. He tousled his hair as he passed. As he opened the door and stepped gingerly into the lane the freezing wind bit into his hands and face but he didn't care. He was angry. Angry with himself for instigating Jacob's abject disappointment, angry with the viewer for his narrow unimaginative decision and angry with the pit that spawned it. It took him almost an hour to walk to the lane end and up to his shop. Up ahead he could hear the noise of the pit and he could see the twinkling lights at the base of the head gear. He realized it was because of the pit that he earned his living, but with every whoop of the pump he cursed its very existence.

Joe Mennem clutched at his jacket collars and held his mouth tightly closed in an attempt to stop his teeth chattering. Every now and again he peered out from his hiding place between the earth closets. This time though he wasn't hiding from anyone —not really anyway. He was looking for someone—looking and waiting as he had been for the last half an hour. The fact that he was there in the concealing shadows was because no one had to know. It was a secret, a secret that was becoming increasingly difficult to keep.

Soon he heard a door open, then close softly. There were gentle footsteps coming closer. He swallowed hard as the darkened figure peered cautiously around the wall. There was a whispered call and a warm hand as an answer. In a trice Margaret Simpson was enveloped in his arms and his lips thawed themselves on hers.

"You're late," he murmured.

"I know. Da's just gone t'bed. Ma made me the excuse of going to the Finches for some thread. I can't be long."

Joe kissed her again. "Come on for a walk. I've changed shifts. I'm not on 'til ten the morn."

He peered out along the lane. It was quiet. He put his arm around her shoulders and guided her out. They walked for a while, out of the village and out across Swinney's fields. Margaret forgot the time. An hour was a minute with him and a minute didn't exist. They talked some and they stopped and kissed. The cold of the night was nothing to them, they were not aware of it.

They came, as they usually did, to Swinney's barn. Joe pulled out the bolt and swung the great door open. Margaret stood silent in the darkness, her body pounding with excitement as it rumbled shut behind her. She felt Joe's arms around her waist and his tongue caress the nape of her neck. After a moment a match burst into life and then a candle took its place. The barn swam with an unreal yellow light. Joe took her hand and led her to where the hay was deep and soft and smelt of summer. He placed the candle on the hub of a discarded waggon wheel then turned and kissed her again.

"Careful with the light," she whispered as she lay back and looked into his dark sad eyes.

"Shall I blow it out?"

Margaret held out her arms and pulled him down beside her. "Leave it on," she said, "I want to know it's you that's loving me."

There was another pair of eyes watching him loving her. They were pushed, wide and unblinking, up against the crack in the warped woodwork of Swinney's barn. They watched every move, drinking in every caress, living every intimate detail as the body that housed them panted in harmony with the threshing figures. Finally Matthew Taylor turned away. He licked at his dried lips then wiped them with the back of his hand. In the darkness an evil smile came to his face and his glazed eyes narrowed as he stealthily made his way back to the village.

The cage dropped and the grey day, even colder than the day before was left to the wind and the desolation of winter. Daniel squatted, silent and zombie-like in the top section with Sid as always, beside him. They were on their way to relieve the fore shift, but Daniel knew, as did all the others that when they reached the Low Main he would have Alfie Mennem and his three strapping sons to contend with before any work was done. He was only vaguely aware of where he was or what he was doing that morning. His mind was numbed by the events of earlier; by the sleepless night, by the screaming and yelling and by his own strength-sapping fury. He was conscious of a throbbing pain in his swollen right hand and as he clenched and unclenched it in the wet, moving darkness, he wondered if it could stand up to any more fighting. He knew the Mennems would hear the news before they rode to bank, if in fact they didn't already know. Their rage would be as great as his had been—of that he was sure and it was bound to come to blows.

It was midnight by the time Taylor had summoned up enough courage to tell him. All three of them were asleep and in fact it was Magaret who first heard the tapping on the window. She shook her father and was again asleep before Taylor had finished his whispered message to him in the lane. Daniel slumped down on a stool near the still roaring fire. His eyes were still sticky with sleep but his mind reeled as it digested the news. A wild anger boiled inside him as his imagination conjured up a scene similar, but reversed, to the one in the bakery a lifetime ago. His instincts screamed at him to drag his daughter from her bed and thrash her, but somehow he could not. An overpowering mental voice said she was innocent; she was not to blame, she had been tricked, seduced by Joe Mennem. He had enticed her to the barn. He had manipulated her pure, unsullied mind. He had defiled her with his filthy body. Yes it was he and not his daughter who had to be punished.

For an hour or more he sat and let his rage eat into his mind. He knew Alfie and his sons would shortly be leaving for the fore shift. He also knew that Joe had changed to back shift and would be alone except for his ageing mother. Silently he dressed himself and when the time was right he stepped out into the night.

The sharp knock on the door brought Mary Mennem immediately to full consciousness. A stream of reasons for the knock ran through her mind in the moment before she meekly shouted, "Who's there?"

"Joe's wanted at the pit," came the gruff answer.

Joe stirred and woke up.

"Who wants him?" his mother asked in a stronger voice.

"The shift's changed back. Y've to do the fore shift like before."

Joe groaned and rolled out of bed. He lit a candle then pulled on his trousers. He grumbled as he peered at the clock, buttoning his shirt as he did. It took him about five minutes to get fully dressed and for his mother to spread some jam on two large slices of bread. Finally he was ready. He unbolted the door and opened it. He had time to place one of his feet on the step before a great fist came hurtling out of the darkness and crashed into his face. A million coloured lights exploded in his head as he tumbled backward. A scream echoed in his mind that came from somewhere beside him as he felt himself being dragged bodily out into the lane. Again the scream came like the backcloth to some weird nightmare as he was picked up under the armpits. He didn't stand long. His legs were already made of rubber, but even before they buckled a searing pain registered at his mouth and his head

195

shot backward with his body following. He could taste blood; he could feel pain and all the time the tiny spark of awareness he had left, kept asking him what was happening. Again he was picked up. He managed to open his eyes. The lane was alive with lights and faces, frightened wondering faces. Men, women and children, puffy eyed from their beds, clutching coats to their necks watching him as he staggered drunkenly, supported by the grasping great hands of Daniel Simpson.

"You filthy bastard Mennem," Daniel yelled. "Tup my daughter would you? I'll teach you Mennem. I'll teach you a lesson you'll never forget!"

Again and again the blows rained on to Joe's face and body until Daniel's rage was eventually sated. He stood over the crumpled bleeding figure, his breath heaving into his lungs. Finally he turned away, his shoulders sagging and his arms dangling loosely at his sides while Mary Mennem, uttering a strange choking whine dragged her unconscious son back into the house.

The cage stopped and they climbed out. Taylor had already relieved the onsetter and was back in form with his jokes and raucous banter as though nothing had happened. Daniel sighed as he squinted along the roadway. He was ready for them wherever they were. They could do as they pleased, It had to come and whatever the result, it had been worth it. He walked in-bye with Sid at his side. Sid had been quiet since they left the village. His mind was full of the sound of his youngest son as he sobbed himself to sleep and the bitterness and injustice of life had him low and depressed. He would have told Daniel about Stell and the viewer. Under normal circumstances he would have had a sympathetic ear; but not today—not in Daniel's present mood. He wouldn't hear, let alone answer.

Eventually the back shift was spread out in the Low Main and the fore shift began their trek to the shaft.

"There he is!"

Daniel swung around. George Mennem, pale and shocked under his grime was bearing down fast on him from behind. He was joined by Alfie, his mouth open and panting. Daniel threw down three of his picks and held the other menacingly

196

across his chest. "Come on George," he snarled, "do what you will, but by Christ I'll cave your skull in for doin' it."

George stopped a yard from him. "What've you done to our Joe?" he screamed. "What've you done to him?"

Alfie pushed forward, his mouth moving but no words coming. George kept him back with an outstretched arm. His eyes blazed into Daniel's.

"I want an answer," he bellowed, "what have you done to him?"

"I effin' well belted him—that's what I did," Daniel snarled, "the dirty little sod was interferin' with the lassie."

George took half a step forward and Daniel raised his pick further into the air.

"Come on!—come on!" he breathed. "Come and get your head stove in."

Sid tried to warn him but he saw them too late. Simultaneously Bill and Fred grabbed at Daniel from behind. A thick strong forearm pressed against his throat and his head was forced backward. The pick was wrenched from his grip and in an instant of unbalance he was flung to the thick muddy floor of the roadway. George took the pick and swung it backward ready for a downward stroke. "I'll kill you Dan Simpson. I'll kill you for touchin' our Joe."

He didn't kill him. The fury that was in all of them was suddenly dispelled by the cold and sobering grip of fear. There was a low, slow rumble from way off that gradually increased in volume as the ground shook beneath their feet. Then the noise stopped and the Earth stopped shivering and the shocked wondering silence that prevailed afterward was broken only by the gentle fall of dust and small stones from the roof and sides of the tunnel.

"Jesus—what was that?" Alfie croaked.

George lowered the pick. He swallowed hard and glanced quickly along to his left and right to where the dimly lit tunnel petered out in darkness. There was no blast of hot air. Perhaps it wasn't an explosion.

Daniel picked himself up as Bill and Fred released their grip. Men and boys appeared from the galleries on each side of the roadway. All were wide-eyed with fear and apprehension.

"Oh, my God—it's the end of the world," Alfie bleated,

"quick lads let's get t'hell out of here."

He ushered his sons forward. Sid tugged at Daniel's sleeve as he followed silently behind them.

"What do you think it is Dan?" he whispered, almost frightened of an answer. "Is it the gas exploded? Mebbe just some bugger's used too much powder for a shot. It's happened before y'know. Young Jakie Jackson nearly blew the whole pit up when he first started on the shots—remember?" His voice had raised its pitch as he spoke and he realized that it was giving away his fear. He didn't want to let Daniel think he was frightened, he just wanted some reassurance that there was nothing to worry about. But Daniel walked in silent grimness back toward the shaft. He could not give Sid his opinion because he could not fathom out what could have caused such a noise or what force had made the Earth shake as it had. The air was still, he had noticed that, but he said nothing, perhaps it was his imagination.

Soon the whole of the back shift joined their fore shift mates and the ways were crowded with moving bodies. When Daniel and Sid arrived at the shaft bottom the crowd that had reached there before them crouched or stood with shocked disbelief on their faces. A few of the youngest lads cried for their mothers and were shushed by a father or elder brother. Daniel's blood turned to ice and Sid let out a low groan. They forced their way to the front. Matthew Taylor was standing by the rapper as always but this time there was no smile on his face, no hearty leg-pulling or laughter. His still clean face was white and his eyes dazed. When he saw Daniel he moved toward him with outstretched hands and clutched frantically at his coat. His voice was hoarse and tight and frightened as he explained what had happened in a quick short sentence. He could have saved his breath. As Daniel looked over his shoulder he could see the tangle of broken water pipes and a mass of splintered wood from the collapsed brattice in the shaft. His heart stopped for a moment at Taylor confirmed that he wasn't dreaming. "The shaft," he croaked, "the effin' shaft's caved in!—we're trapped like effin' rats!"

CHAPTER 7

The immediate transition from noise and activity to almost absolute silence had an aura of unreality about it as the surface workers at the Hester pit stood and gaped in disbelief toward the pump house. Everything had been as normal. The back shift had gone down to relieve their fore shift mates and in fact sixteen men from the fore shift had arrived at bank. Then, for no apparent reason, the great cast iron beam of the pump weighing forty-two tons and the epitome of power and reliability, snapped like a dry twig at its pivot point, sending the projecting half of twenty-one tons tumbling irresistibly down into the shaft. With a roar like thunder it splintered the dividing brattice into matchwood. It tore into the lining of the shaft dislodging stone and timber and journeyed on, carrying away the cage slides, buntons and twisting and breaking the pumping spears with a terrible force that nothing in its path could withstand. Finally, there was silence. Yet, the silence seemed louder than the noise before it. Everyone stood rooted and stiff, unable to comprehend what their eyes told them was fact. One second normality, the next shock, fear and horror billowing through their innards.

It was the slamming of the door to the viewer's cabin that brought John Short back to his senses. That, and the fast running steps of the viewer and his deputy, coupled with their shouts of "Jesus Christ" and "My God in Heaven". He blinked and his frozen mind suddenly thawed and allowed his body to move. It set off a chain reaction. As suddenly as had everyone froze, so they now ran and stumbled and milled up to the black mouth of the shaft. There was jostling and pushing and groans of despair as the significance of what had happened gelled in their minds.

"Get back!" the viewer yelled. "Ease off there! Let's find out the state of things, for the love of God!"

"Harry," he bawled to the under viewer, "make sharp to Newcastle for help. John Short, where's he? Where's the enginewright."

John Short pushed his way forward. The viewer breathed deeply. "Make ready the Gin, the Jack and the Crab—we'll need to go down—quickly now."

"The lads—they're all trapped. They're all in the Low Main," someone shouted.

Jacob Garrett, fighting back the tears shouted. "My da's down there."

The viewer held his hands up for silence. His face was grim and pale.

"Listen lads—listen to me now—we don't know the state of things yet. The beam had gone down the shaft, but most of them would be in-bye—they'll be safe. We'll get them out."

"There was a cage on the way up," the banksman whispered, "there'd be eight in that."

The viewer winced. He blinked and swallowed hard as his brow tightened.

He turned to where John Short had made off. "For Christ's sake hurry with those engines," he yelled.

Robert Garrett was the first in the village to notice it. He rose slowly from his chair and pointed a finger in the direction of the door. His mother, on her knees and busily blackleading the grate, stopped and looked up at him.

"What is it son?" she asked, resting the palms of her hands on the stone floor. "Want the closet?"

Robert shook his head quickly. "Listen," he whispered.

Martha followed the direction of his outstretched arm. "What is it son?—what's up?" she whispered back at him.

Robert swallowed, his sightless eyes fluttering madly. "The pump's stopped. Can you hear? The pump's stopped working."

Martha crouched for a moment. She cocked her head to one side like an alert hound, then pulled herself ponderously to her feet. "Eeh, you're right," she gasped. She lifted her ragged work-pinafore and wiped the black lead from her hands as she walked to the door. "What does it mean son?" It's unusual not to hear the pump."

It had been an unusual morning throughout the village. Jacob Garrett still smarting from his disappointment the night before and hating the viewer like the devil had to be almost forced to go to work. Sid had been sullen and quiet as he prepared himself for the pit and had left without a word. Both Martha and Robert recognized that he was suffering with the boy and they had not tried to make conversation with him. They knew the golden chance that was slipping from his grasp because of the viewer's decision.

Margaret Simpson had tasted the discrimination and abuse meted out to the Mennems that morning. After Daniel's return from the Mennem cottage, Margaret screamed and cursed and thumped her frail fists into his chest, but he brushed her aside as he would an annoying fly. He sat, silent and breathing deeply, barring her way to the door for the rest of the night, and it was only when he finally disappeared from view at the bottom of the lane that Dorothy allowed her, limp and tired as she was, out into the cold morning. She ran to the Mennem cottage, past the cliques of women discussing, analysing, opinionating, on the early morning events initiated by her father. She heard shouts of "dirty cat" and "guttersnipe" but she ignored them.

It was Joe Mennem who filled her mind—and what her father had done to him. And when she finally saw him she could have vomited with shame. Tom Mennem was there with Victoria. He had only heard the news an hour earlier. His cottage was at the far end of the rows and the commotion hadn't carried that far, but someone with a mouthful of bad news burning to get out, had broken the habit of years and spoken to him. His imagination ran riot and he shook with frustration at his disability, his fingers itching for revenge. Yet he consoled himself, knowing that his brothers would feel as he did, and that Daniel Simpson would pay dearly for his attack on the youngest of them.

He did not go to the pit and collect the tallies that morning. He sat almost hypnotized in his battered wheelchair and watched his mother and his wife and Margaret Simpson as they worked to hurry the healing of a face almost cut to ribbons by big and unmerciful fists. Yet as he watched, he remembered with a grim smile, a far off day when the man responsible for the carnage in front of him had saved the life of his eldest brother and that same brother would now be the one to eke out the very last smattering of revenge.

Tom Watson breathed a deep shuddering sigh of relief as the absolute blackness of the shaft, with its frightening sounds of running water and rumble of falling stones, was illuminated by a lantern attached to a slowly lowered rope. From his precarious resting place on a ledge in the shaft, he had sat and prayed and gazed through the eternal night for almost twelve hours and at last rescue was at hand. Never had he experienced terror like it; never had his mind been in such a whirlpool of impatience and wondering. He had been riding to bank with Bob Bewick, Bill Brown, Ralph Robinson, George Sharp and his young son George, also Ralph Robson and Bill Sharp. They were all tired and quiet and looking forward to a meal and bed when the roar came, then the nerve shattering crackle of splintering timber and falling debris. The cage swung wildly and screams intermingled with the deafening clatter of objects raining on to the metal roof and sides of the cage. Then silence, and the agony of uncertainty in the shapeless void.

As the numbness of the initial shock gradually left him, Tom Watson tried to assess his plight. Ralph Robson who had been sitting opposite him was now hanging out of the tangled remains of the cage and groaning softly. Bill Sharp was still on the upper deck and called out that "Old Sharp" was clinging on beside him, but that his leg was badly hurt. The other four were not there. In an instant of catastrophe they were gone, tipped from the relative safety of the cage, to fall down into the depths below. In the darkness, Tom groped out a hand from the cage and felt the rapper ropes. It crossed his mind that perhaps he could climb up them to safety, but it got no further than a thought. From way below him there was a low echoing groan among the gushing water, then a pleading cry for help. "Old Sharp" yelled out. It was the voice of his sixteen-year-old son.

Before he really knew what he was doing, Tom was slithering down the rapper ropes instead of going up. Slowly he manoeuvred himself past the broken jagged timbers, often stopping to mould himself as close as possible to the slimy shaft side as stones and soil and wood careered past him. Finally he came to where the conglomeration of debris, by its sheer volume, had blocked the shaft. He clung to the rope with one hand and explored with the other. The low groaning was very close to him. He touched a shoulder then a head. It was George Sharp, half buried among the tangle of wreckage. Nearby, Bob Bewick gave out a low, bleating cry. Tom Watson comforted them as he clung to the rope. He tried to give them hope for he was sure hope would help ease their pain. He spoke softly to them for hours. Then they were quiet among the constant noise of water and falling rubbish. They were dead.

Tom Watson himself was by this time far from well. He was soaked and cold from the cascade of water and weak from the ordeal of clinging to the thin rope. It was miraculous that his feet found the ledge where he could rest the weight of his body, but he could not rest his mind. Hour after hour he sat in silence and abject fear, occasionally trying to clamber back up the rapper rope, but his weakened body would have none of it. He was forced to wait and hope and pray and cling to the grim ledge near his dead workmates. And then there came muffled shouts from above, and the noise of banging and sawing. At long last rescue, as the feeble light dangled down and struggled to dispel the darkness. "Old Sharp" some sixty feet above him and still hanging on to the battered remains of the cage was first to go. He painfully slotted himself into the loop of the rope, but his leg, left mangled and bleeding for so long, had sapped his precious remaining strength. He was raised only a few yards when he lost his grip and fell out of the loop. With a croak of fear he dropped headfirst down the shaft, bouncing off the cage, then time and time again off the protruding wreckage until he came to rest near his son.

The rope came down again for Bill Sharp. Then it was Ralph Robinson's turn and finally Tom Watson snatched at it and felt the pleasure of its strength in his hands. Almost twelve hours after his initial ascent, he reached the High Main where the rescue party eagerly pulled him to safety.

The rescuers had hurriedly formed themselves from a few surface workers and the men from the fore shift who had ridden to bank. John Short, the enginewright had the Jack engine working and a looped rope ready for descent in record time, but they found the shaft between the surface and the High Main was cluttered with dangerous and hanging wreckage. The only way in was down the narrow parallel pumping staple that joined the High Main seam. From there they cleared a path to the shaft and held their lamps over the gaping black chasm.

"Hello—anybody there?" Short yelled, and his voice amplified and eerie, echoed above the cascade of water and into the depths.

There was a low weak unintelligible answer.

"God! They're alive," Short whispered.

The frail human voice from below was like a starting gun at a race. The Crab rope was lowered from above and a scaffold of timber was built over the shaft at High Main level in an urgent flurry of activity. Finally their work was rewarded when Bill Sharp, black faced and wide-eyed with relief, was yanked over the lip of the shaft, then Ralph Robinson, then Tom Watson.

At the surface, what seemed like the whole village stood silently waiting as they had done since the morning. The night was bitterly cold but they did not seem to feel it. The wind blew its low forlorn blasts from the sea but they did not hear it. Their faces, solemn and rigid, were locked unemotionally toward the head gear and the watchfires that had been lit waved a sickly glow over them. There were strangers there also. Viewers and under-viewers and miners from every one of the neighbouring pits had arrived to give their services. They discussed the problem in low undertones as though to speak normally would be irreverent, for they knew that many men's lives were in danger. The whole of the back shift and all the fore shift with the exception of the lucky few who had ridden were trapped below. Suddenly there was activity and shouting from the pit-head. The crowd stirred and craned their necks. There were survivors in the shaft somebody shouted and the crowd surged forward. It did not seem long before their names were known and they were carried away to a nearby cottage. For the majority of watchers it was a sigh of disappointment that came from them. Each had prayed for it to be their own. A tremendous number of prayers were not answered.

Sid Garrett scurried along the way, stepping over outstretched legs of varying sizes, and repeating the number over and over in his head and when he reached Daniel he gasped out "Eighty-nine down this side!"

Daniel nodded and looked over his shoulder to where Jim Armour the back-overman scribbled on a scrap of paper. "One hundred and ninety-nine, all together," he snapped.

Daniel breathed a slow deep breath. "Sure we haven't missed one?—sure we couldn't make it two hundred straight?"

"Sure Dan," Sid said quickly. "I've checked twice."

He smiled as though that was confirmation of his accuracy. He would have been enjoying himself if it hadn't been for the circumstances that surrounded them all. As soon as they knew about the blockage of the shaft, Daniel had almost automatically taken command, and, just like the old days, Sid was proud to be his assistant. Taking his lead from Daniel he had helped to calm some of the crying boys and reassure the others. He had formed them into two lines, one on each side of the main way and helped to count their number. One young lad had pulled at his jacket sleeve as he went down the line. "Will we get out mister?" he whispered.

Sid looked at the frightened face. The candlelight seemed to colour his skin to a deathly ochre and exaggerate the deep shadows around his eyes.

"Certain we will son. You're a stranger aren't you. You new at the pit?"

The boy blinked back the tears. "I only came down for a look. I came with Billy Turnbull and his da'."

Sid forced a wry smile to his face. He patted the boy's shoulder . "Y'll be all right bonny lad—y'll be late for your dinner but supper'll taste all the better," he said softly.

When he knew how many of them were there, Daniel spoke to them. His voice was loud and firm but carried an undisguisable tone of doubt. "Men, as you know, for some reason the shaft has collapsed and blocked itself. As far as anyone knows we are all here in the Low Main."

His voice dropped in strength, "all one hundred and ninety-nine of us. We cannot stay here though, we've got to move up to the Yard Seam. It is obvious that the water pipes are broken and the pump is no longer working. That means the sump below us will be filling up and may well flood the whole of the Low Main. There's another thing as well, the blockage in the shaft may not be as bad as it looks. At Yard Seam level it may be clear and our way free for rescue."

"D'you think that—d'you really think that?" Alfie whined, the feud between them temporarily forgotten in their unanimous craving for freedom.

Daniel sighed. He wanted to be truthful. He shrugged his shoulders. "I don't know, but we've got to try. We'll form a procession and go up the staple drift then climb up to the Yard Seam. Let's have no panic now—we'll all get there, there's plenty time."

Sid helped Daniel form them up. Even Matthew Taylor strangely silent and sheeplike allowed himself to be led to the queue. Then they set off along the way, each heart pounding, each mind praying for quick deliverance; a pathetic drawn out line of humanity, their shadows dancing in the moving candle-light, shuffling toward hope.

The road began to slope upward as they reached the staple drift and the incline became severe and slippery. They stumbled up it, some scrambling past their slower mates, pulling at their arms and coats, but Daniel's stern authoritative voice brought their panic under control. They reached the staple ladder. The narrow vertical tunnel, like a miniature shaft was dark and foreboding, but they knew there could be freedom at the top. With a silent determination they began the ninety-foot climb. Sid was first to reach the worked out Yard Seam. He waited there until James Armour appeared from the staple, then they both waited for Daniel bringing up the rear. Most of the miners in their keenness had scrambled on ahead.

"Right lads," Daniel whispered grimly as they began to pick their way among the disused workings, "let's see if our luck's in."

Their luck was not in that day. When they reached the vicinity of the shaft the hopeless cursing and frantic cries of their mates told them the worst. And when they saw for themselves, the fear that had been hovering around suddenly gripped with full force at their stomachs. Where the shaft should have been was a solid wall of rubble, spilling out into the way, blocking their last hope of exit. A few of the miners clawed at the stones and swung at them with picks, but it was useless. As soon as a boulder or a piece of timber was dislodged, another took its place. Daniel took off his cap and wiped at his brow and shaven head with the inside of it.

"Christ," he said flatly, "it's patience we need now. They'll be diggin' down to us from up top."

"D'you think they'll get to us Dan," Sid whispered.

Daniel stood looking blankly at the wall in front of him for a moment. His mind was racing. He thought of the countless number of times he had complained about bad ventilation; about the great stike of '44 when he had rallied the men to make a second shaft a condition of their return to work; about the Hester pit and how he had been foolish enough to think that the owners would spend the money to better the ventilation at the same time that the pump was installed. He smiled a grim mirthless smile and shook his head sadly. All they had was a staple from bank to the High Main and another from the Low Main to the Yard Seam, and nothing in between except the main shaft itself! He looked at Sid who watched him with the wondering gaze of someone about to learn something.

"It'll take a while," he whispered, squatting down.

Sid nodded sadly. The young visitor was opposite. Billy Turnbull's father had him and his son squatting beside him, an arm around each of them.

Sid smiled at his worried face again.

"Y'might not get supper son—but breakfast the morn'll taste good."

By Friday morning the rescue seemed to be progressing well. The mangled remains of the cage had been brought to bank and the dangerous loose wreckage between the surface and the High Main cleared. Crowds of miners flocked to help as the news of the accident spread by telegraph and word of mouth all over the country. Organized parties of shift workers were picked and the task of descending to the Yard Seam was begun. Reporters arrived from Newcastle and mingled with

207

the still-waiting crowd of villagers. Since the three men had been rescued from the shaft, hopes had been running high that the rest of the men would be reached in four hours, but that had dragged on to eight and by the time evening came they had still not made the anticipated progress.

William Coulson arrived from Durham that day. He was an expert sinker and had in fact been in charge of the sinking of the Hester shaft. The crowd of officials present at the time were only too pleased to hand over the organization of the rescue attempt to him and his crew, bowing at once to his lifetime knowledge of shafts and their idiosyncracies. All through Friday they slowly worked their way down, heaving out the loose timber and shattered metal, until at about 100 ft. below the High Main their progress slowed almost to a halt. The beam had carried with it an enormous weight of wood and stone and metal. This great volume of rubbish had jammed at this point and formed a matrix almost as impenetrable as solid rock itself.

Another night passed. Another night of freezing uncompromising darkness broken only by the dancing light from the watch-fires. Another night of agonizing impatience for the waiting villagers praying that any second the news would come that they had reached the Yard Seam. Another night of disappointment as the rescuers, on their endless two-hour shifts, hacked at the solid mass beneath them and made little progress. "Jowling" was heard from below during the night and the news of it caused a glad ripple of conversation from the crowd. At least they knew there was still life below. The dull regular hammering from far beneath them proved it, and hearts lifted in hope. By Saturday the situation had changed little. The band of rescuers toiled on, the shaft above them loose and dangerous and giving way, sending rubble crashing down among them. Coulson halted the work at the blockage while timber supports were positioned around the sides. Almost all of the day was taken up. The conditions in the shaft were still appalling. Water, stinging and freezing, teemed down constantly. Debris still rained on to the rescuers injuring more than one of them, yet the struggle continued. At the surface the sickening, gnawing feeling of defeat slowly began to over-power hope. Rumours spread that hunger and thirst would be taking its toll of the oldest and the youngest and that the flood water would be now nearing the Yard Seam. Then counter rumours came, saying that Coulson was only an hour away from them. More jowling was heard. More hope, then disappointment.

Saturday brought crowds into Hartley. By train and coach and on foot came the curious, the morbid and the religious to live at first hand the drama of the men below from the safety of the surface. Barriers were hastily erected around the pit-head. Hartley was suddenly the focal point of the country as the enormity of the situation became apparent. All the time optimistic reports kept coming from Coulson and his men. "Two hours; four hours"—then another two, another four.

Saturday melted into Sunday and more people arrived to savour the excitement of a life or death battle. They seemed caught up and entranced by the drama of it all. The atmo-sphere held some magical ingredient that stimulated, at the same time as it held them in awe. The Hastings Arms did a roaring trade. The bars and staircase and passage were crammed and smoky as people drank and laughed and giggled to cover their relief at the fact that it was not them. Toward evening they swarmed around the pit and it took the police to contain them.

Work in the shaft never stopped. Inch by inch they dug their way down, painfully slowly, on and on, hour by hour, shift by shift, hope by hope. Monday became Tuesday and Tuesday brought the greatest hazard of all to the rescuers. It brought illness to them and despair to the waiting villagers. The oldest enemy of all came snaking out of the debris to meet them and halt their precious progress. It was gas.

The air in the Yard Seam was hot and thick and still. Sid fought off the compelling drowsiness that smoothly and stealthily crept into his brain and with an intense effort he managed to raise his head from where he had rested it on his drawn-up knees. Slowly the fact registered that the singing had degenerated to a few unintelligible grunts from somewhere along the way, but somehow he didn't care any more. The tunnel, lit now by a few remaining scraps of candle spluttering in the darkness, held one hundred and ninety-nine human beings. How many were still alive had been of deep concern to Sid and Daniel, but not now, after so much time they had lost interest. They were interested in only one thing. The dull noise of scraping and banging emanating from somewhere above the blockage meant salvation for whoever was left alive. So now each clung to his life and waited and prayed and sang —but even the singing had become too much for them.

Sid listened to the quick shallow breathing that came from Daniel and watched the silhouette of his head, covered in blond stubble now, as he rested it against a rock behind him. He wondered how long they had been there. He knew it was a long time. James Armour's watch had stopped in the early hours of Saturday morning and it seemed as though an age had passed since then. Suddenly there was a weak agonizing cry from along the way and a figure stumbled drunkenly toward them in the semi-darkness. The face was thin and the haunted eyes screamed out in an agony of realization. It was George Finch carrying his youngest son Billy with his last remaining strength. When he reached Sid and Daniel he dropped to his knees.

"The lad—me little lad," he croaked, tears cleaning little paths down his cheeks. He looked imploringly toward them. "He was just tired—the poor lad was just tired. I told him to rest his head against me."

He held out a hand and stared incredulously at the palm.

"I felt him gan cold," he whispered. "He just went cold. One minute he was warm and then he went stone cold."

His voice trailed away and his brow furrowed in disbelief.

Daniel forced himself to take notice. His mind was in a swirl of shadows and unreality but he took notice. He said nothing though, and neither did Sid. They knew words were useless. He raised an arm and patted George Finch's hand. George picked up his son and stumbled away into the darkness.

Alfie Mennem grabbed at George's arm. His voice was hoarse and frightened in his scrawny throat as he fought off the overwhelming desire to sleep. "Eeh God, George—d'you hear that? Christ son, will they never get us out? That's another poor bugger gone. Finchy's son died in his sleep. I feel bliddy sleepy George. Don't let me go to sleep for Christ's sake."

George swallowed hard in the darkness and he fought to keep his voice calm and normal. Bill and Fred at the other side of him had been silent for hours. They were stiff and still, arms folded in front of them. George had not told his father. He had fought back the urge to scream because he knew his father would feel it worse than he. Above all he wanted to spare him any more hurt as his miserable life drew to its close.

He winced as the waves of sleep rolled silently through his mind.

"Y'll not go t'sleep da'. I'll see to that," he whispered.

"Promise?—promise me George? Don't let your old da' die before they get to us."

George nodded. "I promise," he said numbly.

There was silence for a minute then Alfie gave a low wheezing chuckle.

"So Dan Simpson did our Joe a favour—eh son? He saved him from this lot. At least little Joe's all right—eh?"

"Aye," George gasped. "S'funny isn't it. Dan Simpson saved Joe's life as well as mine and I was ganna kill him for it."

Alfie's voice took on a high-pitched whine.

"We'll not die here George—will we? We'll get out soon won't we?"

George reached over and patted his father's shoulder. It was a thin narrow shoulder, but still firm and sinewy from a lifetime of hard work.

"We'll get out da'—they can't be far away now. Listen, can y'hear them clankin? We'll be out shortly."

He gave a deep shuddering sigh as his body searched for oxygen.

"Reckon we've just about paid off our debt now—eh da'? I reckon me and you's just about free and clear after this bliddy episode. When we get out we'll be able to hold our heads up with the best on them. They'll not dare treat us like shit anymore. Y'll like that—eh da'."

Alfie didn't answer. George turned and shook his shoulder,

211

then again, harder.

Alfie's head slumped loosely forward. Alfie was dead.

The tears welled up behind George's eyes and burst out on to his face. He gritted his teeth as a wave of intense rage burned inside him.

"Jesus Christ Almighty!" he yelled.

He looked to his left at his two brothers, then to his right at his father. He thumped his clenched fist down into the ground beside him. The pit that he had been proud to work in had taken them. After giving it his all it had repaid him like this.

"Blast you—you effin' pit," he bawled.

Then he sniffed and a deep regret took the place of his anger. He imagined how his mother would react when she got the news, and Tom and Joe. Yet another thing to suffer; another memory of misery to absorb and conceal.

"Poor buggers," he whispered.

He gave another deep sigh and rested his head against the stone behind him. He thought about the warm sun on his face and green fields and sound of birds singing. He remembered the smell of baking stotties and rain on the meadow. He remembered the happy laughter of childhood days before the strike in '44. He gave another little sigh as he relaxed and let the peaceful, powerful waves of sleep come and take him.

Sid was pleased that Danel could still be bothered to talk. For some reason he felt more talkative than he had for days and he enjoyed having Daniel answer him.

"It's a queer thing you know Dan," he whispered.

"What is?"

"Well, did you ever wonder what day you'd die on. Did you never recite the days of the week then say 'that's it, it's got to be one of those'."

Daniel gave a loose chesty chuckle.

"You're a silly bugger, Sid Garrett."

"I know, but isn't it queer. We're ganna die down here Dan and we'll not know what day it is we're dyin' on—see what I mean?"

Daniel swivelled his head and looked into the deep worried eyes of his friend. He could see through the thin layer of casualness that covered his terror and he hunted his mind for something to say that would please him.

"Sid?" he said at last.

"Yes Dan?" Sid garbled, almost before Daniel had closed his mouth.

"All my bliddy life I've complained and argued about the rat-traps we've had to work in. Me an' you and thousands like us. We've gone without food and shelter tryin' to force the owners to listen, but in the end they've always won. Now Sid, I've been thinking here, these long hours. Me and you have always stuck together. We've been mates Sid. There's not many a bad bugger like me can take to, but you've been a good marra of mine. When they dig us out of this bastard place—whether we're alive or dead, there'll be hell on—believe me. The miners in this country are ganna say 'Bliddy hell—that bloke Simpson was right, not only do we need another shaft for ventilation—but we need it as an escape—look what happened to that lot at Hartley.' That's what they'll say Sid and they'll say Dan Simpson had a good marra. He was Sid Garrett. He helped Dan all during the big strike. They were the ones that Lovat wouldn't let back into the pit. They were the ones that stuck up for us and for what we deserve."

Sid's jaw dropped and his eyes shone with pride.

"Will they really say that Dan?"

"Aye they will."

Sid blew a low whistle from his dry lips.

"God, that's amazing Dan. I never thought they'd remember my name."

"They will Sid."

For a moment Sid forgot their predicament, but only for a moment, then the sickening foreboding fear crept back.

"Oh, God Dan, they've got to get us out," he breathed. "What about Martha and the bairn—he'll be something great one day Dan—and Robbie—and John, oh Christ I've never seen John for so long."

Daniel gave a long, almost silent cough. His arm came up and he clutched frantically at Sid. He fell sideways and his head slumped on to Sid's shoulder. "Tell Margaret. Tell Doss . . ." he wheezed.

"Dan?—Dan?"

In a flurry of panic Sid scrambled out of the way. Daniel Simpson rolled over and his face buried itself in the clayey mud. He had escaped at last. Sid stumbled to his feet, he tried to pull his mate's head out of the cloying morass, but he hadn't the strength.

"Dan," he screamed, "you can't die—you can't leave me!— for the love of God don't leave me here all on me own."

Frantically he stumbled along the way past the twin rows of still, silent bodies, some as though asleep, others with faces twisted in agony.

"Is anybody alive," he yelled. No one answered. It was silent except for the plink-plonk of dripping water and the dull scraping and banging from somewhere above. He passed Alec Cairns squatting beside the remains of his candle, then Matthew Taylor, a twisted grin on his face and Joe Skinner and Ed Chapman, his two young sons curled up at his feet. Old Billy Charlton was there, eyes open and sightless like some macabre wax-work. Jacky Stobbs sat near by, his father with an arm around his little body and Billy Turnbull with his mate and his father all huddled together. All were dead. Only Sid was left. He turned and made his way back toward Daniel.

"Why me," he bawled along the way. "Why leave me out. Take me—for Christ's sake take me as well!"

And he was taken. He sat himself down beside Daniel and closed his eyes and dreamed himself into eternity.

CHAPTER 8

The crowd was hushed and solemn as it waited for the first of
the bodies to be brought to the surface. It was Saturday, nine
days since the accident and the finale to an heroic, unstinting
struggle which was at the reckoning, to bear no reward. The
hazards and setbacks that Coulson and his men had encoun-
tered during this time had been incredible, as had some of the
incidents at the surface. The gas, discovered on the Tuesday
had not deterred the rescuers but it had delayed them for a full
twenty-four hours while a temporary brattice cloth was positioned in the shaft to assist in ventilating it. The downcast air
was helped by an artificial waterfall and the upcast section was
coupled to the boiler chimneys via the pumping staple. The
work was intricate and slow, but necessary before the rescue
attempt could continue. The crowd, gathered around the pit-
head were at times near to rioting as they swayed and chanted
in an agony of impatience. They yelled for action and results.
They screamed for Coulson's life. A man leapt up on to the
platform around the shaft and attempted to throw himself
down to where his son and grandson were trapped below.
Then came a telegram from the Queen herself, enquiring
about the rescue, then another giving her sympathy. The
Bishop of Durham arrived and tramped around the lanes giving comfort, as did the Lord Mayor of Newcastle. Suddenly
the miners had become a cause for concern. Suddenly their
lives were valuable and people cared. The conscience of the
nation had been pricked and Hartley had become the focal
point of hope, then prayers, then tragedy. It had a sudden
infamy thrust upon it.

Bill Adams was the first to break through into the Yard

Seam. The gas was still thick and dangerous but he managed to crawl along the narrow furnace drift. He found two bodies. He penetrated into the long-sought Yard Seam and found more bodies, then more. A macabre collection of rigid, silent, decaying humanity. The rescue was too late.

John Taylor, a viewer from Backworth told the anxious waiting crowd. His voice was dry and cracked as he spoke to them and their low buzz of conversation stopped instantly as he raised his hands.

"My friends, they have entered the Yard Seam. It was as we expected. All the lads seem to have made their way up the drift and staple from the Low Main. Bill Adams has seen with his own eyes. They are dead. Everyone of them has perished."

The crowd gasped at the news. What little hope they had left had been finally erased. There were cries of anguish and sobbing and the mutter of comforters. "What about the Low Main?" someone shouted, "have they got to the staple?"

Taylor shook his head. "Patience I implore you. The gas is still very bad. It is useless throwing away lives to recover those who are already dead. The work will go on, the pit will be ventilated and made safe and everyone will be brought to bank."

The crowd groaned in unison. It had been an ironic accident —a terrible irony. The pumping beam that had been so necessary to keep down the level of water had been the prime cause but the furnace near the Yard Seam had caused the deaths. The miners had died of Carbonic Oxide poisoning. The furnace, a poor but essential method of ventilation had suddenly reversed its role when the shaft had become blocked. Instead of replacing the foul air it had begun to eat into the precious oxygen and at the same time giving off the deadly gas, taking pay in full for its years of work.

The sight of two hundred crude, black coffins piled five and six high and three and four deep around the mouth of the shaft left no one in any doubt as to the enormity of the disaster. It should have been enough to brace even the most unimaginative of minds for the work that was about to commence but when the first of the bodies appeared at the surface the strongest stomachs squirmed. The body, accompanied by it's 'rider' to ensure its safe ascent, was stiff and dangling grotesquely at the end of the Jack rope. The skin was discoloured and the flesh wasted and reeking in decay. Quickly it was laid out and

216

sprinkled with chloride of lime. A young tally boy who knew almost everyone at the pit peered down at the lifeless face.

"Ben Pearson," he whispered.

Silently the body was wrapped in a shroud and a coffin of suitable size chosen from the pile. The name was chalked on the coffin lid and Ben Pearson was wheeled out on a little trolley across the bridge to the waiting crowd.

"Ben Pearson!"

There was a low "ooh" from the crowd and it parted as Maggie Pearson moved slowly forward. Her two brothers from Blyth took over the trolley and guided it through to a waiting cart. Maggie trembled in her fight to keep back the tears as they silently made their way home.

The next body arrived and then the next and the next. Then they came in twos, lashed together face to face.

"Thomas Gibson and son James," shouted the solemn voice.

Then, "Aaron and Luke, sons and brothers to the previous."

Dorothy Simpson knew in her mind that it had to come and she had rehearsed it over and over, but when the voice said "Dan Simpson", a wave of nausea gripped at her and she felt the strength drain from her legs. But she held on; she controlled herself. She gripped tightly at Margaret's hand and numbly they moved forward, blind to the wide-eyed stares from the crowd that parted in front of them.

Margaret's mind had been in a turmoil of conflicting emotions since the accident. She had seethed with hatred for her father, for what he had done to Joe but as they approached the black coffin that lay silenty waiting for them her instinctive love for him overwhelmed everything. He was dead and she sobbed for him.

When Sid was wheeled out, Martha clung to Robert for support and it was left to Jacob to guide them through. Robert felt along the rough side of the coffin then placed his hand inside. He ran his hand through the dense curly hair and down the bushy beard. He moved his fingers lightly over the cold, closed eyes and mouth. He nodded grimly. It was his father. Then willing hands carried the coffin away to follow Daniel on their last trip to the village.

"Alfie Mennem and son George."

The voice came like a thunderbolt to Mary Mennem but she only blinked back the tears and held her head high as she

217

moved forward. Victoria pushed Tom by her side. When they reached the bridge there was a sudden silence from the crowd. Mary stared unflinchingly into the sea of eyes. This time it was not her who lowered her gaze.

"Bill and Fred Mennem, sons and brothers of the previous."

Mary winced visibly. Tom looked around at the stony, immobile crowd. They hesitated, then four of them moved forward and trundled her family away. Mary nodded and smiled sadly as she turned to follow them.

It was seventeen and a half hours before the gruesome task was completed and the last body returned from the Hester pit. It was dark and it was cold. The crowd had dispersed and the watchfires were low and red. The pit was silent, a final crushing silence. The pit was finished. The pit was dead.

The funeral was the next day. The churchyard at Earsdon was too small to take such a number of corpses and a gap had to be made in the churchyard wall and the adjoining field rapidly consecrated and prepared. It was midday when the carts began to arrive at the cottage doors and already the village teemed with visitors anxious to see the final episode of the awful drama. They were not disappointed. They witnessed an unimaginable event. The coffins were brought from each little cottage and loaded on to the waiting carts. Some carried only one; most had two or three. Mrs. Liddle had seven. One after the other they creaked off toward Earsdon, four miles away and when the first arrived the last was still in the village—a vast snaking column of death.

And so they were returned to the earth where they had eked out their livelihood and perished in the process. The mourners, weary with their ordeal made their way back to Hartley. The visitors went home. The reporters packed their papers and left. A great loneliness smothered the village as the wind blew in gusts from the sea and howled around the silent headgear.

The next morning the remains of the community gathered once again around the pit-head. The Methodist minister preached and they listened in unemotional silence as he stood on the platform near the shaft. His face was pained and his voice

218

solemn and low.

"Brothers and sisters we are gathered here this morning to pay our last respects to some brave men and boys. They were our husbands, sons, fathers, sweethearts and friends and they have departed this life by a dire misfortune. They were men who laboured in the darkness, but Jesus said 'I am the light and the life and whosoever believeth in me shall have eternal life.' Some of these brave lads had laboured through the night and into the morning, the others had descended to relieve them and left the light to work in the darkness. They knew the darkness of the morning, but believe me they saw a sunrise more glorious and more beautiful than any we shall see in this mortal life. They knew the darkness of the morning—they now know the glory of the night. Amen."

"The crowd whispered "Amen".

The viewer appeared from among them. He moved toward the Minister and spoke to him. The Minister smiled and held up his hands.

"My friends, some good news. A relief fund has been set up for your welfare and already monies are pouring in from all over the country. And that is not all. The owner of this pit has also made a generous gesture. All dependants can remain in their cottages for as long as they wish. Let us give thanks to the Lord."

The service continued. Suddenly the weak but meaningful singing of "Oh God our help in ages past" came to a faltering stop. Heads began to swivel. The crowd gasped as Joe Mennem slotted his way past them. His face was discoloured and swollen and a mass of cuts. His right eye was black and the left still puffed and closed. Margaret's heart leapt when she saw him and the crowd gasped even louder as he stopped beside her and pulled her gently toward him. She buried her face against his bony chest then smiled up into his toothless ravaged face. He pulled her even closer. She knew now that everything would be all right. There was nothing to touch them or hurt them any more. They were free.

Dorothy Simpson watched them as they walked arm in arm ahead of her toward the village. She thought of herself and Daniel and what their marriage could and should have been. She felt a deep regret and sadness at the years of coldness and forced tolerance between them. Yet surmounting that, she felt

219

a great release. Daniel was no more and she would no longer have to bear his stifling, overpowering authority. She could now emerge and be herself again and live what life she had left in peace and normality. She too felt a freedom.

Mary Mennem was proud as she walked home with Tom and Victoria. She was proud of her men who at long last had paid their debt. It had cost them dearly but she knew now that they would no longer be objects of scorn. It was meant to be. Perhaps she had known that it was to be like this all along. Her men would not leave the village. It had been a game to them—a contest—and they had all lost. She held her head up high. For the first time in a long time she walked among the villagers with pride.

Martha Garrett was silent as they walked slowly down the narrow muddy pathway. Her hair was untidy and she had forgotten to wash herself that morning. She held tightly on to Jacob's hand and watched Robert up ahead as he was guided by Tom Mennem's chair. He was almost helpless and Martha felt a surge of dread at what the future held for them all. She wanted to cry but she had been wrung dry of emotion. She had a vast emptiness within her. She was afraid.

Jacob tugged at her hand. "Ma," he said, more as a question.

She blinked her eyes away from Robert and looked down at him. "Yes bonny lad?"

"Did the viewer mean you can stay in our house for always 'cos da's dead?"

"Yes son, that's what he said."

Jacob thought for a moment. "Does that mean I can go to school now?"

Martha looked down at the wide-eyed innocent face, his cheeks glowing in the winter air. Suddenly she was not afraid of the future. Come what may she would live her life. She would see Jacob grow up and enjoy with him his achievements. She would look after Robert. Perhaps John would come home. She had much to live for.

"Yes bonny lad, you can go to school," she said softly.

Jacob smiled and gave new impetus to his steps. Fifty yards behind them Septimus Stell struggled to get his stiff, painful legs into motion along the path. But he wasn't cursing. He was smiling too.

THE END
220

EPILOGUE

Much comment appeared in the Press following the disaster at Hartley. *The Times*, the *Illustrated London News* and other influential newspapers of the day asked poignant questions and gave their conclusions as to how to avoid such a catastrophe occurring ever again. They were unanimous in their opinion that a second shaft was an essential and obvious precaution both as a means of improving ventilation and as an escape. The inquest on the 204 who perished endorsed this view. But there were antagonists. A report by J. Kenyon Blackwell, a Government inspector for mines, to the Home Secretary concluded that single shaft pits introduce an element of serious additional danger but pits in operation at that time might be forced to close down if they were compelled by law to provide a second shaft. Several owners bemoaned the fact it would cost £10,000 to sink a second shaft and then see nothing for it but improved ventilation.

Public support for the miners' cause was growing however and Queen Victoria sent a cheque for £200 to the relief fund. The London Stock Exchange raised £500. The Duke of Northumberland sent £200.

At a meeting in Newcastle on 25th January 1862, even before the Hartley miners were buried, Mr. James Mather, a champion of the miners' cause, moved that: a petition be presented to the two houses of Legislature, praying that a special committee be appointed to enquire into the general question of colliery accidents with a view to preventing a repetition of the frightful calamities which have taken place and it is the opinion of this meeting that no colliery should be without two independent means of escape from the mine with a view of securing the safety of the miners.

A Mr. Towers from London attended that meeting. He had been sent by Lord Shaftsbury and Sir Fitzroy Kelly who were highly distressed at the overall plight of the British miners. So, influential men joined the ranks of Press and public agitating for action and on the 12th June 1862 a question was put to the Home Secretary in the House of Commons by a Mr. Dillwyn asking "whether it is the intention of the Government to introduce any measures to amend the law relative to the working of coal mines".

His answer was that a Bill was in preparation which would provide for the construction of a second shaft in cases where it was practicable. The Bill was duly presented and had its three readings in the Commons without debate. On the third reading in the House of Lords, Earl de Grey and Ripon stated in a reply to a question by Lord Ravensworth that "nothing but a strong case of necessity could justify the passing of such a Bill and that he had no doubt that the Secretary of State would in the administration of the Law, show the indulgence which was due to the coal owners for the manner in which they had received the Bill".

Thus Parliament reluctantly submitted and the law of the land was changed. No new mines could be sunk unless at least two shafts or outlets were provided and separated by natural strata not less than ten feet in breadth, and after 1st January 1865 mines existing at the time of the Act were also to be supplied with a second shaft.

Daniel and Sid would have been pleased.